Also by Caroline Flynn

The Forget-Me-Not Bakery
The Winter Berry House

A Wildflower Summer

CAROLINE FLYNN

ONE PLACE. MANY STORIES

HQ
An imprint of HarperCollins*Publishers* Ltd
1 London Bridge Street
London SE1 9GF

www.harpercollins.co.uk

HarperCollins*Publishers*
1st Floor, Watermarque Building, Ringsend Road
Dublin 4, Ireland

This paperback edition 2021

1

First published in Great Britain by
HQ, an imprint of HarperCollins*Publishers* Ltd 2021

Copyright © Caroline Flynn 2021

Caroline Flynn asserts the moral right to be
identified as the author of this work.
A catalogue record for this book is
available from the British Library.

ISBN: 9780008480943

MIX
Paper from
responsible sources
FSC
www.fsc.org
FSC™ C007454

This book is produced from independently certified FSC™ paper
to ensure responsible forest management.

For more information visit: www.harpercollins.co.uk/green

Printed and Bound in the UK using 100% Renewable Electricity
at CPI Group (UK) Ltd

To Jazz.
You'll always be the heart of Port Landon,
just as you've always been the heart of
everything in my world.

Wildflower (def.): a flower that grows in the wild, meaning it was not intentionally seeded or planted.

Prologue

Jason

'You're the greatest son a mother could ask for, Jason, but the truth is, neither of us are getting any younger.'

Jason stifled a groan, trying to keep his voice down lest he bother any of the other six people sitting in the waiting room with them. His mother, however, didn't give a hoot who heard about his advanced age of thirty, or his lackluster love life.

Okay, nonexistent love life. That was more accurate.

'You make it sound like I'm over the hill, Mom.'

'Well, if one of us is, it isn't me, darling.' The laugh lines etching her pale bluish-green eyes grew deeper with her cheeky grin.

When she smiled like that, Jason had a hard time remembering that the woman sitting in front of him was in her mid-sixties. He had an even harder time with the fact that the eyes staring at him with so much sparkle and vitality were failing her, slowly but surely. He welcomed the moments when he forgot that truth, but it only made it harder once the realization hit him again, bowling him over with the same flood of shock and sadness he felt when he'd first found out.

Bettina Forrester had glaucoma. Eventually, she would be blind.

But today was not that day, and Jason reminded himself that he couldn't dwell on what would inevitably happen. Just like he couldn't dwell on what had already happened. The past was the past.

Unfortunately, it wasn't far enough in the past for him to entertain his mother's recurring monologue about finding someone to fall in love with. And that's how she always phrased it, finding someone to fall for, as though he could go into the nearest Wal-Mart and pick someone off the clearance rack. Jason wished it were that easy.

'Did Grandma Mary-Jean give you this much trouble about settling down and getting a ring on your finger?' He regretted the mumbled enquiry the moment it left his mouth. His grandmother was a force to be reckoned with, and there wasn't a soul in Port Landon who didn't know it. The old woman might have only stood four feet ten inches tall, but she could cut a grown man down to size with a quick-witted comment, never once letting her radiant smile waver. And people loved her for it, because they always knew where they stood with Mary-Jean, and they always knew her words and advice came from a place of love.

Jason's mother was no different in that regard. That didn't mean he liked hearing about his lack of a significant other all the damn time, though. He was starting to think she believed he wasn't whole or something, unless he found the piece to make him that way. It certainly wasn't the way he saw it, even if he had to convince himself of that on a daily basis.

'Heck no.' His mother chuckled. 'She and Daddy thought I'd lost my marbles when I agreed to go out with your father at such a young age. Mama told me to hold my horses and wait for someone to come along who had money.'

Jason shook his head. He had heard this story countless times, and he knew the latter comment was true. But it was said in jest. Everyone knew Roderick and Bettina's love story could be summed up in four words: love at first sight. They had married young and never looked back. Even now, so many years later, they only had eyes for each other.

'See, that's what I'm talking about.' He gestured with his hands, as though she had given him a perfect example of what he was trying to say. 'I'm just waiting on a girl with money, Mom.'

She swatted at him. 'Oh, you are not.' She laughed. 'I raised you better than that, and your grandmother raised me better than that, too. You're not holding out for money, son. You're holding out for a girl who will hold your heart and keep it safe, not break it like she did.'

She. Jason didn't remember the last time his mother said his ex-fiancée's name out loud. He couldn't remember the last time he did, either. He reached out for Bettina's fingers, acutely aware of how paper-thin and weathered the backs of her hands seemed.

'I've got to do what's right for Carlie. The casual dating scene isn't any place for a four-year-old to be.' *Or for a man with a four-year-old.*

His mother's gaze narrowed. 'Jason, you—'

Whatever she was about to say—and he had a pretty good idea what it was—it was thwarted by the sound of her name from across the room.

'Bettina Forrester.'

Simultaneously, they turned. A woman in lavender scrubs held a clipboard against her chest, staring out into the sea of faces. The muted green of the waiting room only looked more putrid in Jason's eyes when mixed with the pale purple she wore. Then again, maybe it was just the reason for the follow-up appointment that had him seeing everything within these walls as sickly and unnatural.

We're up, he thought. He stood, holding out a steady arm to his mother. Any other minute of the day, Jason put his effort into being what Carlie needed him to be. A good father, her provider, her hero. Right now, it was time to be what his mother needed. She needed him to be strong. For her, for their family.

He had every intention of doing right by her, too. Even if it broke his heart. After all, he was no stranger to heartache.

The nurse led them down a short hallway, her dark ponytail swaying with each step as they entered a cramped examination room. The furnishings were just as drab and sterile.

'Dr. Evans will be right in.' Her smile was warm, a stark contrast to her swift movements as she headed out the door. The nurse was efficient, good at her job. Jason didn't begrudge her that. For her, this was her place of employment, and she had to keep the revolving door turning.

For him and his mother, it was where their life changed. And not for the better.

'It will be okay.' Bettina had taken a seat beside the exam table. She reached out and patted his hand.

Jason stared at her fingers. Wasn't he supposed to be comforting her? He didn't get the chance to come up with his own consoling words.

'Bettina, you made it here,' Dr. Evans announced before he was barely through the door. 'The traffic's getting quite bumper to bumper out there.'

Immediately, Jason picked up on the fact that the doctor didn't greet her with, *So nice to see you*. He figured that wasn't an accident.

'We did. Not hard to tell that school is out and summer is officially under way.' Bettina patted Jason's hand again, who had taken up residence against the wall beside her chair, attempting to make himself feel smaller than his broad shoulders and six feet of height allowed for. 'This is my boy, Jason.'

Idly, he wondered how old he would have to be before his mother stopped introducing him as a boy, but he shook the doctor's outstretched hand, nonetheless. With Bettina Forrester, the odds were it would never happen. 'Good to meet you.'

It wasn't the first time he'd been within the walls of the North Springs Memorial Hospital. Far from it. He brought his mother here for her regular appointments when his father wasn't able to. It was, however, the first time Bettina had asked him to come into the appointment with her. She was always so keen to keep her health concerns under wraps. If there was one thing Forresters didn't handle well, it was having someone else worry about them, regardless if there was reason to do so or not.

And there had never been a reason to worry, until a year and a half ago. That was when they were introduced to Dr. Evans, an ophthalmologist who held satellite clinics in North Springs. His main office was in Lansing, but he made scheduled biannual visits to the city to accommodate some of his patients. As a doctor specifically trained in the medical and surgical treatment of glaucoma, Jason's mother became one of his rostered patients when a few tests and a dilated eye exam revealed her dwindling eyesight wasn't just from the need for a stronger eyeglass prescription.

'I've got your most recent intraocular pressure tests.' Gone was the talk about the summer sun and the bustling traffic. The doctor was all business, his gaze trained on the manila folder in front of him. He shuffled a few papers around. 'There is slight fluctuation, Bettina, but compared to the values from your last tests, it's relatively stable.' He glanced up at his patient. 'That's a good thing.'

'So, the disease isn't getting worse.' It wasn't a question, and Bettina hung on to his every word, desperate for the answer she obviously wanted to hear. Jason suddenly felt just as overwhelmed by the need to hear some positive news as well.

'Not quickly,' Dr. Evans assured her cautiously. 'As we've previously discussed, your glaucoma wasn't caught nearly as early as we would have hoped, and there is no cure. But it can be controlled.' He held up the papers. 'These tests are telling me that your medication regime is working. I may adjust the dosage slightly, but I'm confident in the progress we're making. As long as we're making progress and the disease isn't, I'm a happy camper.'

Jason wished he could share in the good doctor's sentiment. While it was good and fine that the glaucoma wasn't getting worse in a rapid fashion, it wasn't getting any better, either. It was unfair of him to think it, but he didn't understand how, with all the medical advances made during this day and age, they couldn't cure this godforsaken disease and make his mother better. That's what he wanted.

That's what she deserved.

The follow-up was fairly uneventful after that. It wasn't until after the routine eye testing and the consultation, on their way back out to the parking lot, that Jason realized his chest ached. He had been rigid as a fencepost throughout the entire appointment, waiting for the ball to drop, for the catastrophic news to come. It didn't. But he realized now that he had been expecting it. It was funny; he didn't feel any better knowing there was no bad news. Because it would come. Eventually. Maybe not during this hospital visit, or the next, but eventually. And there was nothing in the world he could do to stop it.

'You doing okay, Mom?' He opened the passenger door of his Dodge truck for her and helped her climb in.

'Doing just fine,' she replied. A quizzical expression clouded her features. 'Why wouldn't I be? Dr. Evans is right, Jay. Things are stable, and that's a good thing. Sometimes stable is all we can ask for.'

Jason held the seatbelt out for her until she grasped it between her fingers. 'I don't want stability for you, I want a cure.'

Bettina tilted her head, a dark lock of her hair falling in front of her face. 'I love you for that, I do. But sometimes we don't always get what we want, my boy. We've just got to deal with the hand we've been dealt.'

Under any other circumstances, Jason knew exactly what she meant. He knew it all too well. But there was a fierce level of irrationalism that came with the unfairness of his mother's sickness. To him, she was an angel, on a pedestal so high no one else would ever reach it. 'I just wish there was something I could do,' he confessed. 'Anything.'

His mother's lips formed a genuine smile. With the seatbelt firmly locked in place, she reached for her son's hand and squeezed it encouragingly. 'There is,' she replied. 'You can open up that heart of yours and allow yourself to find love. It'll happen when you least expect it, but you've got to let it in.' She paused, ducking her head to make sure he was staring into her eyes and paying attention. 'I want to *see* you happy, Jason. That's all any mother would ever wish for.'

Chapter 1

Lily

She had begun this trip with the best laid plans. Everything she needed was packed meticulously into the cramped confines of her car's backseat. Every mile and gas station pit stop was plotted on a printed map draped across the passenger seat. And almost every dollar in her bank account was spoken for in her attempt to get to her destination.

Lily Brentwood was a planner, an organizer. She wasn't a fan of surprises and did her darnedest to avoid them.

But she never planned for this. Amidst all those preparations, she never once thought that her trusty Toyota Corolla—or Cruella, as she frequently referred to it, referencing its dingy white exterior and black cloth interior—would give up on her.

Yet, here she was, standing on the side of the highway, staring at Cruella with a stricken expression as the car's unmoving wheels sat on the gravel shoulder—its engine unwilling to rumble into life.

Lily glanced around. Darkness had fallen hours ago, and any other time she would have welcomed the night. She had always been a fan of the serenity it brought with its blanket of blackness, covering everything it touched and enveloping it in safety until morning arrived. Others might not see nighttime the way she did, too hung up on the shadows to see the beauty that created them, but Lily loved it. It was one of the reasons she had chosen to make the eight-hour drive from her hometown of Sherman to Chicago later in the evening rather than through the bright light of day. It also made it easier for Eden, who was currently fast asleep in the backseat, completely oblivious to the conundrum they faced.

They were only four and a half hours into the trip. Barely halfway there, and obviously nowhere near the city. Around her, silence reigned—save for the chirping of crickets and the odd snap of a branch from the one of the many trees that lined the road. She could just make out the flicker of light from what she thought might be a farmhouse in the distance. In the other direction was the town limit sign she had aimed for when she realized her car was taking the nosedive from suddenly running poorly to not running at all.

Welcome to Port Landon.

She had never heard of the place, but Lily hoped that beyond the sign, somewhere in the not-too-distant darkness, was a town that held everything she needed, which acutely included a mechanic with an emergency line and hopefully a whole lot of mercy.

This was the furthest thing from the city life she had set out for. In fact, judging by the nearby farm on the outskirts of town and the wholesome rustic vibe of the town's signage, Lily would bank on Port Landon being closer in size to the small town she had just escaped from.

Escaped. Goodness, she made it sound like her hometown had held her there, in captivity with shackles and chains. No one had forced her to stay as long as she did, and no one had kept her from leaving.

And now, when she had finally taken that step, good ole' Cruella was going to make it even more difficult.

'Not if I can help it,' Lily muttered. She opened the driver's side door as quietly as she could, not wanting to wake Eden. A soft click was the only sound she heard as the door unlatched, followed by a squeak as it opened, which probably wasn't nearly as loud as it seemed in the silence of the night. Her phone lay under the map. Lily didn't bother consulting the paper, she went straight for Google. It would know everything there was to know about Port Landon and its capability to get Cruella back up and running. This was a curveball in Lily's plans, not the end of them completely. She refused to let the setback hold that kind of weight.

The search engine found two potential hits. One was Forrester's Auto, which boasted being Port Landon's number one repair shop for all makes and models. The second was a small engine repair place that looked as though it conducted its business from the single-car garage in the owner's backyard. Seeing as Cruella wasn't a lawnmower and that Forrester's Auto seemed to be embellishing their claims—they weren't the number one repair shop in town, they were the *only* one—it looked like Lily had no other choice than to call the number in the listing. With each ring, she hoped the twenty-four-hour emergency line wasn't just an embellishment, too.

'Forrester.'

She stared up at the sky, thanking the stars that twinkled back at her that someone answered. Even if he did sound about as awake and alert as the pebbles beneath her feet. 'Hi, I'm sorry to call so late, but I found your number online. My car has broken down just outside Port Landon.'

'No need to apologize. Whereabouts are you?' Every word sounded on the verge of a yawn.

Lily assessed her surroundings again. 'I'm practically leaning against the welcome sign coming into town. I took exit …' She sighed. No one would ever accuse her of being overly observant. 'I'm not sure which exit it was, but I—'

'It's okay, I know where you are.' The man on the phone didn't try to hide his amusement. 'There's only one way in and out of town, for the most part. Will your car run at all?'

'No, it was just making this *wahhh wahhh* sound and then *cccrrrrrr* when I tried to make it go faster.'

'I'm sorry, I didn't get that the first time. Can you do that again?'

'It sounded like *wahhh*—wait a second, are you making fun of me?' Lily's face burned. It didn't matter that he couldn't see her.

'You could've just told me it was making a whining sound, then grinding when you revved it,' he chuckled. 'But I'll give you props, your imitations were spot on.'

'So, you know what the issue is?' The sliver of hope she clung to was stronger than the streak of embarrassment that coursed through her.

'I've got a good idea, but I'll need to come and take a look to be sure. Give me ten minutes, okay?'

Relief—that's what she felt. In ten measly minutes, someone was going to show up, make her car run smoothly again, and get her back on the highway, heading toward her and her young daughter's new life. 'You have no idea how perfect that sounds. Thank you.'

'Don't mention it.'

She knew she should just hang up and let him get on his way to meet her, but the man had restrengthened her hope and made a joke at her expense. The least he could do was tell her who he was. 'I'm assuming Forrester isn't your first name.'

'I'm Jason,' he replied easily. 'And you are?'

'Lily,' she said. 'Lily Brentwood.'

'It's nice to meet you, Lily Brentwood. I'll see you soon.' He hung up without another word.

* * *

It was the only shining headlights she had seen since taking the exit and pulling over in the outskirts of Port Landon. Somehow, Lily didn't think that was considered an oddity in these parts.

12

The spheres of bright light grew larger as the truck drew closer, spotlighting the gravel and asphalt in their blinding streaks of brightness. They rolled to a stop behind Lily's car. Engine still rumbling, the driver's door opened and a man climbed out. Tall and wide at the shoulders, his silhouette reminded Lily of one of those football players in the movies: strong and muscular, outlined in stadium lights as he ascended the field and prepared for battle.

Lily, however, was the one trying to avoid a battle, and she scurried forward, meeting him in the space between her vehicle and his. Her car keys were wedged between her fingers at her side, the only weapon she had at the ready in case he wasn't as friendly as she hoped.

'I'm assuming you're Lily?' he asked as she approached. 'I'm Jason.'

She stared up, shielding her eyes in hopes of seeing him clearly. 'Thank goodness. Can you do me a huge favor and turn your truck off, Jason? The lights are shining into my car, and I'd really like to avoid waking my daughter if I can.' She winced, praying she didn't sound ungrateful, but things would go much more smoothly if she could keep Eden from being rudely awakened.

Jason's expression transformed instantly to something resembling a mix of surprise and mortification. 'Of course. I didn't realize you had anybody with you. One sec.' He bolted back inside the truck and killed the engine. The sudden silence was quickly followed by the immediate absence of light, and the highway was plunged into darkness once again.

Lily blinked in quick succession, waiting for her eyes to readjust. When they did, Jason Forrester was in front of her again. His features were shadowed by his baseball cap, but she was pretty sure not even a worldwide blackout could dim what she saw in his eyes. More comforting warmth radiated from them than she had ever witnessed from anyone's gaze before, let alone from a complete stranger.

'Sorry about that,' he said, pulling his wallet from the back pocket of his jeans. 'If I'd known, I'd have tried to be a little quieter.'

Lily figured he meant it since he was now whispering. 'It's no problem, really. I should have said something on the phone.' She cast a glance at the rear windshield, saw no movement and heard no impending wails. 'She's still fast asleep, so there's no harm done. If she wasn't, trust me, we'd know.'

Jason chuckled. 'I know exactly what you mean. My daughter's the same way. If she's awake, she's going to make sure I hear her.' He held his wallet out toward Lily. 'There's my driver's license, by the way. To prove I am who I say I am.'

Using the glow of her cellphone light, she glanced at the name and Port Landon address on the card, nodding when the photo matched the man before her. She loosened her grip on the keys in her other hand, slightly. 'Thank you for that. How old is your daughter?'

'Four, going on fifteen.'

'Mine, too!' Lily laughed, then clamped a hand over her mouth. If, after warning him to stay quiet, she was the one to wake up Eden, she had a feeling the man standing in front of her would have something to say about it. And he would enjoy saying it, too. 'Well, she's five, but definitely going on fifteen. That's quite the coincidence.'

'Quite. Her birthday's in a couple of weeks.' He stared at her as though he couldn't see her clearly. Like he was curious and intrigued and …

Interested.

Get over yourself, Lily chastised herself. *He's here to boost your car, not your confidence.* Then again, if she was thinking he might be interested purely because he looked at her in some strange way, maybe her confidence was already overinflated.

'Let's see what's going on with your car.' Jason stepped around her and popped the hood with ease. 'I'll be as quiet as I can.' His movements were careful and methodical, proving he meant

14

it. He didn't want to awaken a sleeping child any more than she did.

Lily watched him work, pulling a small flashlight from his back pocket and checking multiple things under the hood. She didn't know a nut from a bolt when it came to cars, so Lily wasn't about to pretend she had a clue what he was doing. He did, though. That was obvious.

The wheels in his head were clearly turning. Jason said nothing as he assessed the situation. When he suddenly stood up and held a finger up in a *wait here* gesture, she didn't know whether he was leaving or just getting something from his truck, or if she should laugh that he felt the need to make the gesture in the first place.

Where in the world was she going to go?

Jason jogged back to his Dodge Ram, pulling the tailgate down to grab something from the truck bed. Upon return, he held what looked like a little computer with two little wires hanging from it.

'That looks serious,' she stated.

'It's a multimeter. It'll tell me if I'm on the right track or not.' He disappeared back under the hood.

The tightness of his angular jaw made Lily think he already knew the answer to that question, and that she wasn't going to like it. He started to tap the little probes on the ends of the wires against something, and Lily stopped watching after that. Jason wasn't looking at her, but there was no mistaking the way he winced at whatever he was seeing on the little digital screen in front of him.

Dread made her stomach plummet. 'You want me to try starting it or something?'

Jason glanced up. 'I'm not sure I need you to,' he admitted. 'One sec.'

Lily pushed away from the horror story that was beginning to unravel under the hood to sneak a peek into the backseat. Hands cupped to peer in, she saw Eden still sleeping soundly in her car seat, head tilted, mouth hanging slightly open. One of her unruly

15

blonde ringlets had fallen across her porcelain forehead. The little girl was completely unaware that her mother's dreams for the both of them were on the verge of disintegrating into dust.

'What's your daughter's name?'

His voice floated on the breeze, dragging Lily back to the here and now. Jason didn't look up from whatever he was doing, but the question hung between them, seeming to grow more compelling the longer it went unanswered. She wondered if it was merely his voice that gave each word that kind of power.

'Eden.' She stole one more glance at the girl as she said her name, then trudged back around to the front of the car. 'What about yours?'

'Carlie,' he replied. 'And she'd have woken up long before now if she was the one in that car seat. The slightest jostle or spoken word and that girl is awake and wondering what she's missing out on.' It was hard to construe it as a complaint when he was grinning like the proud father he obviously was.

'Not Eden,' Lily chuckled. 'She sleeps like she's hoping to claim she's an expert on her job résumé someday.'

'Consider yourself lucky.' Jason's hands had stopped moving. His attention was turned toward her, sharing in the amusement, and the understanding.

'Trust me, I do. Every day.'

There was that look in his eyes again, the one Lily couldn't read. The one she was thinking was something it wasn't. Yet, he was holding her gaze the same way, tilting his head curiously. It was the same angle Eden's head was tilted at, only there was no solace in it. It was gone as quickly as it had appeared.

'So, what's the damage?' She ripped her focus away from him and turned her attention to the car. Where it should have been in the first place. 'Can you fix it and get me back on the road, Mr. Forrester?' She wondered if the formal way of addressing him sounded like the proverbial step back she heard in her own tone. She didn't know, but that was exactly what she needed to do, take a big old step away and get things back on track. Lily didn't need to be standing here in the middle of the night, making friends with the handsome mechanic who had come to her rescue like a white knight in a blue Dodge truck. She needed to get the wheels back in motion and keep moving forward. This momentary standstill had taken too long already.

Jason stood to his full height and unlatched the metal rod that held the hood up, slowly lowering it and pushing on the hood until there was a telltale click to confirm it was latched closed. 'I've got a feeling you're in a big hurry,' he said carefully.

'I'm on my way to Chicago.' Lily said the words, but they were already void of emphasis. She could almost feel what Jason was about to confess before he actually admitted it.

'Not tonight, I'm afraid.' He had the decency to flinch on her behalf. 'Not in this car, anyway. I'm pretty sure your alternator is toast, as well as the battery. And I'll be honest, there are a few things going on under that hood that, if they aren't issues at the moment, they're going to be, real soon. I can fix it, but it definitely won't be tonight. I'll have to order parts in and—'

'That sounds expensive.'

Another flinch. 'It's not a minor repair, unfortunately. I know that's not what you want to hear. I'm sorry.'

'It's not your fault.' Which was true, but Lily yearned for someone to blame other than herself. The problem was, the blame lay at her feet, and for good reason. She hadn't been as prepared as she'd thought, after all.

'I can probably get you back on the road by next week,' Jason assured her.

'Next week?' she squeaked out. Granted, it was Thursday, and since parts had to be ordered, it made logical sense, but that didn't make it any easier to hear. Not to mention, Lily was pretty sure there wasn't enough money sitting in her bank account to pay for the repairs. Another thing she hadn't planned for.

'I can tow it back to the garage in a few hours to get a better idea of what's really going on. Unfortunately, the tow truck is in use at the moment. Two calls in one evening; a big night in Port Landon.' He grinned, but Lily couldn't bring herself to return the gesture. 'In the morning, I can look up the parts and give you a more accurate timeline and cost. How does that sound?'

Lily appreciated the apology in his tone, but she couldn't help but be honest with herself: it didn't sound good at all.

'There's no other option, I'm assuming.' It was her last feeble attempt at hope. There had to be something else that could be done, something that would keep her and Eden heading toward the heart of Chicago instead of sitting at a standstill in the middle of nowhere.

'Afraid not,' Jason admitted. 'But I'll do what I can, and as fast as I can do it, to help you out.'

Defeated, Lily nodded. She couldn't ask for more than that. He was a complete stranger offering the only olive branch he had. She grabbed on to it and gripped it tight. 'I appreciate that. More than you know. Go ahead and tow it, then we'll go from there.' He was her only hope at the moment. She had to have faith in him despite not knowing a thing about him.

Lily didn't harbor hope for anyone, least of all strangers. Yet, here she was, stranded with a man who promised things that gave her the tiniest sliver of it to cling to. She knew how dangerous that could be. How hard. And still, she clung to it like a lifeline.

Maybe there was no hope for her, either.

Chapter 2

Jason

Jason had been completely out of it when his cellphone rang. Being ripped from sleep by the shrill ring left him with a pounding heart and the immediate conclusion that something was wrong, something had happened, to Carlie, to his mother. He wondered if there would ever be a time when his rational side would kick in before he answered the phone and realized his worst fears were exactly that … fears. Not rooted in reality, and the world wasn't ending. He was just on call, as he always was. It was one of the joys of owning his own business.

Having the only tow truck in Port Landon was both a blessing and a curse. Jason was grateful that he could aid his community when they needed him—he would never begrudge the town residents his help if he could offer it, just as they would never turn away from him, either. But on those nights, long after the clock had struck midnight, when folks called his number and sent him into a fearful frenzy, he wished he could bestow that double-edged sword on someone else.

Tonight, he had done exactly that, about two hours prior. A

call had come in and he had taken his best friend, Branch, up on his offer to share tow calls. It was one of the many moments that had occurred over the past six months that he was relieved and appreciative that his friend had moved back to town and decided to work for him. Rarely did Jason pass a late-night call on to Branch. Now, he was glad he had. Sure, his phone had scared the living daylights out of him, tearing him away from the first decent sleep he'd had in days, but there was something about the voice on the other end of the line that made him grateful it was him on the other end of the line.

Until he had to give her the bad news, at least. Then, he felt a flicker of guilt at having to tell the poor woman that she and her daughter weren't going anywhere fast driving the rusted Corolla. The car had died a heroic death, he would give it that. Frankly, he was shocked it had been running at all based on the cracked hoses and worn gaskets he saw under the hood. He had a hunch that automotive maintenance wasn't high on Lily Brentwood's priority list.

Something else was, though. Judging by her eagerness to get back on the road, he thought it was safe to assume that whatever was in Chicago was at the top of that list.

'Is there a hotel nearby where I can book a room, by chance?'

Jason wiped his hands on his jeans. 'Port Landon is hardly big enough for a hotel, but there's a bed and breakfast in town, and it's not too far from my garage. I know the owners. I could give them a call, if you want?' He had his cellphone pulled from his pocket before he'd even got the entire question out. Options were limited. It was the best he could offer.

Lily seemed genuinely surprised by his willingness. 'Oh, um, sure. I can call them, though.'

'It's no problem.' He searched through his contacts for Nancy Bergeron's number. Nancy had been friends with his mother for as long as Jason could remember, and they had even headed Port Landon's community gardening committee when his parents had

20

still lived in town. 'I'm sure they'll have room for you and Eden. I can drop you off there. Give me a second.' He wandered away from her to make the call. Privacy wasn't needed, but he felt bad for waking up Nancy in the same shrill manner he had been awakened. Like him, however, it came with the territory of owning a business that catered to the public. Being available every hour of every day included the hours that were less than convenient.

Nancy answered on the third ring, calling Jason by name. She had call display, then. The woman sounded far more awake than he'd been when he answered Lily's call. Just as he suspected, they had one room available—and only one room, which was pure luck considering the area's population seemed to triple this time of year—and she would be ready and waiting for them when they arrived. He had a feeling she would have made room even if there hadn't been an available bedroom.

As he spoke into the phone, Jason took aimless steps, moving for the sake of doing something. When his gaze rested on the back passenger window, he stopped. The little girl in the car seat faced the window, though her eyes were closed. She reminded him of one of the porcelain dolls his mother used to keep on a shelf in the downstairs rec room, smooth and elegant and fragile. Her blonde corkscrew curls could have been fake, they were so perfect. Carlie's hair was curly, but it was hurricane curly, as his mother had fondly referred to it, every curl doing its own thing, some tighter than others. Lily's daughter was the personification of angelic as her chest rose and fell softly with each easy breath.

Jason knew better than to believe the cherub-like mask—he had been a father long enough to know that even angels delighted in a little devilishness now and then—but, still, the sight of her, with long lashes and high cheekbones that brought out her resemblance to her mama, was enough to give him pause.

He needed to help this little girl and her mother. The desire to be useful propelled him forward. Jason thanked Nancy for the third time and hung up.

'You're all set,' he announced. 'There's a room waiting for you at the bed and breakfast in town.' He turned away from the window.

Lily let out a sigh. 'That sounds great. Thank you for making that call. Are you sure you don't mind giving us a ride?' She ran a hand through her hair, the straw-colored strands loose with a subtle wave.

'Unless you're up for a little nighttime stroll.' His mouth curled up at the corners.

'Only if you come with us to show the way,' she countered.

Humor, he thought. *That's a good sign*. The woman had suffered enough unexpected blows tonight that he wouldn't have faulted her for being a little ornery if she felt so inclined. He definitely preferred the amusement, though.

He shrugged. 'Walking's not really my thing, if I'm being honest. It's—hmm, what do you call it? Oh, right. Exercise.'

'Guess I'd better wake Eden, then.'

'Should I get earplugs from the truck?'

Lily turned, a grin forming on her lips. 'Do you have two pairs?'

He stifled a laugh, shaking his head. 'Nah, I guess if you've got to deal with the high-pitched wails of a rudely awakened preschooler, I won't let you go through that alone.'

'My hero.'

He knew she was kidding, but Jason refused to kid himself. He didn't want to be anybody's hero, regardless of how nice it sounded on her lips.

Lily walked around to the passenger side of the car, then paused. Jason could almost see the wheels of her mind whirling. She looked to him, to the car, then to his truck and back again, assessing it all. 'You're going to tow the car in the morning?'

There it was. He wondered how long it would be before she became really, truly cautious. No one was trusting enough to jump into a truck with a stranger in the middle of the night with the promise of a bed to sleep in and repairs on a broken car come dawn.

Jason didn't move. 'My employee's got the tow truck here on another call. All I have at the moment is my pickup truck.' He pointed back toward the Dodge. 'I'll come back and tow your car once Branch is done with the tow truck. As for Edwin and Nancy's place, if you want to Google the bed and breakfast, be my guest. You'll see the number listed, and I can show you it's the same number I just called on my cell.' Pulling his wallet out, Jason slid a small white rectangle across the hood of the car. 'There's my business card, more proof that I am who I said I was, and I can give you something in writing that attests to the fact I'm going to tow your car to my repair shop and do up an estimate for the repairs required. Does that ease your mind a little?'

In the darkness, it was hard to tell for certain, but he was pretty sure Lily's cheeks flamed red. 'I'm not saying you're a serial killer or a convict or anything …'

He couldn't help it; he laughed. 'No, you're being a protective mama bear, and you're caught between a rock and a hard place at the moment. I get it, Lily, I do. If it would make you feel better, I'm sure you can call the listed phone number for the bed and breakfast and Nancy would be more than willing to come and pick you two up, if that would make you feel more comfortable.'

The silence that ensued made Jason wonder if she was about to take him up on the offer. 'Do you want some kind of deposit for the towing call or something?'

'You'll be at the Bergeron's. I can settle up with you in the morning once I've had a chance to thoroughly look over the car.'

Her eyes narrowed, skepticism reflecting in them. 'Just like that.'

He nodded. 'Just like that.' He would have made the same deal with any other person in the small town. Port Landon did things a little differently, but in the end, people honored their word and they made good on their promises. Jason was a member of Port Landon, through and through.

After a moment's hesitation, her shoulders lowered slightly. 'Let me get Eden, then I'll grab my purse and lock the car up.'

'Don't worry about the car seat. I've got Carlie's in the back seat of my truck.'

Lily opened the car door and ducked inside. Jason could hear her cooing and whispering to Eden, attempting to wake her up without startling her too much.

A little voice asked, 'We here?'

Through the shuffling and moving about, Lily replied to her daughter's question. 'No, baby, we're not there yet. I don't really know where we are, but the convicts here sure are nice.'

* * *

All in all, Eden handled the rude wakeup call a lot better than Jason thought she might. Judging by Lily's raised eyebrows as she tucked the young girl into the car seat in the back of his truck and did up the buckles, she was surprised by her daughter's demure response as well.

Usually when kids met strangers, it went one of two ways—they either played the scared or shy card, or they talked their new audience's ear off. That had been Jason's experience, anyway. Eden's mild reaction to being jostled awake was in part, he guessed, to her blatant curiosity about him. The little girl's eyes, though heavy, rarely left him. She didn't say anything when he gave her a small smile and a little wave. She just watched him from the backseat unabashedly.

He tried not to notice, but Jason thought maybe Lily was watching him out of the corner of her eye, too.

It would have been funny if he didn't wonder about her reasons for it. Sure, she didn't know him and he didn't know her, and he had called in a favor for her—and offered her the benefit of the doubt that she wouldn't somehow skip town and leave him holding the bag when it came to her car and her room at Nancy's bed and breakfast.

But had the woman never had someone offer to help her out without asking for something in return?

Jason hadn't really thought about it, he'd just done it. Offered the help without thinking about it. He didn't think that made him come off like a serial killer, but … her words, not his. He didn't know her story, but he didn't think extending a friendly, helping hand was the wrong thing to do. Everyone needed a little benefit of the doubt sometimes.

'So, you live in Chicago?' He waited for her to close the passenger side door and buckle her seatbelt before he turned the key, letting the engine roar to life. He did a three-point turn in the middle of the road and headed into town, leaving the Port Landon welcome sign glowing in the blaze of his tail-lights.

Lily shook her head. 'I will, once I get there.'

He nodded like he understood, even though he didn't. 'So, you're moving there, then.'

'That's the plan.' Eyes trained out the windshield, she didn't look at him. 'My stuff is in storage right now until I find a decent long-term rental for Eden and I.'

The lampposts of Main Street glowed like fireflies up ahead in the distance. 'Staying with family?'

She turned. 'Playing Twenty Questions?' Her eyes sparkled in the dashboard lights.

'Trying to stay awake.'

'Awake is good when you're the one behind the wheel.' She went back to staring at the road in front of them.

He hadn't meant for it to sound like an interrogation, just a simple search for information disguised as innocent chatter. Badly disguised.

Jason asked himself why he cared. He didn't. Not really. It wasn't his place to be asking questions he didn't need the answers to. He promptly swallowed down any others he might have spoken aloud.

'Well, this is Port Landon.' The Main Street was vacant save for a few vehicles parked along the side of the road. The wrought iron lampposts cast light into the darkened storefronts, offering

25

shadowed glimpses of the items that would be available for purchase once the sun rose and the *Closed* signs were flipped to *Open*. 'It's not much, but it's home.'

'Have you always lived here?'

Lily's question caught him off guard. Not only because she hadn't seemed keen on being on the receiving end, but because it was personal. Related to him, not to her car or her current situation.

'Yeah, I have,' he replied honestly. 'Except for a year when I moved to Grand Rapids for school, I've never left.' He cast a glance in her direction. When Lily's gaze met his, there was something in her eyes that startled him. He couldn't figure out what it was.

'Do you regret it?' Her voice grew quieter. 'Not leaving, I mean?' The startled expression she wore transformed into wide-eyed horror. Lily was swimming in a little regret of her own after saying those words out loud.

On the outside, Jason shrugged. 'Like I said, it's home.' On the inside, he was bemused. There was more to that question than mere curiosity. There had to be.

It has nothing to do with you, he promptly reminded himself. *Leave it alone.*

Unfortunately, Port Landon was a small town, and it took little time to drive from one end to the other. He turned off Main Street and made another immediate left, revealing the massive Victorian home with its fancy gothic era charm. As he expected, the front porch was lit up and Nancy was standing in the front window, her graying hair wrapped in a silk scarf, awaiting Lily and Eden's arrival. Jason's chance to delve further into his conversation with his passenger had passed, which was likely for the best.

'Welcome to the Bergeron's bed and breakfast,' he announced, pushing the gear shifter into park. 'They're good people. You and your girl will be comfortable here.' He leaned forward, peering up toward the sky. The old house had been fully restored and meticulously maintained. It never ceased to amaze him when he

26

saw it, drawn in by its high-reaching peaks and ornate moldings. 'What do you think?'

Lily looked just as mesmerized by the old-world mansion. 'I think, for tonight, it's home.'

Chapter 3

Lily

For weeks, Lily had played this Friday morning over and over in her head, daydreaming about what it would be like. This wasn't at all what she'd had in mind.

The bed and breakfast was great—gorgeous, even. She had never slept in a king-sized four post bed before, let alone one with Egyptian cotton sheets and a plush down-filled duvet. And the pillows, there were so many of them, so soft she melted into them. Eden had crashed almost immediately upon being laid down on the bed, and the mattress was so immense that Lily had slept all night without being pushed out of bed by her daughter's sprawling limbs, a bed-stealing tactic the girl had mastered as a toddler.

Nancy Bergeron was an absolute sweetheart, too. No wonder Jason hadn't thought twice to call her in the middle of the night. Donning a comfy-looking terrycloth robe with striped pajamas peeking out from under it, the woman had incessantly doted on Eden from the moment they stepped onto the front porch. Lily had heard it all before—how she was such a precious child, that her feathery long eyelashes were worthy of envy—but it didn't slow the flood of pride that rushed through her by hearing those things once more. The woman was just as attentive to Lily herself, making sure she had towels and toiletries and a glass of water before being ushered up to her awaiting bedroom. Nancy had to be at least in her late sixties, if not early seventies, and she took her role as hostess seriously, lovingly blurring the lines between innkeeper and honorary mother figure to all who inhabited her home.

But it wasn't where she and Eden were supposed to be. Right now, she should have been hunkered down at the battered table in her hotel room, cheap coffee steaming from a paper cup in her hand while she scoured the rental ads of the *Chicago Tribune*. She should have been watching Eden play with the purple unicorn and carriage she had chosen as a parting gift from Lily's best friend, Danielle, a teary ordeal that had left both women's eyes red and swollen despite the happiness they had both hoped would be found at the end of Lily's travels. She should have been swiping through her phone to see what kind of response she had received from the countless dream job applications she had submitted while gearing up for her first day at her for-now job as a full-time barista at Starbucks the following Monday. After all, no one could waltz into the big city and scoop up a luxurious fashion design career on a whim, no matter how many years they'd yearned for it, or how determined they were to prove to their ex—and themselves—that childhood dreams could indeed come true. There might have been a time when Michael's dismissal of her passion for designing had wounded her, even held her captive behind the steel bars of her own fears and worries, all purely based on the doubts he had helped to root deeply in her mind. Lily's move to Chicago was her chance to escape the ghost of him as well as the lingering deprecation of her talents he had instilled within her. She vowed to pay her dues, start at the bottom, work her way into the industry she longed to be a part of, and be a shining example to her daughter that one's heart was worth following, always, even when it was scarred or broken.

All she had to do was make it to the city.

Instead, she was in a fancy bed and breakfast nowhere close to Chicago, holding the most delightful cup of coffee in a stoneware mug, with a car that didn't run and a hotel reservation that hadn't been cancelled in time and therefore was nonrefundable. The clerk she had spoken with the night before advised her she could dispute it with the manager when he arrived today, and seeing as the fourteen-day reservation in question had tied up a significant chunk of her money, Lily had every intention of doing exactly that. It was the only chance she had of paying for Cruella's repairs. She wasn't above begging at this point.

She was so conflicted by the unexpected turn of events, Lily didn't know whether to laugh or cry. After all, it was hard to be completely devastated when the coffee she was drinking was so unbelievably good. She had a funny feeling the silver lining was going to tarnish real quick once she made her way over to Forrester's Auto later that day and found out just how much her lack of planning had cost her.

'Coffee's pretty good, huh?' Nancy scurried into the kitchen, her arms full of bagged bagels and breads. She went to work arranging them in the oversized basket on the counter. Just another detail that made the country kitchen resemble something out of a magazine. The room was huge, but the hefty island in the middle of the work area and the massive table with ten oak chairs around it helped to rein in the size of it. White-washed cupboards lined two walls, one boasting the stainless-steel sink and matching oven, the other with a long hutch that stretched across it, set up like a shabby chic coffee bar. The fancy coffee machine and multiple kinds of roasted coffees to choose from had been a highlight of Lily's morning.

If she could call it that. The kitchen was vacant save for her and Eden, purely because the other guests had been up and gone for hours before they had managed to drag themselves out of that glorious bed. Even when she had trudged down the rich walnut stairs and saw the sunlight streaming in the windows, she didn't regret sleeping in. She'd needed it, and so did Eden.

Now, with her daughter still in the same pajamas she'd been in last night and her bouncy curls wrangled into two unruly ponytails, and with her coffee cup almost drained and the clock ticking by unforgivingly, Lily needed to figure out her next steps.

Because that's what Lily Brentwood did, she made plans and executed them. It's who she was.

'This coffee is better than pretty good, it's fantastic,' she replied. 'Where's it from?'

'It's from our very own coffeehouse,' Nancy gushed proudly. 'Down on Main Street. You should check it out while you're here. You can tell Allison I said hello.'

Lily loved Nancy's eclectic style. No one else she had ever known could pair a raspberry pink maxi dress with a beaded patchwork shawl and make it work the way she did. Her collection of silk scarves was also impressive. Today's scarf was a deep plum and yellow motif, and her grayish silver locks were pinned in an intricate knot and wrapped in it. With her graceful way of moving about, the woman resembled a hippy fairy godmother.

'Not sure I'll be here that long,' Lily replied noncommittally, more for her own benefit than anything else. 'But I will try. Thank you again, Nancy, for opening your home up to us so late last night.'

The older woman waved a hand before turning back to her meticulous bread arrangement. 'Dear, that's my job. And even if it wasn't, there isn't a thing is this crazy world that would stop me from giving somebody a roof over their head if they needed it. And Jay Forrester knows that.'

'Even for a complete stranger.' She didn't mean to sound so condescending, but there were so many factors about this—they didn't know each other, it had been the middle of the night, she opened her arms and her home without any questions

31

asked—that Lily had a hard time comprehending. The woman was a saint, there was no other way to put it. Luckily, Nancy took no offense to her skepticism.

She whirled around, clutching a bag of English muffins to her chest. 'The Forrester boy is a good judge of character. Must have seen something in you that he liked.'

There was no mistaking the glint in her eye.

Or pitied, Lily thought to herself. 'Well, I appreciate the help he's given us, too. Do you know Jason well?'

'Girl …' Nancy began, dragging out the word and making it sound like they were teenagers about to embark on a juicy gossip session while they braided each other's hair, 'I've known him since he was knee high to a grasshopper. His mother, Bettina, and I go way back. He's as good as they come, darling.'

A good judge of character. As good as they came. Jason was good. Got it.

'If you both are any indication, then I'd guess the same goes for the rest of Port Landon.' Lily smiled before tipping her mug up again.

'Now you're catching on.' Nancy winked, dusting her hands off. She stared at the tower of bread rolls and bagels fondly. 'So, where were you headed when your car broke down, Lily?'

Every time she spoke Lily's name aloud, it made Lily smile. Nancy didn't have an accent, but she pronounced it almost like *Leelee*, drawing it out and giving it a luxurious ring that had never been there before. She had a feeling the woman did that with most things in life.

'Chicago,' she replied. 'But the universe had other plans, it seems.'

'It usually does.' Nancy stopped flitting around like an exuberant butterfly long enough to perch on one of the stools near the island. 'A temporary trip, or a permanent move?'

'Permanent. It's just temporarily on hold until I can get this setback figured out.'

Nancy nodded. 'Good for you. You're absolutely right, it's merely a setback. A broken car can be fixed, and it doesn't stop you from going forward when you're able.'

She was right, although Lily hated to think about when she actually might be able to move forward. Mostly because the answer was undoubtedly a lot different compared to when she wanted to go. Which was now. 'Speaking of that, I should probably get Eden dressed and give Jason a call to see where I stand with the car repairs.'

Nancy stood. 'If you'd like, I can give you a ride to his garage. I have to pick up a few things downtown.'

'Oh, you don't have to do that,' Lily said quickly. Nancy had already done too much for her and Eden as it was.

'No one said a thing about having to do anything,' Nancy replied. 'I want to, and it's only a few blocks away. Afterward, I can either pick you up, or you can enjoy the scenic walk home. See what our tiny town has to offer.' She was already bustling about, grabbing her shoulder bag and plucking a list from the countertop.

Lily had to admit, a walk in the summer sunshine might be good for her. Eden would enjoy the outing, too. From what Jason said last night, there was no way her car was going to be ready for at least a few days, so it would probably be wise to get her bearings in the town she had unwillingly been plunked in.

'Thank you, that sounds nice.' She rose to her feet to rinse her mug. 'I'm a little scared of what Jason is going to tell me, but I guess I've got to face the music sooner or later. Once I know what I'm up against with him, then I can tell you for sure when Eden and I will be out of your hair.'

Nancy fluttered by, her shawl floating in her wake. 'Oh, Lily, it's okay. Trust me, you're the only one counting down the days.'

* * *

Forrester's Auto was a large, three-bay garage with an adjoined office on the edge of town. Nancy was right, only four blocks separated it from the bed and breakfast, and as she had driven Lily through those residential streets and onto the last road that gave way to the treed expanse behind it, Lily found she was looking forward to the walk home amongst the Victorian homes and the flourishing flower beds.

All three bay doors were closed. Hand in hand with Eden, she walked under the green and white Forrester's Auto sign and pushed open the steel door. She barely had the door closed before a loud voice called out to her.

'Hey, can I help you with something?'

Lily whirled and her gaze landed on a man in a Lakers cap, his dark, wisps of hair curling out from underneath it. She clasped Eden's hand tighter. Everything she had witnessed in Port Landon so far seemed so small. Somehow, Lily had wrongly assumed that Forrester's Auto was a one man show. She hadn't expected the office to open up into the garage bays from inside, either. 'Oh, hello. I'm actually looking for—'

'Me.' Jason appeared from underneath a mid-nineties Ford pickup, rolling across the concrete floor on a wheeled stool. 'How are you, Lily? I kind of thought you'd be here before now, so I took a look at your car this morning.' He rose, wiping his stained hands on an equally stained cloth he plucked from his toolbox.

Immediately, guilt swarmed her. Looking around, Lily saw that the first two bays were full, with vehicles jacked up on hoists, waiting to be tended to. She hadn't missed the cars and trucks sitting outside, either. One was Jason's and another probably his coworker's, but some of them were undoubtedly clients' vehicles in the queue for repairs.

He had pushed her car to the front of the line.

'I'm sorry,' she began. 'Eden and I slept in and—'

Jason held up a hand. 'No need to apologize,' he assured her. 'I didn't give you an exact appointment time. Besides, if you can avoid succumbing to Nancy's hospitality, then you're not human.' Jason crouched down. 'Hi, Eden. I met you last night, but you were pretty sleepy. Do you remember me?'

Eden glanced up at Lily, and her mother offered her an encouraging nudge. The little girl turned back toward Jason, shaking her head.

'That's okay. I'm Jason, and I'm going to help fix your mama's car.'

'What's wrong with it?' she asked, swinging her head from him up to Lily's once more.

Lily was a bit surprised by the question. She shouldn't have been, seeing as the girl had been fast asleep throughout most of last night's ordeal, but Eden was a shy child. Rarely did she acknowledge people she didn't know well, let alone ask them direct questions. Then again, maybe she was overthinking it and the question was actually directed toward her. It was hard to tell. Either way, it was Jason who responded first.

'There's a few new parts it needs in order to run good again,' he explained to her. 'If you want, there are some cool toys over by the desk that my little girl left here. You can play with them while I tell your mom about the new car parts.'

Eden followed Jason's finger as he pointed toward the red tote of toys. It took only two seconds for her to shake her head and step in closer to Lily's leg.

'Don't take it personally,' Lily chuckled. 'She's shy until she gets to know folks.'

'Carlie's the same.' Jason nodded toward the farthest garage bay. 'Ready for the not-so-great news?'

She followed him. 'You can just call it bad news, you know. I can handle it.'

Over his shoulder, he replied, 'I like to be an optimist. Because, you know, it could always be worse.'

Lily wasn't sure whether to take that as a ray of hope that it wasn't as bad as he originally thought, or that Jason Forrester was just a glass half full kind of guy, to the point of being slightly exasperating.

In the harsh fluorescent lighting, Cruella looked even worse than Lily remembered. Lifted on the hoist, the rust underneath the car was at eye level, making it a lot harder to ignore. She took a deep breath and let it out slowly. 'All right, I'm ready.'

Jason's expression announced that he didn't quite believe her, but he went on, anyway. 'My original suspicion was correct. The car needs an alternator and a new battery. And, like I said last night, that will take a few days to order in and—'

'And it's expensive,' Lily finished for him.

'It's not cheap,' he agreed.

She eyed him. 'Same difference. What else?'

'I started looking at other things. The transmission fluid lines are cracking, though I don't see evidence of an active leak. The brake pads and rotors are on the verge of worn out. There's a—'

'Wait,' Lily interjected. 'You're telling me these are all things that need to be fixed, too?'

He didn't blink. 'I'm telling you I'm shocked that this car didn't leave you on the side of the road long before last night.'

Lily felt the blood drain from her face. 'Oh, Cruella,' she muttered.

Jason's eyebrows rose. 'Cruella?'

'It's the car's name.' She waved her hand, dismissing the fact. 'Look, Jason, I don't know what to do here. I don't have the money for a long list of car repairs right now. Not on top of paying to stay at Nancy's bed and breakfast.' Heat rose in her cheeks. Her humiliation threatened to burn her up from the inside out. Without realizing it, she shook her head, disgusted by her own helplessness. But the truth was out, and she couldn't take it back.

Jason looked just as uncomfortable about her confession. It only made Lily feel worse.

'Eden,' Jason said softly, resuming his crouched stance to bring himself eye to eye with the girl. 'Can you do me a huge favor?'

The little girl bit down on her lip, uncertain, but she nodded.

'I need something out of that red tote in the office. There's a long metal car. It's a dark reddish-purple color.' He held his hands about a foot apart, showing its approximate length. 'Do you think you could go grab it for me?'

Eden's grayish blue eyes were round as she glanced up at her mother for guidance. Lily nodded, nudging her softly in the direction of the overflowing red tote.

'It's okay,' Lily promised. 'I can see you from here. Go ahead.' Her daughter reluctantly released her hand and dawdled across the concrete floor.

'I knew last night that you didn't have money for the repairs.'

Lily snapped her head toward Jason, slightly affronted. 'Yet, you towed it here and put it before all your other clients first thing this morning.' She didn't mean it in the accusatory manner it came out, but she wanted him to know she realized he had made an exception for her. She needed him to know. And if he had done it all under the ruse of helping a damsel in distress when the truth was that he wanted to make sure he made a little cash for his efforts, she was darn sure going to make him say it out loud. 'Why?'

'What was I going to do?' He raised his oil-stained hands, palms up. 'Leave you and your daughter on the side of the road in the middle of the night? You might not know me, but there's one thing I can attest to on my own behalf, Lily. I'm not that kind of man.'

Lily's throat moved as she took him in—*really* took him in. His hair was as dark as his eyes, somewhere between a deep espresso and an inky black. The smudges on his worn work pants and blue crewneck T-shirt matched his gaze. It looked as though he hadn't shaved that morning, and the stubble only accentuated the rugged curves of his cheekbones and jaw. Leather work boots covered his feet, the yellow laces tied loosely as though he liked to slip them on and off rather than retie them every time he put them on. Jason Forrester was the personification of a working man. A man who worked hard, who wasn't afraid to put in time and effort. The deepest depths of his steady gaze, however, revealed more than that. A warmth lingered there, as she had seen the prior evening. An unebbing compassion that ran deep and free.

She thought of making a quirky comment about chivalry not being dead, but Lily feared it would belittle his random act of kindness. Instead, she sighed and went with the brutally honest truth. 'I appreciate that more than you know, but it still doesn't change the fact that I don't have the money for the repairs. I can pay your towing fee right now, but that's it at the moment. My hotel reservation in Chicago was nonrefundable. I'm appealing it, but until they give me my money back, I have to make what little money I do have last. I'm not looking for sympathy, Jason, but I want to be honest with you—I'm drowning here.'

Dread filled the pit of her stomach like lead. Never one to admit defeat, it was downright painful to have to admit to him, a stranger she hadn't even known existed twenty-four hours ago, that she had taken her first real, honest-to-goodness leap of faith and fallen flat on her face.

Lily knew now that she should have just stuck to planning and organizing and preparing for everything. Absolutely everything. Instead, she had gotten ahead of herself and given herself that little bit of leeway—two weeks' worth of time to make the pieces fall into place without securing the perfect apartment beforehand—to add a dash of excitement and thrill to the move.

There wasn't a person she could think of who would ever describe her as spontaneous, but Lily had wanted to give it a shot. She wanted to live a little, not to mention see the place firsthand that she and Eden would be living in before forking over her money, and be able to look back on the gutsy move and laugh at her temporary reckless streak. She wanted to know she had taken the chance, moved on from the heartache she had endured, and walked away from her safe little life in Sherman with her head held high. She had wanted so badly to hold out hope that it was meant to be.

She never dreamed that it would work out like this.

'It's okay,' Jason said. He reached a tentative hand out as though to touch Lily's shoulder, then stopped only inches away, obviously thinking better of it. It wasn't until she locked eyes with him and saw his shocked expression through blurred vision that she realized she was barely holding back tears.

Could it get any more humiliating?

'Is there someone you can call?' Jason continued. He craned his neck in Eden's direction, watching her dig through the tote of toys.

At once, Lily knew what he was really asking. *Can you contact Eden's father for help, perhaps?* The simple answer was no, but Lily's preferred answer was that she would rather file for bankruptcy and live in a paper sack before she would ever call on Eden's dad, Michael, for anything. Not that she had the option, anyway. With no phone number or address for him, Michael was gone.

She also couldn't bring herself to call her best friend, Danielle. As the only person in Sherman that Lily considered family since her mother passed away a few years ago, admitting that she had crashed and burned before making it to the Chicago city limits would only succeed in making the defeat more real and breaking her best friend's heart in the process. Danielle believed in Lily. Maybe even more than Lily believed in herself. She couldn't do that. To her friend, or to herself. Not yet.

'No.' Lily shook her head. 'This is my mistake, so I'm going to have to fix it, somehow.'

'You really don't do well with asking for help, do you?' Jason arched a brow. No malice laced his tone, just an observation he felt compelled to voice. 'Or allowing others to help,' he added.

'I try to avoid needing other people's help, if that's what you're asking.' She breathed in deeply, feeling confident that she had sufficiently reined in her tears for the time being.

Shoulders shaking, Jason chuckled. 'That wasn't what I was

asking, actually, but I think you answered my question, anyway.' He reached for another rag from the top of his toolbox, this one cleaner than the last, wiping his hands. 'The thing is, whether you want my help or not, I think you might need it.'

Lily glared at him. It was like pulling teeth to have to confess it out loud. 'Well, you're not wrong.'

His mouth pressed into a hard line as Jason fought to contain his amusement. 'Careful, that sounds slightly optimistic,' he joked. 'I'm about due for a coffee break. How about you sit with me for fifteen minutes or so and we can talk this through? I might have a few ideas that'll help you come up with a plan to get you back on the road to Chicago. And if not, at the very least, you've got a few things off your chest and had a decent cup of coffee. I've got apple juice and cookies for Eden. Sound good?'

Everything in her was telling her to turn him down. Yet, that same inner voice was also telling her to do it out of principle, not because she actually wanted or needed to. She didn't know Jason Forrester, but her gut instincts were telling her she could trust him. Knowing she could trust someone and actually doing it were two different things, however. Trusting her gut instincts also seemed to be a recipe for disaster lately. 'Is the coffee from the coffeehouse downtown?'

Surprised, Jason nodded. 'Yeah, why do you ask?'

'No reason,' she said. 'Count me in.'

Chapter 4

Jason

He could tell Lily was going through something. He didn't know what it was, and he certainly had no right to ask. In fact, it would have been simpler to fix the car and leave the rest of it up to her.

In a perfect world, at least. But this wasn't a perfect world, and he wasn't a perfect man.

And that was before she had come two seconds away from crying.

If there was one thing Jason couldn't handle, it was the tears of a woman. Whether from the eyes of a four-year-old girl or a thirty-something woman, seeing those wet droplets of emotion splash onto the cheeks of a lady broke something inside him and weakened him. He could tell she needed help and was likely too proud to ask for it. And as soon as he saw the telltale glint brimming her eyelids, threatening to overflow and essentially drop Jason to his knees, he would have done anything, said anything, if it meant it would prevent Lily one more second of that kind of pain.

Luckily, he had managed to come up with the suggestion of

coffee and a meaningful conversation. Isn't that what women lived for, caffeine and talking about their feelings? He didn't know anymore—it had been a long time since he'd thought about what women wanted in any way, shape, or form—but he wagered it was a good enough guess.

Judging by Lily's acceptance, he had guessed right.

The office attached to the garage bays was a mess. Worse than a mess. Besides the scattered toys and stuffed animals on the floor beside the desk, courtesy of Eden, who looked about as delighted as any child could despite obviously forgetting which toy Jason had sent her in there to find, the entire room was chaotic organization. And Jason only allowed himself to call it that because, in spite of the work orders and invoices piled high on his desk in towering piles and the whirlwind of random auto parts and leftover coffee cups and Post-it notes that clung to every surface, he knew where everything was, what was going on within the walls of his business, and where to turn if he needed answers about something.

He wished things were that easy when it came to Lily Brentwood. He had felt it the moment he pulled his pickup truck up behind her car the night before. Even on the side of the road in the middle of the night, Jason could sense the urgency thrumming through the woman's veins, the vibrancy that lit a fire inside her and propelled her forward toward her goal. He felt just as strongly the disappointment she harbored that her plans weren't working out as she had expected. Disappointment in the situation, and in herself. Maybe that's why part of him wanted to help the woman and her daughter get through this fiasco, even when he knew he should stay out of it. Nothing good ever came from blaming oneself for things beyond their control.

Take your own advice, he silently chastised as he placed a new filter in the coffeemaker and set it up to brew. Just as quickly as the thought entered his mind, Jason pushed it away. This wasn't about him. It was about a woman and her daughter getting where they needed to go, nothing more.

'Do you want to tell me what's in Chicago that you're so eager to get to?' Jason phrased the question carefully, giving Lily the opportunity to shut him down with a simple no. He was just as cautious in his tone, maintaining nonchalance. This didn't need to sound like an interrogation, and he didn't need to know the answer. Even if he was wholeheartedly curious.

Lily took a seat on one of the vinyl chairs near the door. They were rarely used, since customers usually called ahead to see if their vehicle was ready to go instead of waiting around for it, but they were the same battered chairs that had sat in this room when Forrester's Auto was once Robinson's Auto. When the Robinsons sold the business to him, he kept them in the same spot they had been when he was a kid. Both chairs were ripped and worn, but they were a reminder of days gone by. Jason hadn't known he was a sucker for nostalgia until he had tried to replace them.

'Not much, actually.'

The sardonic scoff that accompanied Lily's words forced Jason to turn around. 'What do you mean?' Whatever he had expected her to say, it wasn't that.

'I made a mistake,' she sighed. 'I thought I was taking the bull by the horns and being spontaneous and …' She shook her head. 'Instead, all I was being was stupid and irresponsible.'

Jason listened to the coffeemaker sputter for a second, trying to catch up. 'I'm not sure I follow, Lily. Start from the beginning, maybe?'

'The beginning.' She chuckled under her breath, but there was no humor in it. 'I'm not even sure where that is.'

Defeat emanated from the woman in waves, floating across the room and twisting Jason's insides. 'You were headed to Chicago,' he tried again. 'From where?'

'Sherman.'

Nodding, he mentally calculated that she had made approximately half the trip before her car decided to stop running. 'That's where you're from, then.'

Lily shrugged as though there was no escaping that fact. 'Born and raised.'

Jason didn't wait for the coffee to be finished brewing. He pulled two mugs from the shelf underneath the wheeled cart that housed the makeshift coffee bar and filled them, adding a generous dollop of hazelnut creamer—his favorite—to both. It would be stronger than he usually made it, but he had a sinking suspicion he might need it.

'So, you're a small-town girl, too.' He meant it as a compliment. Jason passed the mug to her and Lily inhaled the scent of it. She didn't try to hide her scowl.

'I guess I am.'

Adding the creamer had been an act of habit. 'Not a fan of that fact, or is it the hazelnut creamer?' He didn't want to sound argumentative, but she wasn't giving him much to go on. He needed to get beyond her one-word answers and find out something that wasn't trivial.

Lily took a sip of her coffee, savored it, then continued. 'The creamer is perfect, thank you. And I never said I wasn't a fan of my hometown. I just ... it was time for a change.'

'And Chicago was that change.' He realized his mistake as soon as he said it. '*Is* that change.'

'That was the plan.'

Jason cast a glance through the open door into the garage bays, but Branch didn't seem to be paying them any mind. Jason knew him better than that, though. They had been best friends since they were kids. Just because it seemed like Branch Sterling wasn't paying attention, that didn't mean he wasn't hanging on their every word.

Eden didn't seem to be paying much mind to their conversation, either—she beamed at Lily a few times, showing off a plastic fire truck or a furry elephant toy before diving back into the tote to unearth more treasures—so Jason took the plunge and continued.

'Mind if I ask what the plan was?'

Everything about the woman tightened immediately. Her features seemed to draw in on themselves, her shoulders tensing as her spine grew rigid as a fencepost. Watching her steel herself against his intrusion of privacy, Jason didn't think she would answer. After a long, deeply silent pause, she surprised him.

'We're starting over, me and Eden.' Lily's throat moved, and she looked anywhere but at him directly. 'Enough was enough, so we were getting out of Sherman. I saved up as much as I could, packed up what we needed, and got rid of what we didn't. Then, we left. I had a job waiting for me on Monday.' She winced. 'Have a job waiting for me.'

Jason nodded, though it created more questions than answers. 'Why Chicago?'

'Because I applied for a handful of jobs there that I wanted, took a job for now that I needed, and was hoping to live in a place that allowed for more room to grow—to *live*—than my hometown did.'

He was pretty sure it was the most honest thing she had said to him yet. However, Jason was also confident that her ideas of how quickly and easily she was going to start over in the big city were a little on the idealistic side. Or, more accurately, the naïve side. 'So, you have an apartment you're waiting to get into?'

'Not exactly.' She offered him a fleeting glance. 'I booked a cheap hotel for two weeks to give myself time to find one. There were lots available to rent in the newspaper and online, and I've spoken to a realtor about some showings, but I didn't want to commit to one until I'd seen it firsthand.'

'You really meant it when you said you were getting out of Sherman, huh?'

He heard her words echo in his mind. *Enough was enough.* There was more to it, he was sure of it.

'I wanted out,' she said simply. 'So much so that I made a slightly impulsive decision for the first time in my life, and it led me here.'

45

'Well, that part ain't so bad, is it?' Jason ducked his head to meet her gaze, hoping for a ghost of a smile. 'There are worse things than being stuck in Port Landon.'

'I'm broke and homeless,' she stated, staring at him as though she couldn't understand through which lens he was looking at her situation. 'My car died, and it's going to be days until I can get my money back from the hotel, if they refund me at all. I've got a job that I'm supposed to be starting on Monday, and a daycare spot that Eden's supposed to be attending. I'm not seeing the upside to all this, Jason.'

'You made an impulsive decision—your words, not mine.' He held up his hands in mock surrender. 'And didn't plan for all the curveballs the universe could throw at you. There's no shame in that. You're not the first person to act on impulse and have it not work out as planned, and you certainly won't be the last. The upside is that your car broke down here, in a town where folks know what it's like to make mistakes. We won't hold it against you.' He flashed her a grin, hoping to lighten the mood. 'Not to mention, I just happen to know how to fix your car, and Nancy just happens to be good friends with my mother. She's not going to kick you out, Lily.'

'I don't expect anybody to help me out for free.'

'Good, because that's not what anybody's doing,' he reasoned. 'Around here, people like to help other people out of the goodness of their own hearts, but I've got a funny feeling you don't expect that, either.'

Lily worried her bottom lip, obviously weighing her response carefully. 'I don't mean to sound ungrateful, I just don't want to put anyone out. I don't need anyone's charity—'

'It's not charity,' he interjected. 'You said you'd pay me for the tow call and Nancy for the room. Maybe once you appeal the hotel's refund policy and deal with the things that are waiting for you in Chicago, things won't seem as bad as you think they are. That said, you've got no one else you want to call.' He phrased

46

it that way because her current fighting arguments were making him think there might be someone she *could* call, but no one she would. 'So, the best I can do for you is fix your car whenever you're ready for me to do it, and make sure you guys have a place to stay while I do it. If you've got a better idea, I'm all ears.'

Lily opened her mouth, no doubt to maintain her independence once more, but she was cut off by a shrill cheer from the other side of the desk.

'Found it!' Eden scrambled to her feet and raced toward Jason, a metal diecast car clutched in her hands. She had finally remembered her original task. 'The car!'

Setting his coffee down beside the coffeemaker, Jason crouched down to meet the little girl eye to eye. Gone was her initial shyness, replaced by an exuberance that simmered at the surface, reminding him of a pot about to reaching its boiling point. 'That's the one! Does it look familiar?'

Eden stood before him, her face contorted in confusion and thought. He had to raise a hand to cover the amusement on his face. She was so expressive, so alive with wonder. It was what he loved most about Carlie at this age, too. Eden shook her head vehemently. 'No, it's yours!'

Jason reached out and let his fingertips trail along the top of the classic car model. It wasn't meant to be a child's toy per se, but Carlie got a kick out of it, so he had let her keep it in the toy bin. He expected Eden would find some joy in it, too, once she realized what it was. So would Lily.

'How about we show your mama? See if she recognizes it.'

Eden scurried across the floor to her mother, arms outstretched to show off her prize. 'See it?'

Lily smiled at her daughter, holding the squirming child at bay as Eden held the car up in front of her eyes.

'I see it,' she assured her, 'But I'm not sure I understand why Jason had you go get it, baby.' Her gaze flicked to him in silent askance.

'Because I want you to hold on to it for me for a bit.'

'Why?' She didn't take the car from Eden, and Jason doubted the little girl would let go of it if she tried. But she stared at it, searching for whatever made it so important.

Jason pointed casually at the toy. 'That is a replica of a 1974 Panther de Ville Saloon,' he replied. 'Cruella's car in the cartoon movie, *101 Dalmatians*. My daughter adores that movie.'

Now, Lily was staring at the car intently, as though it might do tricks at any moment. 'Then why do you want me to hold on to it for you?' she asked, bemused.

Jason shrugged. 'I want to trade my Cruella for yours.' He was enjoying this, seeing the realization dawn on her face that it was an awfully intriguing coincidence that she broke down there and ended up on his proverbial doorstep, quite possibly the only place in the world where someone else harbored a beloved car named Cruella, albeit for different reasons. 'Temporarily,' he added. 'While I fix yours, while you stay at Nancy's, and while we wait to see what happens with your hotel refund. Can we at least agree on that much?'

He could see how much it pained her to have to consider his offer. Jason respected her independence, and her will to stand on her own two feet. Hell, he admired it. But even the strongest folks needed a little help sometimes, and what made them stronger was knowing when to ask for it. He didn't know much about her, and his gut told him she had been let down enough in life that she found it hard to know when to accept generosity.

But Jason knew himself better than anyone. No matter what, he was a man of his word. He could at least show her that not everyone was an impending disappointment to be avoided, before she went on her merry way toward the city.

Lily gingerly touched the front fender of the model car. 'Agreed,' she said. 'Temporarily. But I've got to ask. Why do you have a toy from *101 Dalmatians*? It doesn't look like something a preschooler would choose.'

Jason held her gaze, thinking. Debating. 'I've got to get back to work, but let me show you something first.' And he did need to get back to the countless repairs that weren't going to fix themselves. But after that miniscule victory, Lily's leap of faith, he decided to take a leap of his own. Mostly because he didn't think his mind was going to get back to work nearly as fast as his hands, even if he knew it should.

And that made him wonder if convincing Lily to stay in Port Landon was really miniscule at all.

Chapter 5

Lily

Lily disliked how correct Jason's summation was. She didn't have any other options. It hurt to know she brought this on herself, but somehow, it didn't sting as much when the offer of help was coming from someone whose kind eyes sparkled the way his did.

She scolded herself for the thought. *The guy's being nice about it, but he wants the profit from his efforts, nothing more, no matter how glittery his eyes might seem.*

Besides, she sure as heck didn't want anything more, either. There was no denying Jason was attractive, in a rugged kind of way, but Lily didn't need another man with alluring eyes and all the right words to make her believe things that weren't real. She had done that once and all it had left her with was a shattered heart and more debt racked up than she knew how to deal with.

Jason had a daughter, anyway. He didn't wear a wedding ring, but that didn't mean anything. Maybe he didn't wear one because of his job; lots of people did that. The man was probably happily married and living in some quaint little cul-de-sac with two point five kids and a puppy.

Goodness, what has gotten into you? She did not need to be thinking about this. About him. Lily had sworn off men at the same time she swore off her hometown of Sherman, and that was that. It might have been a man who broke her heart, but it was the town that had reminded her of it everywhere she turned.

She had effectively gotten away from both. Now, if she could escape the painful memories as easily, she would be well on her way to freedom.

Except, she wasn't on her way to anywhere. She was in Port Landon for the foreseeable future. And even if the kindness she had experienced thus far wasn't completely genuine, she reluctantly agreed with Jason—the town didn't seem like the worst place to be stranded.

Time would tell, though.

'Where are we going?' Lily had let Eden keep the model car in her hand as they followed Jason out the office door and behind the building. To her surprise, another detached two-door garage stood behind the business. It didn't match the steel siding of the building in front of it. It was newer, resembling a garage that would be in someone's backyard or attached to a residence instead of hidden behind a repair shop.

She was starting to question her serial killer theory from the night before. 'Should I be concerned that there's no one around to hear us scream for help?' Lily was joking … mostly. Still, she glanced around and mentally calculated the distance to the office door.

'I think I'm the one who should be concerned that you still think I'm a criminal.' He chuckled. 'I'm obviously doing something wrong.' Jason pulled a key from his pocket and unlocked the door at the side of the garage. Cheekily, he stepped back and waved a theatric hand, gesturing her and Eden inside. 'Ladies first.'

There was no mistaking the mischievous smirk he wore. 'You think you're so funny,' she said, shaking her head. 'Not a chance. Convicts go first.'

Laughing, Jason disappeared into the dark garage. A second later, the overhead fluorescent lights blazed brightly. 'How about now?'

She stepped inside. Immediately, Eden lurched forward, placing her small hands on the black fabric cover that hid a car from view.

'What's this?' Eden exclaimed just as Lily heard the toy in her hand bang against the covered car.

'Oh gosh, Eden, be careful!' One hand around her daughter's middle, she hauled the little girl away from the vehicle. For all she knew, there was a multimillion-dollar supercar underneath the thin material, just waiting for its fancy paint job to be scratched by the innocent movements of a five-year-old.

A line of lights blinked on at the back of the room, and Jason stepped forward. 'It's okay, Lily. She can't hurt it any more than it already is.'

'Sounds like a challenge to me,' she quipped. A challenge she wasn't prepared to pay for. 'What are we doing in here?'

The garage was one huge room, harshly lit and so spotless that she wondered if Jason ever came in here. The back wall was lined with multiple red toolboxes that were the same height she was. The floor was concrete, just as it was inside the repair shop, but rubber matting stretched across the surface, muffling her footsteps as she wandered around the covered vehicle that took up most of the left side of the garage.

'You asked me why I had Cruella de Ville's car,' Jason replied. 'I figured rather than tell you, I could show you.'

'Show me what?'

'Eden, want to help me pull this cover off?' Jason's fingers gripped the edge of the black fabric, but he waited.

'Yeah!' Eden took a step, then stopped, second guessing whether she should or not. Her pleading gray eyes were round as saucers.

'It's okay.' Lily motioned for her to go on.

In one fell swoop, and with the echoed laughter of her daughter as Jason picked her up in one strong arm, they tugged the cover past the cab, unveiling the car hidden beneath. Dropping the cover to the floor, a few pieces of rust flaked off with it. Lily wasn't sure whether to cringe at the falling pieces or the overall state of the classic car itself.

She pointed. 'Is that—'

'Cruella's car!' Eden cheered.

And it was. At least, she thought it was, or would be if it were restored to its former glory. As it stood, the car that sat before her was rusted badly along the fenders and missing a headlight. And those were only the things she could describe. Pieces and parts rested against the tires, awaiting their turn to be installed. Regardless of the disrepair, there was no mistaking it.

Jason Forrester owned his own Cruella.

'Not quite.' Jason patted Eden's head, smiling from ear to ear. 'It's actually a Panther Lima, not a De Ville,' he explained. 'And it's a 1981 model. They weren't produced in '74.'

'Looks pretty close to the car in the movie to me,' Lily said.

Circling it, she was in awe. Having a car in front of her like this wasn't something she experienced every day. Heck, she didn't know if she had ever seen one like it before in real life. Despite its age and weathered appearance, it was a sight to behold. 'And you just happen to have one of these cars sitting in your garage.' It wasn't a question, though her voice raised at the end of the sentence, sounding dubious. It all seemed too surreal, too convenient.

Jason chuckled, watching Eden run her hands along the chipped paint near the door handle. 'Trust me, when you referred to your old car as Cruella, I was thinking the exact same thing. I had to show you this old girl.'

There was no mistaking the adoration in his eyes as he stared at the classic car. Lily didn't think he saw the rust or dents or flaking paint when he looked at it. In his mind, he saw the gleaming beauty it had once been and could be again, all shiny paint and polished steel. 'Why is it sitting out here, covered up?'

Jason glanced up from the car. His expression made Lily feel like he just noticed she was still standing there. Wherever he had been a moment ago, it wasn't there, with her. 'It's my grandfather's,' he explained, then flinched. '*Was* my grandfather's. He's in a nursing home in North Springs now, with dementia.'

'I'm so sorry, Jason.'

A somber nod was his response. 'He signed over the car to me when I first got my driver's license, long before his illness.' He spoke so fast that Lily's chest constricted, pained that he felt he had to prove he had been given the car while his grandfather was still of sound mind.

'You've had this car since you were sixteen?'

'On paper.' Jason crouched and boosted Eden, whose hands were cupped against the murky glass windows trying desperately to see inside. Knowing the little girl's vivid imagination, Lily figured she was probably checking for spotted puppies or one of Cruella de Ville's red heels. 'She was in Grandpa's garage when I was growing up. His most prized possession. I can still remember when he hauled it home on a trailer. My grandmother was livid—she'd known nothing about it until it showed up in the driveway.' He stifled a laugh.

'Oh, I'll bet that was an interesting conversation.' Lily could almost picture it. She was pretty sure Jason was, reliving every moment and cherishing it as it played out in his mind.

'You have no idea,' he chuckled, shifting his weight as Eden squirmed in his arms. 'Grandma Mary-Jean didn't know it at the time, but I'd known all about it. To be honest, I'm thirty years old and I still haven't told her that.'

Lily's eyes bulged. 'You're scared of your elderly grandmother?'

'Petrified,' he laughed. 'The woman's the best thing ever, but she's as feisty as a wildcat.'

For the first time since her car broke down the night before, Lily realized she was enjoying herself. Normal conversation with someone about normal things. It was hardly a mundane topic seeing as the car and its previous owner meant the world to this man, but the back and forth was easy, unrushed. It was hard to believe she hadn't known Jason Forrester existed twenty-four hours ago. 'So, you're going to fix it, then?'

Lowering Eden to the floor, Jason tilted his head. 'Grandpa and I always talked about it. You know how it goes, though. Life gets in the way, time passes, and before you know it, the opportunity is gone.'

Another ache pierced her chest. 'You can still do it, though,' she said, softer this time. 'You've got the car, and those are obviously parts for it.' She pointed at the pieces leaned against the cracked tires. 'You could still make it shine.'

This time when his gaze met hers, it was like he was trying to figure her out. 'Who's the optimistic one now?' His smile was crooked as he waved a hand. 'Trust me, I'd love to restore her. Time is a factor, unfortunately. And every time I tell myself I'm going to get started and actually do it, I talk myself out of it or something comes up.'

'Oh, come on, it can't be that hard.' She leaned down and pointed at one of the parts resting on the floor. 'You just put this metal piece over the rusty piece, and slap some paint on this here front thingamabob …' She grinned at him. 'See, piece of cake.'

He took the bait, his ever-tightening features easing into softer contours. 'Wow, I didn't know you were so mechanically inclined.'

Lily raised her eyebrows, thankful for the shift to a more lighthearted topic. 'What, like it's hard?' She stepped to the left, pressing a finger against a curved piece of sheet metal. 'You just put this whatchamacallit—'

He crossed his arms, amused, and closed the gap between them. 'The caustic panel,' he corrected her.

'That's what I said. You put the caustic panel here, and replace this rounded thingy—'

'Spheric widget.'

'Right, the spheric widget,' she continued. 'Then, you put the—'

Lily was hoping she could remember all the part names he was teaching her for future reference, attempting to convert them to memory when another voice echoed through the room.

'There you are.'

Both she and Jason whirled around as though they had been caught red-handed. Doing what, she wasn't sure, but having the sudden interruption in their unexpected playfulness made Lily's cheeks burn. The expression on Branch's face as he stood in the doorway only added to her embarrassment. He seemed to be just as confused by their close proximity as she was. She didn't remember Jason moving closer, but now there was less than a foot between them, with her pointing at car parts and his gaze sparkling as he named them for her.

She took a step back as though she had been scalded, which probably made her look even guiltier than she felt.

Branch adjusted his Lakers cap. 'Benji's on the phone,' he advised Jason. 'About tomorrow's shift. Want me to tell him you're busy?' He emphasized the last word, drawing it out like it meant something more. Like he knew it was something more.

Jason remained unfazed, though he took a step back, too, tucking his hands into his pockets. 'I'll be right in. Just got to cover up Cruella again.'

Uncomfortable in the sudden tension, Lily blurted, 'Jason was just showing me the … I mean, he was teaching me about caustic panels and spheric widgets on this old car.'

Branch's eyebrows rose. 'Say what now?'

'The caustic panels,' she sputtered, desperate to make him understand that it had been a harmless venture out to the garage. With one finger, she pointed at the curved metal piece to clarify.

Jason's coworker stared at her as if she had grown a second head. 'The caustic panels,' he repeated slowly, testing the words out on his tongue.

'Yeah,' Lily said, nonplussed. She stabbed a finger in the direction of the round piece beside it. 'And the spheric widget.' Her gaze snapped from Branch to Jason, just in time to see Jason's pursed lips burst open and release a loud, unabashed laugh.

Realization dawned on her. 'Oh my gosh, you were making it all up!'

Jason buckled over, laughing even harder when Eden rounded the corner of the car, spurred on by his genuine amusement, and began to laugh with him. 'I didn't know you were going to actually use the information I gave you!' he managed to get out. Tears glittered at the corners of his eyes.

Undoubtedly seven shades of crimson, Lily stared at him with widened eyes. With Eden joining in, and Branch trying hard to stifle his own laughter, she was outnumbered, three to one. It shouldn't have been funny. It shouldn't have been absolutely, positively hilarious.

But it was. Even to her.

Her first strangled chuckle bubbled up from her throat. 'Oh, Jason, you are going to pay dearly for that.'

It only made them laugh harder. By the time it died down, Lily was sure her sides were going to split in two. She hadn't laughed like that in ages. Especially not at her own expense.

'Give me a second and I'll be right in to talk to Benji,' Jason announced finally, reaching for the black cover.

Branch gave a slight nod, but he stayed rooted in the doorway. Lily could see the faint upturn of the corners of his mouth from where she stood. 'Haven't seen that old car in ages, Jay. You never did tell me, what's the special occasion?'

Something passed between the two men, silent but clear. Lily didn't understand it, but judging by Branch's bright eyes, alight with unmasked humor, he did. In the aftermath of their unadulterated laughing fit, the seriousness of their unspoken communication caught Lily off guard.

'Tell Benji I'll be right there,' Jason said again, the faintest edge in his voice this time.

His coworker chuckled and disappeared out into the sunshine, closing the garage door behind him with a loud click that echoed in the ensuing silence.

Jason went about covering up the car. Lily was surprised at the sadness she felt, watching as it disappeared once again beneath the opaque black fabric, hidden away from the world. A car with that much class—that much history—deserved to be on display for everyone to see.

Especially when it meant as much to Jason as it did.

'Why did your coworker ask you if it was a special occasion?' The moment the question left her lips, she regretted it. Not because she wasn't curious, but because her gut told her there was history between the two men, and that his coworker's question had ruffled some feathers. She didn't relish the idea of adding to it.

Jason continued to drape the fitted cover over the car. 'That was just Branch being Branch. I don't show Cruella to many people, that's all. I doubt half the town even knows I still own her.'

'Can we drive her?' Eden piped up, tugging on Jason's shirt hem.

Instantly, Lily felt bad, hoping the simple question didn't pour salt in a proverbial wound. Her daughter's innocence shone like a diamond. What it must be like to look at a rusted old car through the eyes of a child and see the shiny showstopper it might someday be. The way her daughter referred to the car as *her* rather than *it*, mimicking Jason's term of endearment, wasn't lost on Lily, either. 'Eden—'

'You know what?' Jason ran a hand through his hair, offering the little girl a crooked grin. 'Someday I'll fix 'er all up and we can take her for a spin. It might take me a while, but someday we'll be able to drive her around town. Sound good?' He held out a hand, which Eden promptly high-fived.

'Yeah!' she exclaimed.

Lily cringed inwardly. It was obvious that Jason meant well with his response, but she could already bet that Eden was going to ask again and again about their upcoming ride, waiting as impatiently as a five-year-old could for someday to come—a someday that they wouldn't be in town to see.

'There's no rush,' she added, seeking out her daughter's hand and hoping to level out the empty promise. 'Jason's got lots of work to do, Eden. For now, looks like you've got your own Cruella to hang on to. As long as it's still okay that you've got it.' She added the last part, giving Jason an out in case he had rethought his kind gesture.

Pulling the final corner of the cover into place, the Panther Lima disappeared. 'Of course, it's okay,' he replied.

'Your daughter won't mind?'

He paused, mulling over his response carefully. 'Honestly, Carlie's only here every second weekend. She lives in North Springs with her mama.' He cleared his throat, and when he spoke again, the tinge of sadness was gone from his voice. 'You hang on to her, Eden. That way, it'll be a fair trade when I get your mama's car back to her in working order.'

'Okay.' Eden stared down at the toy in her hands like it was a cherished memento she was never going to let out of her sight. To her, maybe it was.

Lily, however, wasn't focused on the toy at all. She was still a few sentences behind, processing the bombshell she hadn't expected. Jason's daughter didn't live with him full time, and he wasn't with Carlie's mother anymore. Not only that, but there was no mistaking the pain that coated every word as he had admitted it. Lily could hear the truth just as clearly as if Jason had enunciated every syllable himself—the split hadn't been amicable, and he would give anything to have his daughter around each day. Her heart broke for the man standing in front of her, and she reached out and touched Eden's silky curls, suddenly desperate to confirm she was still there, within arm's reach.

'Well, it sounds like I'm needed in the shop.' Jason dusted his hands off. 'We're good, then? I mean, you'll let me know when to order those parts, once you've talked to the hotel about a refund, and we'll see what Nancy has to say about you two staying at her place?'

Lily found herself nodding before she had even fully thought it through. While she could only pray that the manager of the Starbucks would give her a few days' leeway to deal with this mishap and that the daycare spot could be held, she reminded herself that it wasn't like the recruiters in Chicago that she had submitted design job applications to were blowing up her phone. She shrugged. 'We're good. Besides, I need time to get you back for making me look like a fool in front of your coworker.'

'Branch,' he corrected her. 'Call him Branch. He's been my best friend since we were kids—coworker sounds way too formal. And, as funny as it was to hear you say those made-up terms out loud, it'll be even funnier to watch you try to retaliate. Bring it on, Lily. I'm ready.' He held up his hands, waving his fingers inward.

Lily chuckled at his *bring it on* gesture. So, that was that, then. She was going to stay in Port Landon with the hope that she could come up with the funds for this ruggedly handsome man to fix her car. This ruggedly handsome man who made her smile and laugh.

Jason might be ready, but she wasn't sure she was.

Chapter 6

Jason

Before yesterday, Jason had all but given up on a lot of things. One of them was Cruella.

His grandfather loved that car. Still did on the days when he could remember her. Even as an adolescent, Jason understood the love a man could have for a vehicle—he had felt it right alongside his Grandpa Wes.

Jason wasn't lying. The day Cruella showed up in the driveway on a trailer, his grandmother had been on the verge of a conniption fit. It wasn't that she had anything against the car, but his grandfather had failed to mention it, knowing Mary-Jean would bombard him with a list of other things that the money could have been used for. Other rational, more logical things. Wesley Forrester had saved her the trouble, deciding it was easier to ask forgiveness than permission. What his grandfather never realized, Jason thought, was that his grandmother understood the relationship between a man and his car, too. More than once, Jason had caught her watching him as he tinkered away on the old Panther, hood up and hands blackened with grease, and he had seen the

61

same adoration in her eyes that Grandpa Wes reserved for only three things in life—his wife, his car, and Jason himself.

It's how Jason ended up with Cruella in the first place. Even before his grandfather was diagnosed with Alzheimer's, it was an unspoken agreement—or, if it was spoken of, Jason had never been privy to the actual conversation. Wesley's beloved grandson would get the car they had spent so much time dreaming of, and so much energy planning to completely rebuild.

A complete rebuild that didn't happen in time. Thinking about it, even all these years later, got to Jason. He stored Cruella away in his garage, carefully and lovingly, in exactly the same state of disrepair she'd been in when his grandfather was admitted to the nursing home in North Springs, purely because it hurt so much to look at her.

Until today. He knew that's what Branch was getting at when he asked what the special occasion was. As Jason's oldest friend, he knew what the Panther Lima meant to him, and he knew that every time he headed into the garage to unveil the car and get to work on restoring it, he rarely got the cover off before giving up and deciding it was just too hard to do. In his mind, it would always be his grandfather's car, and alone, he would never do it justice.

Then, a woman called him in the middle of the night because her own Cruella had broken down. Jason didn't know what drove him to show her the Panther Lima, or to give her little girl the model car and practically promise her a ride in the real car someday, but he had. He'd done all those things, and he didn't know why he wasn't riddled with the usual guilt that accompanied the reminder of all the times he'd said he would work on it and didn't.

Branch seemed to think he knew, though.

'You're interested in her,' his best friend told him once he made it back into the repair shop. Lily and Eden had ventured off, intent on walking back to the bed and breakfast rather than taking him up on his offer to drive them there. It was a relatively short walk, and the warm summer sunshine was a bonus, but he had felt compelled to offer, anyway.

Once they'd left, he retreated inside the shop and headed straight for the phone in the office. He had known what was coming when he faced Branch, therefore he put off his friend's assumptions by calling Benji back. The phone call hadn't taken long enough for Branch to get sufficiently distracted by his work, evidently.

'You're out of your mind,' Jason grumbled, passing by him. 'I called Benji. He's not coming in tomorrow. He's got an appointment with the bank about buying McGee's farm.'

Benji Carson worked at Forrester's Auto part-time on paper, but the kid—he was in his early twenties, but both Branch and Jason referred to him as a kid regardless, being the youngest in their trio—had been working full-time hours since Jason's other mechanic quit last fall. It had been a blessing when Branch returned to Port Landon last December and decided to stay permanently after rekindling a relationship with his high school sweetheart. His mechanical aptitude was welcomed and desperately needed in the repair shop. Not that Benji couldn't keep up. Quite the contrary, actually, but the kid was still working through his automotive technician apprenticeship, and he still had one more semester of trade school to complete in Lansing. Benji had big dreams though, for a man his age, and he had every intention of staying in town. If and when he was ready to make his full-time employee status official, there would be a place for him at Forrester's Auto.

'Good for him,' Branch replied, grunting as he tugged hard on a wrench. The rusted bolt relented under the force. 'The more power to him. The more power to you, too, by the way. About time you noticed somebody else. After Natalie—'

'Branch.' He turned what he hoped was a withering look on his friend. 'Trust me, you're reading way too much into this.'

'I'm just saying, no one would blame you for getting back out there and trying to meet someone.'

Jason sighed heavily. Branch made it sound like he needed to put together his résumé and cover letter and start submitting applications to worthy individuals or something. Like there was a vast pool of candidates beating down the door to meet a single father with a four-year-old daughter. Like there was a market for men who had forgotten how it felt to trust someone openly and completely with their heart. Hell, maybe there was, but he wouldn't know about it since he had purposely steered clear of the dating world since Carlie's mother left him two years ago. But if there was such a market, Jason wasn't interested in being tagged as available.

'You're barking up the wrong tree.' Picking up the tools he had discarded when Lily showed up, he ducked back under the chassis of the car he'd been working on. 'I'm helping someone who's car broke down. That's my job.'

When his friend didn't respond, Jason thought maybe he had gotten the hint and let the conversation drop. That was, until he peered out from beneath the wheel well and saw Branch standing there, staring at him with raised eyebrows as he wiped his hands with a rag.

'You showed her the Panther,' he said easily. 'That's got to mean something.'

Jason pointed toward the white Corolla in the next bay. 'She calls her own car Cruella. I showed her the Panther because they had the same name, nothing more. It's a joke.' The last sentence tasted horrible on his tongue. Branch was well aware that there was nothing regarding his grandfather's car that Jason would joke about.

'That's why you gave her kid the toy car?' Again, more disbelief clouded his friend's gaze. 'And offered to call Nancy for her?'

'What would you have done?' Jason snapped. Not out of anger, but frustration. This conversation was going nowhere, as were

Branch's allegations. 'I told her I'd wait until I heard from her to fix her car. Money's tight. So, yeah, I offered to talk to my mom's friend for her. To help her out. They're in a town they've never been in before.'

Branch dropped the rag on the toolbox beside him and tossed his hands up in surrender. 'And is that what you're going to do? Wait until you hear from her before you order those parts?'

Jason stared at him. Damn him for knowing him so well. Too well.

'That's what I thought.' Branch reached for the work order he'd been working on. 'I never said you made the wrong call, man. All I'm saying is that I think you saw something you liked in Lily, and that's not a bad thing. Even if your mind can't admit it, maybe you're more ready than you realize to give someone new a chance.'

'Thank you for that riveting inspirational speech. Can we get back to work now?'

Leave it to his best friend to find a second chance at love with his old flame six months ago and then think he was some kind of relationship expert on all matters of the heart.

The part Branch was forgetting was that Jason's ex-fiancée, Natalie, hadn't just uprooted the life he'd had with her. She had uprooted the life he had with his daughter. His pride and joy. Seeing Carlie every second weekend wasn't nearly enough time to be the father he wanted to be for his child.

Natalie had admitted to herself, and then to him, that Port Landon wasn't enough for her, that she wouldn't ever be happy in the small town. Which, through Jason's eyes, meant he wasn't enough for her and that he would never make her happy, either. They just weren't looking for the same things in life, she'd said. She loved him, she'd said, but couldn't hide their incompatibility. Then, she had taken with her the one thing that meant everything to him and moved to North Springs. It wasn't like they'd crossed state lines and he never saw Carlie again—Natalie wouldn't do that to him, or to Carlie—but there was nothing that compared to coming home to his exuberant little girl every night, without fail, and having her under the same roof.

Natalie had taken that reality and made it a dream that would never come true.

The worst part was that he didn't have a clue what he could have done differently to change the outcome of their three-and-a-half-year relationship. She had been born and raised in the city, and had tried and failed to pretend that she didn't want to be a part of that world again. Natalie said numerous times that it was no fault of his own. That there was no blame placed at Jason's own feet for what happened between them. She had said it as though she was giving him some kind of gift. Like reminding him that he was a good man who sadly wasn't good enough for her would make it hurt less.

But Natalie was wrong then, and two long years after walking away from him and his small-town life, she was still wrong.

Jason Forrester was not looking for love, in any way, shape, or form. He had everything he needed—his own business, his weekends with Carlie, his own house, and his hometown.

All the things that no one could take from him, just the way he liked it.

Branch, thankfully, took the less than subtle hint and backed up a step. 'Just think about what I said, will you?' He snaked an arm behind his shoulder, rubbing his neck. 'You had a boatload of advice for me back in the winter when I was unsure what to do about my feelings for Kait,' he reminded him. 'I've been there, and I get that it's sometimes easier to give advice than to take it. All I'm asking is that you don't stay closed off from the idea of moving on forever, all right?'

'I'm not closed off,' Jason replied quickly. Too quickly.

'You're definitely closed off.' Branch nodded toward the worn front brake rotor Jason was in the midst of replacing. 'Get back to work. You've got to call Nancy and make a deal with the devil in the name of the woman you don't give a damn about.' His friend trudged back to his own garage bay, snickering under his breath.

* * *

He waited until Branch had gone home for the day before Jason made his way into the office and lowered himself into the ancient office chair behind the desk. He really needed to get this place organized.

It was funny; each garage bay was neat and organized. He knew where every tool was in the shop, and everything had a specific place. But the office, now that was another story. Somehow, paperwork and office supplies didn't rate nearly as high on Jason's radar to warrant spending a Sunday—the only day he took off from the garage whether he had Carlie or not—sorting through and organizing it all into a well-oiled administrative machine.

At the moment, it seemed like a much better idea than calling Nancy. He loved the woman to death, and she had been a godsend when his parents moved to North Springs and sold their three-bedroom bungalow to Jason. Nancy had supplied them with enough cold cut sandwiches and casseroles to feed a small army while they piled boxes into the moving truck. Which was good, because a small army of Port Landon residents is what accumulated at the Forrester house on moving day. She had also been a well-needed shoulder to cry on and ear to be lent for his mother when her diagnosis was confirmed, and Jason was thankful for her devotion to Bettina every day since.

What he struggled with, however, was Nancy's inquisitive nature. The woman wasn't scared to probe about tough topics or someone's romantic affairs. Or their romantic affairs that were tough topics. She was as sweet as honey and as solidly reliable as an old oak tree, but Nancy Bergeron loved love, and she sometimes saw it in places it didn't actually exist.

It wasn't hard to see the similarities between her and her sister, Sonya Ritter.

'Jason, sweetheart, it's so good to hear from you,' Nancy gushed by way of greeting. 'I'm afraid Lily's not here at the moment—'

'That's actually who I'd like to talk to you about,' he interjected, knowing he wouldn't get a word in edgewise if he let the woman get on the topic of her current houseguest. He figured Lily must have decided to take him up on his suggestion and check out Main Street. The mere mention of the Portside Coffeehouse's dark roast coffee was enough to send her heading in the right direction. He didn't think the idea of taking Eden on a walk along the docks or down to the ice cream shop near the pier was a hard sell, either. It was a serene suggestion in an otherwise chaotic time. Jason was glad she had decided to give herself a few hours of reprieve. 'Lily's car is going to take a few days. I won't get it up and running until next week.' *At least*, he added silently.

'As I told the lovely girl already, Jason, she's the only one counting down the days until she leaves.'

Something twisted in Jason's gut. He stamped down the unexpected wave of disappointment, not wanting to think about someone—anyone, not just Lily—counting down until they got to escape Port Landon. 'I'm not sure if she mentioned it, but she's having a bit of trouble with the cancellation from the hotel she'd booked a room at. Until they issue her a refund—'

'She's short on funds,' Nancy finished for him.

He winced. 'Sounds that way. Though, she's assured me she can pay to stay at the bed and breakfast if you—'

'Jason—'

'—have the room for them.' He cleared his throat, convinced he sounded more involved in their well-being than he should. Maybe Branch was getting to him, after all.

A long pause followed his statement. As Jason leaned back in the rickety office chair, feet up on the disorganized desk, he swore he heard the woman's smile slowly spread across her face.

'I won't let her leave, Jason,' she replied. 'Perhaps that'll give you time to give her a reason to want to stick around more permanently, hmm?'

Jason swallowed down a sigh. Was everyone convinced he was so desperate that he had to cling to the first new person in town that he came across?

'I'm just trying to help her out. She needs her car and a place to stay. I can handle the car. I'm just asking if you'll supply the roof over her head while we figure everything else out.'

A haughty chuckle sounded in his ear, and it was a beat too late that he realized he had said *we*, not *she*.

'That, I can do,' she said. 'Depending on how long she is staying, perhaps Lily could help me out around this big old house. It wouldn't be full-time or anything, but I'd love the company. Almost as much as I'd love for you two to *figure everything else out*.'

The emphasis on the last four words made Jason regret his choice of phrase immediately. 'That's up to her, I suppose.' The way the conversation was going, he figured he had better start tossing the ball in Lily's court and remembering to stay on the sidelines where he belonged. Although, he wasn't sure it mattered what he said; folks seemed to be hearing what they wanted to hear lately. 'Do you want me to broach the subject with Lily?'

He couldn't be sure, but Jason swore the woman covered the phone mouthpiece and let out a delighted squeak, making him wish he hadn't offered at all. 'You just leave that up to me. I'll handle everything. You've got an ally in me, my dear.' Nancy hung up before Jason could get past the sputtering phase of his disbelief.

He had no idea what she thought she was his ally against, or why he would even need one in the first place, but something niggled at Jason's brain. Nancy Bergeron might be his ally, but he was pretty sure they weren't fighting the same battle.

Chapter 7

Lily

The small town of Port Landon was beautiful at the end of June.

Lily couldn't remember the last time she had taken a moment to herself and stopped to smell the roses. Literally. The flowerbeds in the front yards and along the brick sidewalks of Main Street were magazine-worthy. They beckoned to Lily with their vivid bursts of color. Before she realized she was doing it, she had bent down and inhaled the vibrant blooms.

'They're so pretty.' Eden couldn't stop staring at the flowers, either. Her little fingers touched the velvety petals, her infectious grin lighting up at their silky softness.

'They really are, baby.'

The whole town was, to be honest. Lily hailed from a small town of her own—mind you, it was slightly bigger and less geared toward tourism since Sherman wasn't actually on the way to anywhere—but Port Landon reminded her of the bygone-era towns she saw on television. The ones where Mom and Pop shops lined the picturesque streets and everything looked like something out of a postcard. The ones where everyone knew everyone's name and no one was ever on their own when it came to hard times or mishaps.

The ones where dreams came true and people found happiness. Found themselves.

Ugh, you're doing it again.

Lily guided her daughter away from the abundant flowers that leaned toward the warm sun and walked further down the sidewalk. Judging by the shadows starting to stretch across the cement, they had been playing tourist for longer than she had intended. Lily needed to get back to the bed and breakfast, back to reality, and talk to Nancy. Nothing was going to get solved by meandering the downtown street and strolling along the boardwalk while boats motored to and fro in the harbor. Eden loved watching them, though, pointing excitedly and staring in wonder as the boaters waved to her and the water churned in their wake.

But it was all a smokescreen, she reminded herself. Her mind was playing tricks on her. This little town was no different than any other. Still too small, still too isolated, and far too laid back for the life she planned to give her daughter and herself. This was a stepping stone, albeit a picturesque one. Her journey didn't end here. It couldn't.

The universe must have decided she deserved a break last night. In hindsight, she should have seen the car troubles coming. She didn't remember the last time Cruella had an oil change let alone a full service. But, for the vehicle to break down outside of Port Landon, for her to find Forrester's Auto on Google and wind up talking to Jason, a man who was so overwhelmingly willing to extend a helping hand …

She thanked her lucky stars for that. For him.

'Ready to head back toward home?' she asked Eden. The little girl's face screwed up, confused, and Lily quickly recanted her choice of words. 'I mean the big white house, with the big comfy bed. You okay if we stay there again tonight?' *If Nancy has the room for us*, she silently added. Planning to settle some of her debts with her gracious hostess when they arrived there, Lily hoped it would be enough to show some good faith and secure a few more nights of accommodation.

'Yeah.' Eden shrugged like it was no big deal. 'Can we go see Jason again tomorrow?' The slight lisp her daughter spoke with made his name come out almost as *Jathon*, and it put a smile on Lily's face every time she heard it. Between that and the fact that Eden hadn't let go of the toy car yet, clutching it in her tiny fingers as she'd dawdled along the docks and licked at an ice cream cone—which had forced Lily to part with almost five dollars of her only cash, but Eden's excitement to taste the bright pink bubble gum flavor had been worth it—from the Old Port Ice Cream Shoppe. She would bet double or nothing that the little girl would curl up in bed and tuck the car in beside her.

Hand in hand, they took leisurely steps down the brick sidewalk, glancing in the storefront windows as people strolled by them, just as unhurried as they were. 'I'm not sure. He's really busy working on people's cars so they can go places and do things.'

'Like our car?'

'Yes, eventually. But we have to wait our turn, and we have to wait for the money to pay for the repairs. We might be here for a little while.' Lily had been about to say they would be in town for a few days, but Eden was so smart, so observant, she didn't want to commit to a timeline that might not hold up. A little while was safe; maybe a few days, maybe a few extra. A week at most.

She hoped.

'We get to stay?' Her daughter's curls bobbed with the swift turn of her neck. She stared up at Lily, surprised.

'Not forever.' She squeezed Eden's hand. 'But for a little while.'

The little girl lit up like a midday sun. 'Okay.'

'You like it here, huh?' Lily kept her tone nonchalant, casting glances at the bank and then The Port Diner as they passed. Inside, however, she was tied in knots. She had dealt with her daughter's tears for the first hour and a half of the trip out of

Sherman yesterday, and she didn't relish the idea of tearing her from a place she'd taken a liking to again.

With the air of a girl twice her age, Eden seemed to mull over the question. 'Yeah,' she said again. 'I like Jason. He's nice.'

Lily's knotted stomach plummeted. That wasn't what she had asked. 'Yeah, he's nice for helping us.'

Like a beacon in the night, she spotted a sign she recognized. The Portside Coffeehouse might as well have had angelic rays blazing from its front windows because, in that moment, it was heaven on earth to Lily. Not only because the decadent scent of perfectly roasted coffee beans wafted out onto the street from the opened doorway, and not only because there was a piece of paper taped to the window with *Help Wanted, Apply Within* in thick block letters written in black Sharpie marker, but because it was the perfect escape from the unexpected turn in their conversation.

There was no way—no way at all—she was confessing the truth to her daughter. The reckless, ridiculous truth. After everything she had been through, after less than twenty-four measly hours ...

Eden wasn't the only one who liked Jason Forrester.

* * *

The interior of the Portside Coffeehouse was everything Lily hoped it would be. When she first inhaled the sweet scent of their coffee at Nancy's house earlier that morning, her mind had conjured up an image of what a place that served such rich, delicious coffee might look like. The kind of people who might frequent it. The way the spot might be decorated.

Scratch that. The coffeehouse wasn't everything she had hoped for—it was more. It was perfect. She had stepped out of a picturesque small town and into a hip and trendy hole in the wall type of café she would expect to find settled amidst high-end stores and boutiques in the middle of a city. Tall bistro tables with ornate stools popped up across the dark walnut floor, the deep crimson of the stool seats matching the vinyl that covered the booths lining the right side of the room. The brick walls added a creative flair, and the ordering counter, though stainless steel and industrial, gave the whole scene a dash of color and character with the sporadic chunky vases of fresh daisies set up near the cash register. Lily let out a sigh, thrilled at finding a spot in Port Landon that made her feel instantly like she would get through this temporary setback on her journey.

With the help of a place that served amazing caffeine buzzes, anything was possible.

'Hey there. What can I get for you?'

Lily tore her gaze from the electric fireplace on the far side of the room—its faux flames were flickering, but no heat came from the unit—to meet the bright eyes of a tall woman in a black T-shirt. The luster of her auburn ponytail caused envy to sear through Lily; her own blonde locks would never possess the same kind of shine. 'Hi. We'll just be a sec. You've got a food menu, too, right, not just coffee?'

'If I don't have it, I can tell you where to get it nearby,' the barista assured her. She pointed at the two handwritten chalkboards behind her. One listed more caffeinated drinks than Lily's imagination could ever dream of, the other boasted an array of soup, sandwiches, as well as scones and biscotti.

'Eden, do you want some mushroom soup?' It was the only thing Lily saw on the board that her daughter might actually eat.

A vehement nod followed. 'With crackers.'

That went without saying. The little girl wouldn't touch any soup without a handful of soda crackers crushed in it. 'Deal. What do you say?'

Eden flashed an oversized cheeky grin. 'Please and thank you.' With her slight lisp, Lily loved the sound of her daughter's polite words.

'It looks like a bowl of your mushroom soup for her, and I'll get a bowl of the Italian wedding soup.' She pulled her wallet from her purse, eyeing the dwindling roll of bills. 'Better add a medium dark roast coffee with milk, too, please.'

The barista paused, but then she nodded, tapping the cash register buttons. 'Coming right up. That'll be …' *Tap, tap, tap.* 'Thirteen dollars and forty-three cents.'

Lily handed over one of the remaining twenties. 'Thank you.'

The barista slid her change across the counter, then went about pouring Lily's coffee into a paper cup. She asked, 'Did you—' just as Lily blurted, 'Is there—'

Both women stopped, then chuckled.

'I'm sorry,' Lily said. 'What were you going to say?'

Still grinning, the barista placed a plastic lid on the cup and offered it to her. 'I was going to ask if I heard you correctly, that your daughter's name is Eden?'

'Yes.' Glancing down at the girl for a brief second, her eyes narrowed. 'Why do you ask?'

'Does that mean you're Lily?'

Shocked, she nodded. 'It does. How do you know that?'

The barista's ponytail swayed as she went about spooning hefty helpings of homemade soup into takeout bowls. 'News travels fast around these parts,' she explained. 'Not much gets by us.'

It was probably meant as a joke, but the comment made Lily's insides churn. 'I'm not sure whether I should be wary or impressed.'

The barista didn't turn away from her work, just chuckled to herself. 'It's not as ominous as it sounds. Or as impressive, honestly.' She glanced over her shoulder toward Lily. 'Nancy's sister works here. I heard about your car trouble when Sonya came in first thing this morning. And how adorable Nancy thinks your daughter is. She's excited to have a child staying at her place, I think.'

Lily hoped that meant she heard about the car's inability to run and not Lily's inability to pay for the repairs. 'Ah, that makes sense. It's much less creepy when I know how complete strangers found out who Eden and I are so quickly.'

Setting the bowls on a copper tray, the barista placed it in front of Lily. Then, she held out her hand. 'I'm Allison, the owner of this fine establishment. There, we're not complete strangers anymore.'

Lily couldn't stop herself. She laughed. What was with the people in this town? Everyone seemed to have a knack for making her smile. They were all just so darn likeable. It actually helped to ease Lily's apprehension when it came to the fact that she liked Jason. It wasn't him, solely, she found attractive, then. Everyone in Port Landon gave off the same friendly vibe. It wasn't just Jason, it was everyone. Everything. There was something freeing about realizing that, and Lily clung to the notion like a lifeline.

Shaking Allison's hand, she replied, 'Nice to meet you. Interestingly enough, I was actually looking for the owner of this fine establishment. What a coincidence.'

'Very interesting. What about?'

Eden rocked back and forth on her heels, staring at the bowl of soup on the counter with unabashed longing. Lily didn't blame her; it had been hours since she had eaten a late breakfast.

'I saw the sign in your window.' Lily pointed toward the door.

Eyes widening, Allison lit up like a Christmas tree. 'You want a job? You're serious?'

'Gravely,' she replied. It wasn't a want at this point, but a need. 'You've heard about my car troubles and that I'm staying at Nancy's bed and breakfast. I'm a hard worker and I learn fast. I don't know what you're looking for, but I'll be honest, I'd be grateful for whatever I can get.'

'You and me both,' Allison chuckled. 'No one's exactly knocking down the door to work now that the weather's so nice. But my cousin, Paige, is getting married and I'm her maid of honor. The preparations are swamping me. Makes me feel kind of bad for all the wedding baloney I put her through when I got married.' She leaned against the counter. 'You're wanting something temporary, I assume.'

'Unfortunately, yes. If that works for you, I mean. I understand if it doesn't.'

Allison waved a hand. 'When you walked in here, I was just excited to meet you and Eden, the two ladies who rolled into town under the mask of night and gave good ole' Sonya so much to talk about this morning.' There was no stopping the woman's relentless grin. 'But if you're saying you can save me from becoming the worst maid of honor in wedding history by helping out here and freeing me up a little time, even for a little while, then you and I have got some talkin' to do.'

'Let me get Eden set up at one of the booths with her dinner, then I'd love to chat. Thank you, Allison.' Lily wasn't sure what she had expected, but Allison's exuberance and infectious personality wasn't it. The woman was a busybody, in constant motion, and she radiated kindness from her every pore.

She was also, evidently, Lily's new boss at a job she hadn't been actively looking for. She needed to call about the Starbucks job in Chicago and figure out how—or rather, if—this was all going to work out. Still, despite the uncertainty about everything, she found that she was excited. This wasn't Chicago, or part of her plans, but the coffeehouse would be something new. And wasn't that what she had been searching for when she left Sherman?

Once again, Port Landon was full of surprises.

Chapter 8

Jason

The more he thought about it, the more Jason became convinced that he had to see Lily.

Not because there was some tug pulling him toward her, urging him to attempt to renew her faith in old-fashioned generosity—although a hint of that might be true, even if he didn't dare to admit it out loud.

It was a valid reason to want to see her again, but nothing was more pressing than talking to her before Nancy Bergeron got to her. After all that talk about allies on the phone, who knew what kind of things the woman would say if she was left to her own devices.

No, it was better if Jason explained his conversation with Nancy to her himself, leaving out all the romantic suggestions and unwarranted innuendo she'd mentioned and letting Lily hear it straight from him that sometimes Nancy could be a little much. It was better to take her anecdotes with a grain of salt.

Once he closed up the repair shop for the evening, he headed to the bed and breakfast. There was a chance he might be too late, that Lily might have returned from downtown already and spoken to Nancy. Regardless, he had to try.

Under the ruse that he could advise her that he had sourced the parts needed for her Corolla and he was ready to order them whenever she gave him the go-ahead, he could find out what the older woman had said. Frankly, he didn't need Nancy making this harder than it needed to be by suggesting things that would only make things awkward.

God, maybe he was the one making this harder than it had to be.

Either way, he pulled up to the curb in front of Nancy's shortly after five-thirty, just in time to see Lily and Eden strolling up the sidewalk from the other direction. Coffee cup in Lily's hand, chocolate cookie in Eden's, he knew where they had been. And they looked happy. With the treetops creating a canopy of leaves above their heads and the little girl skipping along beside her mother as the sun gave their skin a warm glow, the Brentwood girls looked like any of the other carefree tourists heading back to their lodging for the evening.

Jason found himself smiling along with them. Leaning against the side of his blue Dodge pickup, he waited, letting them get closer before he interrupted their distant chatter and the sweet sound of the songbirds hidden amidst the trees.

'You two look like you're settling in well.' He pushed away from the truck and met them on the sidewalk, ruffling Eden's curly hair. The preschooler beamed up at him, taking another oversized bite of her cookie.

'Hey.' Lily held up her coffee cup in salutation. 'Yeah, thank you for suggesting a walk downtown, by the way. I think I'm a little more at ease because of it. Even with the caffeine buzzing through my bloodstream.' A wry smirk formed on her lips. 'Your little town is beautiful, Jason.'

Pride swelled in him. *His town*, like he held the key to it and had bestowed it upon her in the hope that she would see it for what it was. Not just a town, or a pitstop, but a home. His home. The notion that she saw what he did, even for a minute, only made him prouder to be a Port Landon resident. 'It's pretty great, huh? I told you, not a bad place to be stuck.' He nodded toward the cup between her fingers. 'Or to grab a cup of coffee, I see.'

Something darkened in Lily's gaze, the usual ocean in them growing stormy. 'Oh. Yeah, I mean, I know I'm strapped for cash at the moment and that I probably shouldn't have—'

'Whoa, whoa, whoa.' Hands up, Jason cut her off. 'I never meant it like that at all. Do you see the smile on her face?' He pointed toward Eden, who was staring adoringly at the remaining chunk of cookie in her hand like it was the Holy Grail. 'Because I saw the smile on yours as you two were heading this way. If a simple coffee and a walk in the sunshine will give you that, you'd better spend the couple dollars and enjoy it. You've had a rough go of it, so don't be so hard on yourself.'

Her throat moved. 'I just meant, though, because of the repairs—'

'Oh, that.' Jason waved a dismissive hand, pretending it wasn't a big deal. 'But that's actually part of the reason I came here. I've got a proposition for you.'

Lily raised an eyebrow, squinting into the slowly sinking sun. 'I'm not sure how to take that,' she laughed.

He didn't realize the innuendo until it was too late. This is what he got for trying to make light of the whole ordeal. 'What? No, it's not what it sounds like. I should have said that Nancy has a prop—'

'Why don't you two come in off the sidewalk and I'll make some sweet tea!'

Jason whirled around to see an array of colorful patchwork fabric and silky scarves. The force of Nancy Bergeron seemed to flood the quiet street like a sudden tsunami, bursting out from the front door and onto the front porch. The abundance of flimsy material that seemed to float around her only accentuated her wild gestures as the woman waved them frantically toward the house.

Beside him, Lily buckled over, laughing harder. At Nancy or his obvious backpedaling, Jason wasn't sure. God, first he mistakenly made it sound like he was about to propose some kind of scandalous clearing of her debt, and now Nancy was showing up and determined to flutter about like some kind of misguided angel.

Maybe he should have just got in his truck and gone home after work.

'Something funny?' he asked.

Lily wiped the tears brimming her eyes with one hand. 'You just … your face, Jason.' She laughed again at her own nonsensical description. Whispering, she continued, 'You looked utterly mortified, and then Nancy shouted from the porch … oh my goodness, I lost it. I'm sorry, but that was funny.'

He stole a glance at Nancy, who was still waving her hands to gain their attention. He turned his back on the woman, muttering, 'I'm so glad you find this hilarious.'

'You're the one who was laughing at me earlier, Mr. Pretending To Teach Me Something. Returning the favor is the least I can do.'

Okay, she had him there. But that *had* been funny. This, with Nancy, as comical as the hippy woman looked as she relentlessly beckoned to them on the front porch, was a potential catastrophe in the making.

Oh well, he could survive Nancy's good-natured meddling for a little bit, as well as her flamboyance. 'Touché,' he replied, attempting to keep his amusement at bay. 'But just keep two things in mind, Little Miss Spheric Widget. The first is that no matter what that lovely but maddening woman says or does, I was just trying to help you. I swear I meant well.'

Lily sobered immediately. 'And the second?'

Jason paused. 'Nancy is tenacious. Once she gets an idea about something or someone—or *someones*—there's no stopping her.

I talked to her earlier, so I know what we could very easily be walking into.'

'What?'

They both turned to stare toward the porch. Under his breath, Jason muttered, 'Get ready for some sweet tea with a side order of thinly veiled, poorly executed matchmaking.'

* * *

It had been years since Jason had stepped foot inside Nancy's house. He'd been to the front door many times, dropping off her Buick Enclave after either doing an oil change or putting on the winter or summer tires. But he had been a kid the last time he made it inside the looming house, and that was because Nancy was known to give the best Halloween candy during trick-or-treating. He still remembered the year he and Branch changed into new costumes partway through the evening just so they could go back to her house and get more full-sized candy bars.

Nancy probably remembered it, too, seeing as she had called Branch by name and the dunce had answered, giving their identities away. Nothing got by Nancy. Funnily enough, she had tossed two more candy bars into their bags anyway, chuckling as she did so. Probably an award for their efforts and ingenuity.

The house still looked the same as he remembered, all antique wood and intricate moldings. The massive piano still sat near the window by the front door, a masterpiece of maple and expert workmanship. At the moment, that masterpiece was where Eden's attention lied, and she pressed one ivory key, then another, creating an offkey masterpiece of her own.

It was no wonder Edwin and Nancy Bergeron's bed and breakfast had always been a beloved destination when folks visited Port Landon. Even after her husband passed away five years ago from cancer, Nancy kept the sprawling house. She lived for the social interaction that came with her hostess duties. The maintenance and upkeep were hired out without Edwin's help, but, if anything, Nancy had thrown herself into the hospitality business even more since she lost him. The house was her companion now, and it gleamed with pride of ownership.

Almost as much as Nancy's eyes gleamed as she stared at him and Lily across the dining room table.

'So, Jason tells me you're going to be staying for a little longer than expected.' Nancy poured amber tea into the starburst-etched drinking glasses, but there was something about the way she held her mouth, lips pressed to hold in her delight, that reminded Jason of a cat that had just eaten the canary.

'If that's okay with you,' Lily replied quickly.

'Of course it is,' Nancy said.

Jason leaned forward on his elbows. 'I was trying to tell you outside, Nancy and I already discussed this.'

'You're more than welcome to stay here as long as you need to, dear.' The older woman set the pitcher down and settled into her chair. 'As I told Jason, I wondered if perhaps you and I could come to a bit of an arrangement.'

'Would this be the proposition?' Lily's eyes sparkled over the rim of her glass as she glanced in Jason's direction.

He fought to keep his expression neutral. 'It would be.' So, this was an inside joke now, was it?

'What kind of arrangement, Nancy?' She focused away from him, but Lily's amusement remained.

While Nancy didn't understand what was passing between them, she looked about ready to burst, satisfied that it was. Jason fought the urge to wince—he and Lily were giving her ammunition to use in her quest for romantic connection without even realizing it.

'I need a little help around here,' she stated simply. 'Just some cleaning and tidying up as the guests come and go.' She held up her hands, revealing long fingers that were thin-skinned and slightly gnarled at the knuckles. 'These old hands aren't what they used to be, and I'm a little slower than I was thirty years ago. Slower in physical speed, I mean,' she added with a poignant stare. 'My mind's still as sharp as ever.' She winked.

Of course, the all-seeing, all-knowing Nancy Bergeron was letting them know she picked up on everything, no matter how seemingly trivial.

If Lily was affronted in any way, she didn't show it. 'You want to hire me?'

Nancy waved a dismissive hand. 'Call it a trade-off,' she replied. 'Help me out with a few housekeeping duties as long as you're here, and we'll consider it even on the room rates.'

A loud, plunging sound of multiple minor keys being pressed at once echoed off the walls from the living room, offering a doom and gloom ambience to Nancy's offer. Jason held up a hand to stifle his laughter, finding the correlation oddly suiting.

'That's very kind of you, Nancy. Really, it is. But I plan to pay you every penny of your going rate for the nights we stay here. That said, I would be more than happy to help you out as long as I am here, and as much as I can. It's the least I can do considering how generous you've been to Eden and I.'

Nancy arched a brow. 'Sounds like I'm not the only generous one, dear.'

'No, I'm the grateful one.' Slowly, her mouth lifted at one corner. 'Wow, I guess I'm going to be pretty busy for the next week or so. Just the way I like it.'

The way she said it piqued Jason's interest. 'I don't think Nancy plans to run you off your feet.'

'I don't mean that,' Lily said. 'I'm actually thrilled to help you out.' She locked eyes with Nancy, giving her a gracious smile. 'But I also met Allison today,' she added. 'From the coffeehouse. We got to talking and she agreed to hire me while I'm here, too.'

'Oh, that is wonderful!' It was official, Nancy had gone from about to burst, to exploding wide open with excitement.

'Wait, you're going to work for Allison?' Jason was struggling to keep up.

'She said she needed someone to help her out while she's dealing with her cousin's wedding preparations or something,' Lily explained. 'Besides, I've got to pay back all the nice folks who've helped me since yesterday. That includes you, tenfold.'

'Sounds like you've got things all figured out.' Nancy looked as though she couldn't have been happier if the Queen herself had arrived in Port Landon and decided to stay at her bed and breakfast.

Another tinkling of the piano keys rang out, higher pitched this time, sounding like the theme song for a skittering, drunken mouse on the run.

'I'd hardly say I've got anything figured out. But I may as well keep busy while my car is being fixed.' She cast a glance at Jason. 'I'll be able to pay you back a lot quicker this way.'

He couldn't fault her logic. If the roles were reversed, if he had the plans that she did, he'd probably be looking for a way to make a quicker escape, too.

But, though he would never admit it out loud, Jason was thinking that Nancy, as eccentric and misguided as she was, was right. It did sound like it was all figured out. Lily and Eden had a plan to stay in town. Eventually, they would get in their repaired Corolla and head off toward Chicago. But for now, they were a part of Port Landon's community.

He didn't understand why that made him so happy, but he smiled, nonetheless.

* * *

The sun had disappeared by the time Jason managed to say a sufficient number of *I really should be going*s to allow Nancy to let him leave. He had drunk enough sweet tea that he would be on a sugar high long into the night, and enough chocolate chip biscotti to feed an entire army. Not to mention he had sat at her kitchen table and talked, just talked, for the sake of talking, for hours.

Jason couldn't recall the last time that happened.

Sure, he dropped by Branch's place on Crescent Street now and then, but he always feared he was interfering in his downtime with Kait. Besides, he saw Branch at work every day. Showing up on his doorstep too often would signal just how much loneliness plagued him, and he didn't need his best friend deciding that they needed to talk about that.

Between Eden's humorous musical serenade that made his ears want to bleed, and Nancy's incessant efforts to remind both Jason and Lily of the things they so obviously had in common despite only knowing the woman for a day, there had been a lot of laughs and easy conversation. Jason thought he would hate having to sit there while Nancy dropped her not-so-subtle hints and pretended that their three-person chitchat session was something more than a meeting of acquaintances, but he had enjoyed himself. He was exhausted from fending off the constant insinuations, but he had liked the company.

And he liked Lily. What he knew of her, anyway. She wasn't one to put forth more details than she felt she needed to, but Jason respected that. He could relate. It was comforting to know there was someone else who didn't feel the past needed to be rehashed over and over again on an endless loop.

But there was a past there, he could tell that, too. Something Lily wasn't interested in discussing. Something her eight-hour trip to Chicago was meant to erase. Though he hadn't tried to outrun his own past—his past had, for all intents and purposes, run from him instead—Jason could relate to that as well.

'She's a little over the top, but I think she means well.' Lily had followed him out onto the front porch, hands in her pockets.

Jason glanced over her shoulder, but no one followed. Nancy had miraculously disappeared inside the deepest depths of the house, leaving them alone with only the golden glow of the porch light to chaperone. Imagine that.

'Yeah, but if she's going to continue to channel her inner Beethoven, she's going to need some lessons—or you're going to need some earplugs.'

'I'm talking about Nancy!' Lily chuckled. 'You leave poor Eden alone. When she grows up and becomes a famous pianist or composer, we'll both be looking back on this night and laughing.'

'Or still cringing,' Jason argued.

Lily rolled her eyes. 'Oh, come on, like you wouldn't have let Carlie keep playing the piano. I'm fostering her abilities.'

'I wouldn't have let Carlie within ten feet of that thing,' he reasoned. 'Besides, I'm still holding out hope she'll remain in love with the cars in the garage and become a world-famous automotive mechanic or painter or something. You know, like her good ole' dad.'

'You're world famous, are you?' Lily asked wryly.

He held out his hands, gesturing to their serene surroundings. 'Here in Port Landon, I am. If you've got an issue with your vehicle, I'm your guy. Seeing as Port Landon is about as big as my world gets, I guess you could say I'm world famous.' Jason grinned, mighty impressed to have come up with such an iron clad argument. 'In a small town, Lily, everybody's famous.'

Headlights shone up the length of the street. A few seconds later, a dark green Ford Taurus passed by. The windows were tinted and he couldn't see the driver, but the car horn honked in greeting. Jason waved. 'That'll be Ronnie Durvayne, on his way home from work. He cleans the bank and walk-in clinic after hours.'

'You really are famous.'

Jason saw the way her eyes sharpened, the way her smile widened. 'I've been trying to tell you,' he laughed, nudging her back. 'Stick around, maybe you will be, too.'

He had meant it so innocently, the words rolling off his tongue without thinking them through. But he saw the way Lily shifted from one foot to the other.

'For a little while,' was all she said, in a tone void of the humor that had been there moments ago.

Jason cleared his throat. He needed to get back on solid ground. 'So, you're good, then? Feeling okay about helping both Nancy and Allison out?'

She shrugged. 'I have to be. Allison said I was more than welcome to bring Eden with me since my circumstances are a little unorthodox, but I'm worried about her. Nothing worse than a bored five-year-old.'

'Nothing scarier, you mean.' He offered her a quirk of his lips. 'Allison wouldn't offer if she didn't think it'd work out. I'm sure coloring books and the antics of Sonya and Allison will be enough to keep her occupied for a few hours. If it's not, there are a few people here in town that have babysat Carlie before. I could give you some names.'

In the bronze lamplight, she stared at him as though the words coming out of his mouth were foreign or unintelligible. 'Your generosity knows no bounds, does it?'

'Just being a good neighbor, that's all.'

'We're not neighbors,' she pointed out.

Jason took a step closer, pointing down the street. He whispered, as though he were about to tell her his deepest, darkest secret. 'That's what you think. I live around the corner, third house on the left. Trust me, we're practically neighbors.' He was close enough that when Lily turned to peer up at him, his eyes were only inches from hers.

So was her mouth, he noticed a heartbeat later.

Too close. Jason retreated a step, needing to break the sudden pull he felt, a tether between her allure and his intrigue.

'Thank you,' he whispered after a long pause, not realizing the words were out of his mouth until Lily's eyes rounded, alarmed.

'For what?' Was that a tremble he heard in her voice?

'For trusting me,' he replied quietly. 'For letting me help you, with Nancy and with your car. I know it can't be easy when you don't know me.'

She was still as a stone. 'It's not like I have much of a choice.'

'And that only makes me more grateful. We'll get this figured out. I won't let you down.' His throat moved as he swallowed, and it looked as though her pale eyes were trained on that movement, eyelids fluttering with each rapid blink.

'Have a good night, Lily.' He backed away, not trusting himself to speak again and having already said too much, and headed for his truck.

Chapter 9

Lily

Growing up, Lily had never been one to stand by and have someone show her how to do something. She preferred to learn by doing, by using her own bare hands and putting herself through the process in order to convert it all to memory.

When she first learned to drive, she had coerced her mother into taking their old Chevy pickup out on the gravel backroads and letting her get the feel of the steering wheel under her palms rather than reading the driving manual the licensing office issued her. When she had seen her first fashion show on television and become enthralled with the fabrics and buttons and accessories, she had retrieved her grandmother's old sewing machine from the attic and learned how to operate it through trial and error rather than looking up tutorials to reveal how other people created their fashion masterpieces.

Helping Nancy at the bed and breakfast was no different. With nothing to do but wait out the weekend—and hope that the discussion she had with the hotel manager in Chicago led to a refund so that the Corolla parts could be ordered and arrive in good time next week—Lily decided to dive headfirst into her new role as Nancy's assistant. Her conversation with the Starbucks manager hadn't been nearly as positive, though she had been granted a little extra time to figure out when she would be available to start her new job. At the moment, dealing with bedsheets and vacuums was much more appealing than the thoughts of her disastrous trip.

Yesterday had been a busy Saturday, rivaling any Saturday she had ever experienced at the restaurant she waitressed at in Sherman. Not because her job hadn't been hectic at the restaurant—anyone who ever waited tables before knew that was impossible—but because Jason was right about Nancy's tenacity.

'I can see you practically twitching from here, wanting to be left to your own devices and do what needs to be done,' she had said, tossing linens into an oversized hamper on wheels. 'Let me show you where the cleaning supplies are and give you the basics, then I'll leave you be. If you have questions, you can ask.'

Lily could have hugged the woman. If she hadn't known any better, she would have thought Nancy was vying to become her favorite boss on the first day.

Now, a day later, the difference one day made was astounding. Yesterday morning, Lily had felt like an outsider looking in, like she was merely fumbling through the cleaning and folding and tidying up in hopes that maybe she'd done one out of five tasks right. She quickly realized that Nancy was just happy to have help, and she wasn't picky about how crisp the corners of her folded fitted sheets were or whether the throw pillows on the sofa were plumped to perfection. Today, Lily felt more confident in her abilities, and she knew where things were kept and what needed to be done. It was a good feeling.

The house was huge. Lily had already known that, but it wasn't until she ascended and descended the stairs for the millionth time and pushed the vacuum across the floor of the long stretch of hallway both upstairs and down that she really appreciated the sheer immensity of the home. Four bedrooms upstairs, two on the main floor, along with a massive kitchen, dining room, and living room with an entryway. Add in the three bathrooms and the unfinished basement and attic, and Lily wasn't sure she would ever see the whole place before she left town.

Speaking of the difference a day made, Lily figured she shouldn't have been surprised. After all, one day she had never heard of Port Landon, and now she was in the thick of it. She had never heard of Jason Forrester, either. Now, she found her thoughts returning to him while she worked away under Nancy's employ. The acrid scent of floor cleaner was no match for the scent of hazelnut coffee creamer still lingering somewhere in her memories when she thought of him.

I won't let you down.

As Lily navigated through the century-old home, she heard his choice of words. Was haunted by them, yet uplifted by them. They made no sense coming from the mouth of a man she didn't know, yet were so full of conviction that she comprehended every syllable as though it were etched into her psyche, leaving its permanent mark. She didn't understand his reasons, but she believed that he meant it, nonetheless.

Whether or not he was able to live up to the precedent he set was another matter. After all, Lily was sure that Michael had uttered those five words more than a few times himself. A simple promise to make, but a harder one to keep. But she had believed him as well, taken his promises as more than just things people said. Michael, however, had meant it about as much as he had meant *we're in this together*, and *we're a family*.

Just words. He was the father of her child, but that hadn't meant much to him in the end, either.

Lily had loved Michael Pennington since her senior year in high school. He was the football star, the teenage boy who looked the part, acted the part, and played the part. It wasn't until many years later that Lily realized just how flawless his acting skills had been. But the wild-eyed girl she had once been was too blinded by love to see the truth about him—that it was all a show; a well-rehearsed play that Michael starred in every day, playing the hometown hero and the knight in shining armor.

It was hard to be a heroic knight, however, when life got in the way. Real, everyday life didn't need princes on white horses who said all the right things and made sure things looked perfect from the outside looking in. Real life called for stand-up folks who worked hard to provide for themselves, and their families. Real life included more than a day-to-day search for the next big thing, the next easy way to make quick cash and avoid the trials and tribulations that came with working for that perfect façade. At the end of the day, though, façades were just that—fake. Smokescreens. Dirty windows that gave a blurred view inside.

And any theatrical play, no matter how well rehearsed, will fall apart if a new character is introduced that was never in the original script.

A shudder crept through Lily despite the mounting heat of the day. She couldn't think about this, about him. Any reminder of her naivety and his betrayal should have been long gone—that was one of the main reasons for the move to Chicago. No constant, tangible reminders surrounding her, forcing her to stay rooted in the mistakes her foolish heart had made.

The problem was, no amount of distance could allow her to outrun her memories, and no amount of cleaning would ever erase the smudges left on her heart by his hurtful words about her own dreams in life, ones she now kept to herself for fear of someone belittling them once again.

It didn't mean she had to revisit those memories, though. Lily tossed the reusable end of the mop into the washing machine, then set it up to wash. She might not have ended up exactly where she had been headed when she left Sherman, but she was away, and there was distance between her and those painful reminders. It was a silver lining, and possibly the only one she was going to get. Being grateful for the little things was the only way to get through the trying times.

Besides, not for the first time, Jason was right—there were worse places to be stuck than a pretty little harborside town in a timeless Victorian home with a steady stream of sunshine bursting through the windows, daring her to be anything but grateful.

Goodness, there he was again, lurking at the sidelines, waiting for a chance to wind up back at the forefront of her mind. Regardless of whether Jason Forrester was right or wrong, a stranger or an old friend, Lily had no need to be thinking about him. At all.

Yet, she continued to. She wondered about a man who offered up his time, his effort, and his connections to someone without batting an eyelash. It had been a matter of days, not weeks or months, and he had already bestowed upon her a place to stay and a list of babysitters in the area if she needed it. That wasn't even including the actual car repairs she had originally called him for.

Nice guys finished last—wasn't that how the old saying went? It pained her to think that maybe his old-fashioned kindness was just as much his downfall as his strength.

Not only did she wonder about him, Lily found herself curious as to why his daughter's mother no longer lived here, why they were no longer together. And just as quickly as the thought skittered into her mind, Lily shut it all down with the shake of her head.

She should be ashamed of herself. Not only was it none of her business, but she had no business thinking about Jason in any capacity, let alone his romantic life.

'The last load of laundry is in,' she announced, rounding the corner to see Nancy huddled at the kitchen table with Eden. A stack of creased and wrinkled coloring books was piled between them, and a rainbow of crayons littered the tabletop. 'And the bedrooms are all made up. What are you two up to?'

'It's been ages since we've had a child stay here,' Nancy replied excitedly. 'I'd forgotten all about these books until I saw this little one doodling on the grocery list I'd left out.' She patted Eden's hair affectionately.

Lily's heart swelled. Every time Nancy referred to the owners of the bed and breakfast, she used a plural form. Jason had done the same thing on Thursday evening when he brought her here for the first time, referring to the place fondly as Edwin and Nancy's home. Even though Nancy had explained that Edwin had passed away, she and the rest of the town included him as though he were still a part of everything they did and achieved.

What a love like that must be like.

'Yikes, sorry about the list, Nancy.' Lily peered over her daughter's shoulder. 'What are you drawing, baby?' The coloring page boasted the black outline of a butterfly, awaiting an artist's creative touch, but Eden was adding to the picture, filling in the white space with an illustration of her own.

'Cruella.' Eden glanced up at her, beaming. 'That's Jason, and me, and you.' She pointed each stick figure out. 'When we drive her.'

Her. So, Eden was holding on to Jason's affectionate terminology, then. 'That's nice. Good job, Eden.' It was too late to stop the explanation from reaching Nancy's ears, and by the time Lily's gaze snapped up to meet hers, the woman's cheeks were as rosy as the silk scarf that kept her unruly hair at bay. In an attempt to ward off whatever she might say next, Lily reached around to her back pocket and retrieved the tea towel she had rescued from the dryer. To distract Nancy, she held it up, revealing the torn threads and ragged hem. 'Looks like a thread got caught or something while this was being washed.'

'Oh, darn.' Nancy stood, touching the ripped fabric with a bright pink fingernail. 'Another one bites the dust, it seems. I'll bet it got caught on the zipper closure of one of those pillow covers. I knew better than to toss those in the wash with such delicate items.'

Her disappointment was obvious. 'If you've got a sewing machine, or even a needle and thread, I can fix it for you,' Lily offered.

'You can sew?' Nancy's surprise was just as evident.

'It's one of my favorite things in the world to do,' Lily confessed.

Nancy narrowed her eyes as though seeing her guest in a new light. 'There's an old machine upstairs, collecting dust in the hallway closet. I couldn't mend my way out of a paper sack, but if you want to give it go, I won't stop you, Lily.'

Beaming at the chance, Lily nodded. 'Let me see what I can do.'

'That would be lovely, dear. Now,' Nancy shifted her attention back to Eden, still coloring furiously with a purple crayon. 'You really should tell me more about these drives you're going to take in this car.' Nancy was practically busting at the seams with glee. Each mischievous side eye she sent Lily's way was even more wolfish than the next.

Permission was all Eden needed. 'We're gonna take Cruella out and drive her … really fast!' Her gray eyes gleamed, wide and anticipatory. 'Super duper fast!'

'Okay, speed demon, time for a change of scenery.' Lily pushed some of the crayons back toward the empty box on the table. 'Maybe I should go outside with you and help you burn off a little steam. What do you think?'

Nancy stood. 'The park isn't far from here,' she reasoned. 'By the looks of the weather forecast, you'd best bask in the sunshine while you can. They're calling for rain tomorrow.'

Lily raised an eyebrow at Eden as though deciding the afternoon plans amongst adults. 'I'm game for the park if you are.'

The little girl's arms flew up and she cheered, letting her mother know just how game she was for the idea.

'Crayons and books away first, munchkin, then we'll hit the park.' She turned to Nancy. 'Thanks for the suggestion. I think I've got most things caught up right now, but if you need me, I'll leave my phone number. And I will get to that tea towel when I get back.' Lily reached for a stray crayon and wrote her cell number on one of the discarded coloring pages, tacking it to the side of the fridge.

'Don't worry about me, you lovely girl. Just get to the park before it's too late.'

Lily was about to comment that she was pretty sure she and Eden could walk fast enough to outrun tomorrow's rainclouds, but the older woman offered Eden a hasty kiss on the top of her head and disappeared in the flutter of tunics and shawls before she had a chance.

Lily smiled. In the span of Thursday to Sunday, Nancy Bergeron's personal brand of eccentricity had become somewhat comforting. Normal, even. It was enough to make Lily wonder what other crazy, outlandish things could become normal if she just gave them a chance and let them in.

* * *

Walking through the streets of Port Landon was quickly becoming one of Lily's favorite pastimes. She didn't think she would ever tire of seeing the meticulously maintained lawns that stretched out before looming brick and restored Victorian homes. She didn't think she would ever fully get the intoxicating scent of the flower gardens mixed with the harbor that drifted in the air out of her nostrils. The water couldn't be seen from the bed and breakfast, but there was no denying its presence.

As she rounded the corner onto Main Street and the playground came into view, there was no denying another presence, either.

At first, she didn't recognize him. His clothes and hands were a lot cleaner than when she had seen him at the garage, and the smile he wore was bigger than any she had seen on his face to date. But there was no mistaking Jason Forrester for anyone else. His dark, closely cropped hair and the shadow of beard on his

97

chiseled features were his and his alone. Paired with his striking eyes, he was unmistakable.

The brightness within him was new, though. Something seemed warmer about him, more radiant. A heartbeat later when a little girl with curly pigtails dove into his arms and he swung her high into the air, Lily knew exactly what—or who, rather—was the reason for the gleam in Jason's eye.

Hand in hand, Lily and Eden walked across the lush grass toward the bed of sand where the monkey bars and towering play structure stood.

'Fancy meeting you here,' she said by way of greeting, followed by a shy wave.

Genuine shock marred his face. 'Lily, hey.' He set the little girl back on her feet, and she peered between Lily and Eden with a muted curiosity. 'Good to see you.'

'You're out enjoying the sunshine, too, huh?'

'Carlie and I come here every Sunday afternoon that she's in town, without fail. It's second nature for us.'

And just like that, Lily figured out why Nancy sent her and Eden there. *Just get to the park before it's too late.* Her haste had nothing to do with storm clouds. 'I should have known,' she groaned.

'Excuse me?' Taken aback, Jason's forehead wrinkled.

'Nothing. Just something Nancy said.' Lily waved a dismissive hand. 'So, this is little Carlie, I presume?'

Jason squeezed the girl's shoulders affectionately. 'The one and the only. Car, this is Lily, and her daughter, Eden.'

'Hi.' Carlie's greeting was directed toward Eden, who stared at her just as inquisitively. She offered Lily only the briefest of glances, and Lily's breath caught in her throat as she saw Jason's dark, onyx eyes staring into her, not at her. The resemblance was uncanny. And unnerving. 'Wanna play in the castle?' she asked Eden easily.

Eden, known for her initial shyness, shrugged. But she followed the girl's gaze and stared at the play structure longingly. Sure enough, there was a castle that sat at the peak of it, and a series of ladders, stairs, and ropes could be used to embark on the journey to the top, depending on the child's capabilities. 'I don't know.'

Carlie was a tad bit shorter than Eden, but otherwise Lily didn't think there was much else that would indicate the year's difference in their age.

Jason's daughter obviously assumed she knew the reason for Eden's hesitation. 'It's not scary. It's fun.'

A pair of large gray eyes looked up at Lily, seeking wise words of encouragement and reassurance. Lily didn't get the chance to offer it.

'Come on, I'll show you,' Carlie insisted. Her hand looked so small as she held it out for Eden to take that Lily almost teared up at the cuteness of the gesture. 'It's not scary.'

'Promise?' Eden pinned her with a serious stare.

'Pinky promise.'

As though it was enough to seal the deal and right all the wrongs in the world, a bright smile spread across Eden's face as she curled her pinky finger with Carlie's. Together, the two preschoolers scampered off toward the ladders and stairs of the looming castle. Lily wondered if her daughter even remembered she was still standing there.

'I wish a pinky promise was a binding agreement in adulthood the way it is as a child.' Lily stared after the girls, fighting the innate urge to holler out, 'Be careful!' All those steep steps and dangling knots of rope looked downright dangerous when viewed through a mother's eyes.

'Who says it isn't?' Jason argued with a cheeky grin. 'You're obviously pinky promising with the wrong crowd.' He waved her toward a bench closer to the play structure. Lily followed, only because it meant fewer steps to run toward the castle if she needed to.

'Some people drink with the wrong crowd, some people smoke. Me, you've deemed a rebellious pinky promiser. I'm not sure whether to be thankful or disappointed.'

Leaned forward with his elbows on his knees, Jason laughed. 'Yes, because rebel is exactly the word I would use to describe what I know of you.' So much sarcasm in one meager sentence.

'Well, maybe you don't know enough about me, yet.' The challenge escaped her lips before she thought it through. A beat too late, she realized how her comment might have come across as flirtatious. Lily didn't flirt, hadn't in years. She didn't think of herself as someone who could, or even wanted to. Heck, she didn't know if that was what she was even doing. 'So, I take it Nancy knows you and Carlie come here on Sundays.' A change of subject was needed.

Amusement curled on Jason's mouth, but he took mercy on her and let the conversation shift. 'Everybody does, I think. We've got a little routine. Chocolate chip pancakes in the morning, arts and crafts after breakfast, the park in the afternoon, then we stop at Allison's coffeehouse on our way home for treats before I have to drive her back to her mama's house.'

Lily heard the swan dive in his tone as he spoke of having to return his daughter to her mother, as though she were some kind of property they shared between themselves and not a living, breathing, vibrant young girl. She felt his sadness in her own chest just as much as she heard it with her own ears. 'Arts and crafts, huh?' It was a feeble attempt at putting the smile back on his face, but she tried, anyway.

Jason's fingers steepled as he stared across the grass, watching as the girls laughed with each other. Carlie reached out and helped pull Eden onto the first landing. 'Always,' he replied, grinning. 'Sometimes it's with markers, sometimes it's paint and glitter that I can't get out of my living room rugs for weeks, but Carlie always creates me a new picture to stick on my fridge, replacing the one she made the time before.' He cast a glance at Lily. 'You'd think she was Picasso the way I keep every one of them in a plastic case. Maybe they'll be worth something someday.' He laughed but it was humorless.

Lily's heart crumbled completely. Jason didn't need an elusive *someday* to roll around so that those artistic works could be worth something—they were worth something to him now. They were worth everything.

Suddenly, she felt more than merely sorry for him. She felt like an intruder for showing up and interrupting the only one-on-one time he got with his beloved daughter. She couldn't imagine what it must be like to know there was a time limit on their time together, that someone was waiting in the wings to take her away for another excruciating two-week period and that the hourglass would once again be tipped and he would be left with nothing else to do but wait.

'I'll bet they're beautiful,' Lily said. 'Carlie sure is.'

'She is, isn't she?' No hesitation, just a stated fact. The corners of Jason's mouth lifted. 'Good thing she takes after her mama in that regard. Looks like Eden takes after you in the same fashion.'

It took a moment for what he had insinuated to sink in, but when she realized Jason had just complimented her, Lily's cheeks heated.

Was he putting forth a little flirtatious charm, too?

Based on his momentary deer in the headlights stare, she figured it was safe to assume he hadn't meant to say it aloud. Or hadn't meant it the way it sounded. Whatever the reason, Jason had surprised himself as much as he had surprised her.

Lily was saved from having to come up with a coherent response when she heard a snuffling sound from behind her. She turned just as a large brown and black dog ambled around the corner of the bench and licked her hand.

'Oh!'

Jason stood quickly. 'Jazz, easy girl. Don't worry, Lily, she won't hurt you. She doesn't have it in her.'

Lily rose to her feet as well, noticing the way the dog's short tail wagged so fast that her whole body shook. There was so much excitement and adoration in those soulful brown eyes that

Lily believed him without knowing a thing about the animal—the dog couldn't possibly have an aggressive bone in her body. 'Whose dog—'

Jason pointed. 'Where there's Jazz, the rest of the Beckett clan isn't far behind.'

Lily crouched down to give the dog an affectionate scratch behind the ears. Sure enough, a trio was headed their way. A man, a woman, and a young boy.

'Should have known you'd be here before us,' the man announced to Jason.

'Dad had an emergency at the clinic, but we waited for him,' the boy chimed in. He resembled the older man considerably, his eyes creasing into the same amused glare as he stared at his father and added, 'You're welcome, by the way.'

Jason snickered. 'You two better cool it or Carlie's going to come over here and start making you sing the Get Along Song, like last time.' His hand didn't touch Lily's back, but Jason snaked an arm behind her as though making sure she was included in their circle. 'I don't know if you've met these fine folks yet, but Lily, this is the Beckett family. Cohen, here, is the town's veterinarian. The comical one, there, is Bryce, his son and the town's resident jokester.'

The young boy bowed, obviously honored to be bestowed such a poignant title.

Jason continued to point each of them out, then nodded his head toward the dark-haired woman beside Cohen. 'And this is Paige. She owns the bakery downtown and will be the newest member of the Beckett family in a few short weeks' time. Becketts, meet Lily Brentwood.'

'Oh, you're Lily! Allison mentioned you!' Paige exclaimed.

'Allison? Wait.' Her mind was struggling to keep everyone straight. 'So, are you the cousin that's getting married, then?'

'That would be me,' she chuckled. 'And you would be the godsend who's helping out at the coffeehouse tomorrow so that

102

Allison doesn't lose her ever-loving mind. It's so good to put a face to the name.' Her sincere excitement was almost jarring, enough that it forced Lily to wonder just exactly what Allison had said about her.

'Trust me, Allison is just as much a godsend to me,' she countered. 'Congratulations, by the way. You two must be getting so excited to have the big day coming up.'

Cohen wrapped an arm around his fiancée and squeezed her against his side. 'Don't know about her, but I'm counting down the days.' Leaning down, he kissed the top of her head.

Lily had to hold back the sigh she felt bubbling up in her throat. It wasn't only cute as a button to see a grown man unafraid to admit his feelings for the woman he loved, it was refreshing. Seeing firsthand that that kind of love still existed was like finding another thread of hope to clutch to, another foothold in a rut she had yet to climb out of.

There was no denying the devotion in Paige's eyes when she glanced up at Cohen, smiling brightly. 'It'll all feel more real once my dress finally shows up from New York.'

'You don't have your dress yet?' Lily didn't mean to sound so abrupt, but if it was only a few weeks until their wedding … yeah, she would have definitely been a bundle of nerves by now.

'There was some kind of holdup with the cream satin or something,' Paige explained with a wave of her hand. 'They assure me it's been rectified and is on its way, though, so it should be here any day now.' The pitch of her voice rose in anticipation.

'Cream satin. Now, *that* is exciting,' Lily agreed. 'Unveiling your wedding dress for the first time …'

'Custom made, just for me …' Paige chimed in with starry eyes.

'Uh oh,' Jason interjected. 'Looks like we've lost them, Dr. Cohen.'

'Don't worry, their feet will land back on the ground eventually,' Cohen teased. 'This isn't the first time I've heard this spiel.'

'Oh, stop, both of you.' Paige playfully swatted at Cohen's arm. 'It's nice to have someone around who appreciates the finishing touches of a perfect dress.'

Lily beamed, holding up her hands. 'Believe me, you don't need to explain yourself, Paige. I have a soft spot in my heart for fashion.'

Paige's eyes widened. 'Oh, a girl after my own heart! We're going to get along well, you and I.'

'Bonding over a love of silk and satin. Sounds like my kind of friendship.' Laughing, Lily realized just how true that was. She didn't remember ever meeting anyone with whom she had spoken so easily about her love of wedding fashion and dress designs. Rarely did she admit her passion to anyone because the few times she had, someone either belittled her big dreams or dismissed her ideas completely. That someone had mostly been Michael. The town of Sherman, however, wasn't a place for someone who wanted more, someone who wanted something beyond what was considered the norm.

Port Landon didn't seem to be that way at all. It was small, sure, but there was more within the town limits, and it had little to do with what the town had to offer. It was more about who the town had to offer, not what. People were more open, it seemed. To change, and to outsiders. To the folks who thought outside the box. Heck, she wondered what would have happened in Sherman if a resident had ordered a wedding dress from New York instead of shopping as local as possible. A scene that resembled storming the castle with pitchforks, probably.

'So, did you two come here … together?'

Paige's question broke through Lily's thoughts, slamming into her with the force of a transport truck. 'No,' she stated immediately.

At the exact same time Jason uttered the same word.

An awkward pause followed, short enough that Lily was able to find her breath and keep taking in adequate air, but long enough that a slow, knowing grin spread in unison across Paige and Cohen's faces.

'Right,' Paige replied, squinting at the two of them as though trying to see them a little more clearly. 'Well, that answers *that*, then.'

At a sudden loss for words, Lily looked to Jason, hoping like crazy that he would set his friends straight. To her surprise, she realized that his shoulders were moving slightly and one hand barely covered his faint grin.

The man was chuckling to himself.

'Eden and I didn't know Jason was here with Carlie,' Lily explained. She felt compelled to set the record straight, and fast. 'Nancy said—'

'Oh God, Nancy sent you here?' Paige almost doubled over. 'That explains everything.'

Did it? Lily's head was starting to spin. She had forgotten that everyone seemed to know everyone around here. Nancy's antics were obviously widely known and part of an inside joke Lily was struggling to understand. 'Right, you know Nancy.'

'Not well,' Paige admitted, 'but I know Sonya, her sister. Those women are cut from the same cloth.'

'The same meddling, frustrating, motherly cloth,' Cohen chimed in. He offered a wry grin to his fiancée. 'We had our time in Sonya's overwhelming clutches. Looks like Nancy has chosen you two as her next unwitting victims.'

'That's not ominous sounding at all.' She stared at the couple. They looked so happy together, and so amused at whatever was unfolding before them. 'Should I be concerned?'

'No need.' Paige waved a hand. 'Sonya and Nancy are just being Sonya and Nancy. They must see something you don't.' She reached for her fiancé's hand, squeezing it. 'If it's any consolation, it took us a while to see what they saw, too.' With that, Paige offered Lily and Jason a wink, then led Bryce and Jazz toward the play structure. Cohen followed, but only after sending one more wolfish grin in their direction.

'Don't worry, eventually someone else will wind up in their crosshairs,' he called out. 'But until then, good luck, you two. You're going to need it.'

Chapter 10

Jason

Monday was a long day. Every time the office door opened, Jason kept expecting it to be Lily, showing up because she somehow knew that he had gone ahead and ordered her car parts even though she told him to wait until she had the money in hand.

He didn't see her, though. Didn't hear from her the entire day, yet she was there, never too far from his mind.

So were the memories of Sunday's trip to the park. Located near the veterinary clinic, Jason was used to seeing Cohen Beckett and his family there. They knew his routine with Carlie, just as the rest of the town did. But it was the first time he had heard firsthand about Sonya's antics toward them. It left Jason slightly worried and conflicted.

They must see something you don't. Paige's words were clear and concise. She knew exactly what she was talking about. He had heard rumors about Sonya Ritter's unrelenting desire to pair up Cohen and Paige when the latter first came to Port Landon from New York City. She had fallen in love with the town's bakery that was up for sale at that time, and then fallen in love with Cohen.

Whether Sonya had anything to do with that, no one knew for sure, but the older woman had seemed to know there was love in the air long before Cohen and Paige caught the scent themselves.

The rumors were true.

That was the part that worried Jason most. Not that Sonya's sister, Nancy, was going to try to push Lily and himself together— it was already obvious that the woman had latched on to the notion from the very first introduction. What niggled at him was that he wondered about what Nancy was seeing. If it was actually there. If there was a … connection. Was that a good word for it? Was that even what it was?

He didn't know if he would recognize it himself. Or let himself recognize it, maybe that was more accurate.

He had scoffed, then, thankful the garage was vacant. With Branch gone home for the evening and the office empty of clients awaiting their repaired vehicles, it had left Jason alone with only his thoughts for companionship. Normally, that bothered him because it was his first day without Carlie. The day following a weekend with his little girl usually resembled a hangover for him. Not alcohol induced, but an emotional one. The void of her presence after a few short days was wide and vast, and he had become accustomed to succumbing to and then healing from the hangover each time Carlie came and went.

That particular Monday, however, had been a double whammy. Between missing his daughter and questioning himself about Lily Brentwood, Jason didn't know which way was up.

The following day was no different, other than the fact that Branch, as annoyingly observant as ever, noticed Jason's preoccupation.

'You know, if you think you can fix that coolant leak through telepathy, you're sorely mistaken, my friend.'

Jason hadn't realized he'd been staring blankly under the hood of the F-150 in front of him until his friend's voice broke through the haze. He shook his head and stepped back. 'If only it were that easy, huh?'

Branch didn't see the humor in his halfhearted joke. Leaning against the lifted truck, he eyed Jason squarely. 'Something's up. What is it?'

'Got a lot on my mind, I guess.'

Branch raised an eyebrow. 'A blind man could see that. Be more specific.'

Jason sought out the rag he'd left on the edge of his toolbox so he wouldn't have to look Branch in the eye, then tossed it back down with a shrug. 'Nothing, just Carlie and—'

'And Lily.'

Jason whirled around. 'Yeah, her car,' he replied cautiously.

Branch adjusted his Lakers cap, leaving a dark smudge on the beak. 'You can lie to yourself, Jay, but do me a favor and don't lie to me.'

Something twisted inside him. Jason didn't lie to anyone; it wasn't who he was. Hearing his best friend request so matter-of-factly for him to be honest with him—and knowing he had a right to request such honesty—was a punch to the gut. 'I'm not lying to anyone, I'm just—'

'Not telling the whole truth.' Branch's mouth curved upward at the corners. 'Why's it so hard for you to admit you like the woman?'

'We've been through this. I don't even know her, Branch.' Jason didn't know if that was meant to be the reason he found it so hard, or if it was his argument to prove how far in left field Branch's notion was. By then, he was so confused, he didn't know if he even wanted to know.

Crossing his arms, Branch sighed. 'You know enough about her to be thinking about her when you should be working,' he replied. 'And I didn't think there was anything that could slow down your breakneck speed, so that's got to count for something.'

'You wouldn't understand,' Jason countered.

'Why, because Kaitie and I have known each other since high school? Because I barely remember a time when I didn't know her?'

Maybe he did understand, after all. 'Exactly. I don't know how to explain it.'

Branch let out an exasperated laugh. 'Why do you feel like you have to explain it at all? Just because you haven't known Lily since you were a kid, doesn't mean you can't relate to her now. There's no rulebook for these kinds of things.'

'I'm not looking for rules, I'm looking for logic. She's leaving town soon, and I'm helping her do it.'

Branch leaned in, smirking. 'Funny, there was a time when I said I was leaving town, too.' He slapped Jason on the back. 'Seriously, it's not going to kill you to admit you like this girl, even if it doesn't make sense. Stranger things have happened around here.'

'Just what I want to be; the next strange thing to happen in Port Landon.' Jason laughed it off, but his friend's words of encouragement helped. So, he wasn't completely crazy for wondering if Lily had been flirting with him on Sunday.

'There are worse things to be,' Branch assured him. 'Like scared, for example. Scared of taking a chance.'

'I'm not scared of taking chances,' Jason argued.

'Good.' Branch pointed toward the door. 'Then, take one. We're out of coffee, and there's a woman you might know working at the coffeehouse downtown. Go talk to her. It'll be more productive than standing here staring at the truck radiator.'

Jason glared at him. How in the world had they gotten to a point where his best friend—his employee, for all intents and purposes—was sending him, the owner, on a coffee run? 'And say what, exactly?'

Branch scoffed, pulling a ten-dollar bill from his pocket. He held it out to Jason. 'You'll have to figure out that part on your own, Jay. But while you're at it, get me a large dark roast coffee.' When Jason took the money, shellshocked, Branch headed back toward his bay. 'And make it snappy, will you? I'm jonesing for the caffeine the way you're jonesing for the chance to say hello.'

* * *

Driving to the Portside Coffeehouse was the easy part. Once Jason finally found a parking spot on Main Street—which was a feat of its own considering the number of people milling about that afternoon despite the overcast skies and sporadic rain showers—and parked his truck, he was no wiser as to what he would say once he entered the coffeehouse. All he could do was order Branch's coffee and hope the rest of the words came to him before he looked like a fool.

He didn't quite understand the point of the quest, anyway. What was it Branch wanted him to do, walk in and profess his undying love for Lily? Pretend he was a smooth talker and nonchalantly ask her out so he could wine and dine her?

Jason wasn't that kind of guy, and that wasn't what this was. He didn't know a thing about wine, had nowhere to go after eight o'clock to dine, and he certainly wasn't harboring an undying love for anyone. He saw Lily as more of a kindred spirit. Someone who seemed to understand without verbalizing it. It didn't mean he was interested in her in any way beyond that.

Even if she was taking over his thoughts.

Laughter rang out as he stepped inside. Only a handful of folks sat at the bistro tables, and their chatter was muffled and hushed. Another laugh carried from behind the ordering counter. It took Jason a second to realize that the gleeful sound was coming from Sonya Ritter herself. As Allison's right hand, he wasn't surprised to see her manning the shop in her absence. But he didn't think he had ever heard the older woman laugh so unapologetically that her bob-style hair bounced with each intake of breath. With her raspy voice and straight to the point demeanor, the deep laugh sounded foreign and uncharacteristic. A moment later when another chortle erupted, Jason finally got a glimpse of what—or who—was the cause of it.

Lily. She was perched behind the counter, donning a black T-shirt with the Portside logo on the breast pocket that matched Sonya's perfectly. And she was playing Rock, Paper, Scissors with Eden, who stood before her with a mischievous grin on her face.

'She's a master at this!' Sonya cried. 'You don't stand a chance, Lily!'

A second later when Lily's gaze met his, Jason didn't stand a chance, either. Her pale blonde hair tied up in a simple pony-tail, her face fresh without a hint of makeup, she looked lovely. Carefree, even. He wasn't sure he had seen her this relaxed since they met.

At least, she'd looked relaxed until recognition set in.

'Jason, hey.' Lily's hands stayed outstretched and unmoving. Eden, still firmly rooted in the rules of the game took it as a sign of Paper, and her Scissors motion quickly earned her another win.

'Scissors! You lose!' The little girl pretended to chop her moth-er's fingers hungrily, then pivoted and high-fived Sonya beside her.

Sonya didn't miss a beat; not the high-five or the locked gaze between Lily and Jason. There wasn't a thing that happened in Port Landon that the older woman's eagle eyes missed. Ever.

'Hey. Training is going well, I see.' He held up the ten-dollar bill as though it explained everything. 'Branch sent me in.' Immediately, he hated himself for his explanation. He didn't want her to think he was only there on someone else's behalf, but he was leery of letting her think he was there on *her* behalf, either. He was even warier of Sonya thinking that. 'How's it going?'

He stifled a groan. At this rate, he wasn't going to need anyone's help to sound like a fool.

'Jason!' Eden waved emphatically from behind the counter. Barely able to peer over it, she gripped the edge. 'We're working.'

Jason leaned down on his elbows, resting his chin on his arms. He couldn't see her mouth, obstructed by the edge of the counter, but her smile reached her grayish eyes. 'I can see that. And how many times did you beat your mama at Rock, Paper, Scissors?'

'A hundred times!'

'You're on fiyah!' Barely raising his chin, he untucked one hand from beneath it and held it up, earning himself his own boisterous high-five. 'Good job.'

'On fiyah!' Eden mimicked, letting the pitch of her voice trail upward on the last syllable.

Laughing, Jason raised his head. She was too much. 'Think I can get a coffee for my friend, Eden?'

'Mom, coffee!' The little girl bounced away from the counter and pushed her mother toward it.

Sonya let out another hearty guffaw. 'The girl's something,' she chuckled. 'Isn't she, Jason?'

'She really is,' he agreed, shaking his head at Eden's outlandish antics. In a matter of days, she had been uprooted and temporarily planted in a place where she knew no one, and she just seemed to roll with it, taking in every minute and enjoying it rather than questioning the reasons.

Lily had stepped up to take his order, but that didn't stop Sonya from closing the gap between them, either. Leaning in, she eyed Jason. 'I wasn't talking about Eden,' she whispered.

The woman pushed away from the counter, her mischievous eyes staying securely locked on his until she reached for Eden's hand and led her into the back room. 'Eden, come help me get another sleeve of paper cups. Holler if you need me, Lily.'

There were other people in the coffeehouse but be damned if Jason could hear them through the blood pounding in his ears. And he couldn't see them because, in that moment, all he could see was Lily, her face flushed crimson and her eyes wide as saucers. She had heard Sonya, then.

'What did Branch want you to order for him?' she asked.

Jason's hands pressed against the countertop. When he spoke, his voice hushed. 'Don't let Sonya get to you. She's like that with everybody, I swear. You heard Cohen and Paige yesterday. The woman's a menace. Two large dark roast coffees, please, ma'am.'

'Call me ma'am again and I'll put salt in it instead of sugar.' Her lips pressed together to suppress a grin, but she looked thankful to have something to do.

'And if Allison's got any of that flavored creamer stuff back there, I'll take a shot of—'

'Let me guess, hazelnut?' She smiled without taking her eyes off the coffee she poured.

'Did you learn that mindreading stuff during your training yesterday?'

'Nah, just observant.'

There was something about the way she said it, so confident and sure, that made Sonya's overbearing comment drift into the background. He didn't remember the last time anyone paid enough attention to remember his favorite coffee creamer. He kind of liked the sentiment. 'Things are going okay here? You're getting the hang of the whole barista thing, it looks like.'

'What, like it's hard?' She finished pouring the coffee and added a healthy splash of hazelnut flavoring to one cup before sliding them both across the counter. 'I'm kidding. Goodness, you should have seen me earlier. Someone ordered a double-cupped non-fat sugar-free vanilla latte and I almost ran out the back door.'

'Wow, what ever happened to a regular old cup of coffee?'

'Finally, someone who gets it!' she laughed. 'Don't get me wrong, I'm thankful for the job, and I'll be doing the same kind of thing once I get to Chicago, but if you can lose your breath trying to place your order, your cup of coffee is a little too complicated.'

'I guess we're just not connoisseurs in such things,' Jason reasoned.

'There's nothing wrong with simple.'

'That's good, because I'm a simple man, Lily.' He wasn't sure if he had meant it to come out as playful as it did, but the way his choice of words had stilled Lily behind the counter, the way she stared at him as though she was trying to figure him out, he was glad he'd said it. The idea that she was thinking about him, the way he had been thinking about her, held an allure he wasn't quite ready to contemplate, though. 'So, anyway—'

A shrill ring interrupted his attempt at recovering some safe ground. Even Lily looked surprised at the sound, ripping her gaze away from him to reach for the cordless phone on the counter. Another ring rang out, but no lights lit up on the phone's display.

'I think it's … yours?' Jason instinctively patted his shirt pocket for his cell. It wasn't his ringtone, though, so it had to be hers.

Flustered, Lily pulled her phone from the back pocket of her jeans. Sure enough, it was lit up and the sound grew louder. Whatever she saw on the screen had her eyes widening at the sight of it.

'Dang it,' she hissed. 'I've got to take this.' Lily held up a finger, then ducked into the back room. Sonya and Eden emerged a moment later, with the former shaking her head as she took up her post at the counter.

'That girl's far too apologetic over a phone call,' she said. 'Especially when she hasn't taken a break since she got here this morning. Your friend caught on quick, Jason. She's wonderful.'

His mouth opened, then closed, then opened again. 'She's not … I mean, Lily's a smart cookie.'

He didn't know what to say. Lily wasn't his friend, but she wasn't not his friend, either. She wasn't his anything. He was just fixing her car so she could ride out of town on her white horse. Or, in her white Corolla. Same difference at this point, since both a trusty steed and a reliable vehicle would get her where she wanted to be. Which wasn't here. 'Anyway, I just wanted to update her about her car—'

'So, you'd better wait till she's done on the phone so you can.' Sonya didn't miss a beat, waving toward an empty booth.

A few minutes ago, Lily's confidence had made everything else drift into the background, but Sonya's surety regarding what he had and hadn't yet said brought his surroundings crashing into the forefront of his mind. He should have known, but realizing that the meddling woman had been eavesdropping from some-where beyond the doorway of the back room rubbed Jason the wrong way.

'Sonya,' he groaned, 'You and Nancy might mean well, but you're barking up the wrong tree.'

'Maybe.' She shrugged theatrically. 'But maybe not. I'm just saying, don't ignore what's right in front of you.' The only thing missing from her pompous response was, *So there.*

'There's nothing to ignore.'

'And there's everything to see,' she countered, eyebrows raised in silent challenge.

He might as well have been talking to a brick wall. Honestly, how in the world was he supposed to make Sonya Ritter and her sister see things his way, when he had no idea what exactly *his way* was? God, he was confusing himself. Defeated, he set the coffees down and raised his hands, surrendering. 'You win,' he replied. He was fighting a losing battle. Saying anything more would be futile, anyway.

Reaching a hand out, Sonya patted his arm. 'It's not about winning or losing, Jason. It's about the journey of the race. And you can't run the course with your eyes shut.'

He glared at her. 'I don't know what you think I'm running from—'

'Oh, Jason, dear, if you don't know that, your eyes have been shut a lot longer than I realized.'

He was relieved he had let go of the two coffee cups, because his hands clenched just as tightly as his jaw. So, this wasn't about Lily at all. Not completely, anyway. 'Sonya, you are—'

'Sorry about that.' Lily bounded around the corner, shoving her phone back into her pocket. The tension between Jason and Sonya was obviously written in his tight features. She stopped in her tracks. 'What did I miss?'

'Sonya wants Jason to run with his eyes open.' Eden's voice was small amongst the coffeehouse chatter, but the matter-of-fact tone she used, coupled with Lily's furrowed eyebrows and genuinely puzzled expression eased Jason's tension and caused a bubble of laughter in his throat. He didn't mean to laugh. The conversation was far from funny. But he had honestly forgotten the little girl was still peering up at him from the edge of the counter. And Eden's summary was spot on, even if it was slightly misinterpreted.

'The weird part is, she's not wrong.' He chuckled, pulling the coffee cups into his hands again. 'But I really should be going. Branch will never let me hear the end of it if his coffee's cold by the time I give it to him.'

'Remember what I said.' Sonya pointed a long, painted fingernail at him. The strength that emanated from her belied her age.

'No need to worry about that,' Jason assured her. 'You make it hard to forget.' He cast a glance in Lily's direction. To hell with the ruse about car parts. He just wanted to get away from Sonya's watchful eye. 'See you later, Lily. Bye, Eden.' He gave the little girl a bright smile and a wink, then headed back out onto the bustling sidewalk.

The air, though warm and humid, hit him with the force of a man who'd just broken the surface after being plunged into the deep sea. It was fresh and cleansing on his tongue as he breathed it in, filling his lungs. Sonya's riddles had all but drowned him in his own confusion, only adding weight to the pressure on his chest that kept him submerged. It was that feeling that had pushed him out of the coffeehouse. Not because he couldn't take in an adequate breath, but because he didn't need Sonya's misguided anecdotes creating friction where there didn't need to be. Lily didn't need that kind of drama, either.

'Jason?'

He whirled around, almost crashing into a couple of pedestrians who hadn't expected him to stop. Muttering his apologies, he watched as Lily let the door close behind her before she closed the gap between them. Her ponytail swayed, the light hue of her hair seeming bright in contrast to the gloom of the dull gray overcast skies.

'Are you okay?' she asked. Hands in her pockets, she kept her gaze fixed on him.

Whatever he had expected her to say, it wasn't that. 'Of course.' He resisted the urge to question why she would think otherwise, instead choosing words that would offer him a little more insight. 'Are you?'

'Of course.' The corner of her mouth lifted.

'And Eden? She seems to be taking this all in her stride.'

She rocked on her heels. 'Yeah, she's good. Getting tired of wearing the same three outfits, but she'll be fine.'

It had slipped his mind that it wasn't just Lily's belongings that were in storage somewhere in Chicago. Eden's stuff was there, too. And when their eight-hour trip turned into an extended stay, all the Brentwood girls had was what had been in the Corolla at the time. 'You know, Carlie has got enough clothes at my place to wear something different every day for the next three months. Toys, too. Her pants might be a little short on Eden, but they're close enough to the same size. I could bring some stuff by tonight, if you want.'

She wrapped her arms around her middle despite the warm dampness that hung in the air. 'You don't have to do that, Jason.'

'I don't,' he agreed. 'But I don't mind, nonetheless.'

It was only a pause, for a fleeting moment. One breath. One heartbeat. But it was heavy with intrigue, and with what he could only interpret as hope. 'I would like that,' she said.

The flood of relief that accompanied her reply was Jason's first indication that he hadn't expected her to accept. The fact that his next words came out choppy was the second. 'Okay. That's great. I'll, uh, see you tonight, then.'

'Sounds good. Eden goes to sleep around seven-thirty.' She flashed him a crooked grin. 'I'll have the sweet tea ready,' she added, pointing toward the cup in his hands. 'Enjoy your hazelnut coffee.'

Lily disappeared back inside the coffeehouse.

Jason stayed rooted in place, thinking of how, only moments ago, he had walked away in a bid to protect them both from

Sonya's theatrics. He meant it; Lily didn't need any more drama. She didn't need anybody, either, and she was content to struggle through the hand she had been dealt on her own. But, just then, the way she had given in and let him help—let him *in*—he wondered if maybe Lily Brentwood wanted to need someone a little bit, even for the moment.

If the flicker of anticipation at seeing her tonight was a sign, Jason wondered if maybe somewhere, deep down, he wanted her to need him a little bit, too.

* * *

Soft light drifted out onto the street from the bay windows of the bed and breakfast, shining like a beacon in the slowly fading dusk. It was only a few minutes past seven-thirty, but the cloudiness of the day gave everything it touched a dull, darkened appearance, the sky included.

There was nothing dull or dark about Nancy's house, though. Jason would never comprehend how something could be so old and yet look so modern, wearing its age so well that it renewed its youthful glow effortlessly.

On second thought, he took that back. He did comprehend, but it took the context being vehicles for him to fully understand. There was nothing more beautiful than a seventy-year-old car or truck being restored to its glory of yesteryear.

He pulled the wheeled luggage bag of Carlie's clothes from the bed of his truck, setting it down on the sidewalk before he hauled the trash bag of toys and dolls over the side as well. He hadn't asked Carlie's permission, but Jason didn't think she would miss the Barbies and Littlest Pet Shop figurines considering the mountain of toys still piled in her bedroom at his place. If she did, he didn't think Carlie would begrudge her new friend borrowing them for a bit. His little girl was nothing if not generous, and her big heart made him proud beyond words.

One of the luggage wheels dragged as he lifted it up the few stairs, then across the newly painted front porch. Idly, he wondered who Nancy had hired to do it. The paint was dry, but the faintest scent of acrylic clung to the damp evening air.

'Come on in, dear. No use lingering at the door.'

Jason hadn't realized Nancy was there, watching him from the window. 'I wasn't lingering.'

'But you weren't knocking, either.' A satisfied smirk danced on her lips as she pushed away from the window and opened the door for him. 'Nervous?'

Why in the world would he be nervous? 'I wasn't,' he replied. 'But you're making me wonder if I should be.' He dragged the bags inside.

Closing the door behind him, Nancy chuckled. 'Because of your run-in with Sonya today?'

He couldn't even feign surprise that she already knew about that. She and her sister were thick as thieves. They would be burning up the phone lines to keep each other in the loop as to how far their ridiculous efforts got them. Without asking, he knew Lily hadn't mentioned anything about it.

'I'm going to tell you the same thing I told your sister, Nancy—'

She held up her hands in mock surrender. 'Okay, okay.' Nancy all but sang the word as she reached for the beaded hem of her thin, gauzy shawl and flipped it over her shoulder. 'You win!'

He caught on immediately that she had mimicked his words to Sonya from earlier, no doubt on purpose, but Nancy had already floated out of the room and into the kitchen. The sound of footsteps on the stairs met his ears a moment later.

'Jason?'

His gaze followed the direction of Lily's voice. 'Down here.'

She appeared on the curved staircase, bounding lightly with each step closer to him. 'I thought so. So did Eden, which is why she's adamant that she gets to say goodnight to you before she goes to sleep.'

'Oh. Sure.'

Lily shrugged. 'I'm sorry. I think I'm choosing my battles wisely at this point, but maybe I'm just giving in too much? I don't know.' Defeat was in every syllable, her shoulders sagging slightly. She was tired, he realized, and more than just physically.

Kicking off his shoes beside the door, he met her partway up the stairs. 'It's okay,' he promised with a soothing voice. 'She's testing boundaries, that's all. And pushing your buttons, by the sound of it.' His hand was on her arm before he realized he had reached out for her. 'I'll go say goodnight. If you want, you can hide the bags of clothes and toys downstairs till tomorrow, in case she uses it as another reason to stay up later.'

The sigh that escaped Lily's mouth would have been humorous if Jason hadn't experienced exactly how she was feeling many times before with Carlie and her own battle of wills. 'Thank you, Jason.'

He gave her arm a tender squeeze, then ascended the rest of the stairs two at a time. Kids were funny like that—angelic and perfect, and all parents had to do was follow the unwritten rules to help keep them that way. Unfortunately, children made him think of that 80's movie, *Gremlins*—cute and cuddly as long as you followed the rules, but if you fed the gremlin after midnight or got it wet, all hell broke loose.

'Eden?' The hall was brightly lit, and Jason couldn't recall which rooms had lights on when he had pulled up in front of the house.

A ripple of high-pitched laughter sounded from the room at the end of it. Door ajar, the only light came from a low-wattage bulb in a bedside lamp.

As he peeked in past the doorway, Jason wouldn't even have seen her if he hadn't been looking for her. The little girl was positively miniscule in the middle of the oversized bed, surrounded by big, fluffy pillows and plush blankets. She could have been a porcelain doll amidst all the crisp white linens and fabrics.

'You're not giving your mama a hard time, are you?' He smiled, and the ancient wooden floorboards creaked beneath his feet. Jason's back creaked just as much as he lowered himself onto the foot of the bed. 'All ready for bed?'

Her face illuminated, Eden dug beneath the mountain of covers and revealed the model car he had given her to hold on to. 'Yep!'

Laughing, he raised a hand and high-fived her. The girl had her priorities straight. 'Looks like you're taking good care of Cruella. Thanks for that.'

She held it up, showing it off. 'She's a beaut.'

It was all Jason could do to hold in the rollicking laughter that threatened to bubble up from deep inside him. There was no telling where she had heard that line from, but he had to admit, she'd picked the perfect moment to blurt it out. 'She sure is,' he agreed. 'And she needs her beauty sleep, just like you. Listen to your mama and close those peepers, okay?'

'Peepers?' Eden giggled.

He grinned wryly. 'Yeah, peepers.' He motioned to his eyes, then shook his head. 'Jeepers, creepers.'

The giggling transformed into a full belly laugh, making Jason feel like he had just won some standup comedy contest he hadn't known he was a part of or even wanted to win.

'All right …' He stood and carefully tucked the Panther replica under the covers with her. 'Goodnight, giggle monster.'

'Night, Peepers!'

He was still shaking his head and choking on his own laughter when he got to the doorway. Fingers on the light switch, Jason stopped.

On the top of the antique armoire beside the door, a spiral-bound sketchbook sat open, pencil laid across it as though left there in hopes of picking up where she left off. She, meaning Lily. It was an assumption, but as he took a step closer and let his fingertip trail along the edge of the intricate drawing, he spied the elegant *LB* scrawled in the bottom corner of the page.

The drawing looked like something he had only ever seen on

television, a series of scratches and lines and shadows so carefully and lovingly put to paper that there was nothing else they could do except become a masterpiece. The dress design that occupied the page in front of him was long and trailing, something meant to be elegant and luxurious. But it was more than that. There was something unique and alluring about the dress, something that took the simplicity of it and turned it on its axis. Not over the top, but not muted, either. The design was beautiful, and flawless. Not that Jason knew a damn thing about fashion, but if this sketch was anything to go by, he was pretty sure Lily knew a lot about it. It was more than a soft spot for fashion, as she had told Paige. He lifted the corner of the sketch, curious about the other drawings that lay hidden beneath it.

'Looking for something?'

Jason snatched his hand back as though the paper beneath his fingertips had burst into flames. Lily stood in the doorway, only a step away, her head tilted to one side. Arms crossed, she didn't look angry, but he could see her fingers flexing, itching to tear the sketchbook out of his reach.

'Did you draw these?' It seemed silly to ask, but he felt compelled to hear the confirmation straight from her lips. He wanted her to own her artistic talent. 'These are amazing, Lily.' Again, he reached out and lifted the corner of the page.

Lily's arm jutted out and plucked the sketchbook from the armoire. Muttering a curt, 'Thanks,' she stepped away, clutching the book to her chest. 'I'll be downstairs, okay, Eden? Goodnight, baby.'

'Night, mama.' The little girl's voice was so thick with exhaustion, Jason wondered how long he had been standing there, lost in those charcoal drawings. Obviously a while, since he hadn't even heard Lily's footsteps as she padded across the creaky floorboards in the hallway.

He heard every step as she ushered him out of the room and closed the bedroom door so only a sliver of light filtered out into the hall, then scampered toward the stairs, disappearing downstairs without another word.

Sifting through her sketchbook had been some kind of line he shouldn't have crossed, then.

A cacophony of colorful curse words drowned out his thoughts as he followed in Lily's wake.

By the time he reached the bottom step, Lily had already made it out onto the front porch, leaving only the screen door between them so he would know which way she went. It squeaked deafeningly as he pushed on it. Jason wondered how in the world Lily seemed to move so silently throughout the house when everything he seemed to do made so much noise.

'I wasn't trying to upset you,' he reasoned, settling into the wicker chair opposite the one she occupied. The sketchbook, now closed, was tossed on the glass-topped table between them. 'I wasn't snooping, either. I just saw the book and ... those sketches are good, Lily. Really good.'

'Thank you,' she repeated, staring at the closed book. Her arm lay across the table, and she fumbled with the corner of it, smoothing the edge. 'I don't share my designs very well, I guess.'

Jason blew out a breath. 'If I was that talented, I'd be shouting about it from the rooftops.'

'You're famous in a small town,' she reminded him. 'You don't have to shout it. Everyone already knows your talents, and they respect you for it.'

So, that's what her hasty retreat was about, then. Not that he had seen the sketches, but that he might not give her or her ability the respect it deserved. 'I just fix cars, Lily. Judging by that drawing, you create masterpieces.'

There was a slight narrowing of her eyelids. 'You'd create masterpieces, too, if you had the time to build your Cruella.'

The sudden blast of confidence hit him squarely in the chest. 'Perhaps. Tell me about those.' He motioned toward the sketchbook. He was genuinely interested, but he also didn't want to talk

124

about his grandfather's Panther, currently covered in his garage. Not yet. 'If you want to, I mean. That's obviously not something you just idly doodle. It's a finely honed skill, I'd say. Is that the dream, Lily? The one that keeps you going every day?'

The corner of her mouth lifted as she stared affectionately at the book. 'It's everything,' she admitted. 'I was young the first time I saw a fashion show on television, with models sashaying their hips as the overhead lights beamed down on the luxurious outfits they wore. Seeing the way the designers were applauded for their efforts and their creative minds, and the way the audience oohed and ahhed over the clothing, like nothing else mattered, it was something I'll never forget.' Her gaze flitted up to meet his briefly, before drifting away again. 'It wasn't until my mother got remarried and I went with her to try on wedding dresses at a boutique that I felt satin between my fingers and saw the way silk lace and pearly beads could transform a woman into a princess. I was only eight or nine, but from then on nothing else mattered to me anymore, either.'

Eyes focused somewhere beyond the porch railing out onto the darkened lawn, Jason wondered if Lily even remembered he was still sitting there with her. If she could even see him beyond the vivid memory she was so lost in. If she realized she had given him more insight into her own life in the past two minutes than in the past week. He recognized the look on her face, so wistful with a sense of contentment—wherever she was, it was exactly where she belonged. It was the same feeling he had amidst the tools and automotive parts and the scent of gear oil.

'So, you're a wedding dress designer.' He tested the title on his tongue. 'That's your passion.'

'I'm a wannabe wedding dress designer,' she corrected. 'Right now, I'm a barista.'

It pained him to see the way she guarded herself against her own dreams. Like she could protect her heart from breaking if she didn't attain them. Jason had lived through enough to know that wasn't possible.

'Have you ever created any of your designs? You know, sewn them and held them in your hands?' He had a feeling he already knew the answer.

'A few.'

'Then you're a wedding dress designer,' he said. 'Ain't no wannabe about it.' After a pause, he added, 'I don't suppose you've got any of your masterpieces with you that you can show me? Ones that aren't on paper, I mean.'

Lily shook her head. 'No, everything is—wait. Actually …'

'I'd love to see it.'

The corners of her mouth curled upward. 'It's not what you think.'

'Doesn't change the fact that I'd love to see whatever you've made with your own two hands.'

Jason remained still and quiet as Lily scrutinized him. She must have deemed his keen interest as genuine because she stood up. 'Give me a sec.' His curiosity skyrocketed as she disappeared inside. He heard each muted thud of her feet hitting the stairs as she scrambled upstairs. He was grateful for the moment to compose himself, stamping down his shock that she was really going to share one of her designs with him.

The bounce in her step as she descended the stairs had him wondering if he wasn't the only one anticipating the big reveal. The screen door squeaked open, then thwacked closed behind her. Lily stood on the porch, hands behind her back. Her cheeks were flushed and she seemed to be almost vibrating, but Jason didn't think it was all from nerves.

'It's not a real wedding dress or anything—' Lily began.

'There's no need to play it down, no matter what it is,' Jason interjected softly. Had her passion been belittled so many times that she had taken to doing it herself before someone else got the chance? She wouldn't be hearing comments like that from him, no matter what garment was behind her back. 'I'd love to see what you've got, Lily.'

126

Taking in a deep breath, Lily let it out slowly as she unclasped her hands and held out the handful of silvery blue fabric.

In his hands, Jason held the material gingerly, surprised by the softness of the satin and the intricate stitching. It wasn't long enough to be a dress. As he held it up, he realized his mistake. It was a dress. For a child. And it was familiar. No parent of a little girl would fail to recognize it.

'Holy cow, is this Cinderella's dress?' Jason exclaimed.

Lily laughed immediately. 'That didn't take long.'

'I've seen that movie more times than I can count,' he admitted, running his thumb over the gauzy tulle that filled out of the skirt of it. 'If I didn't know what it was, there'd be something wrong with me. Lily, this is incredible. A mini reproduction of the ball gown in the movie. To a tee.'

The pink in her cheeks deepened. 'Eden wanted to be Cinderella for Halloween last year. You don't want to know how many times *I* had to watch the dancing scene in order to get the details right.' Waving a hand, she dismissed the recollection, but her eyes were alight. She was in her element. 'It doesn't really fit Eden now, but she told me she packed it in case she had to go to a ball in our new home. Said she'd trade it with one of the other princesses for one that fits.'

'Okay, she's officially one of the coolest kids I know,' he chuckled. 'Guess she's right, you never know when you might attend a ball gown trading bazaar in the big city. Got to give the kid credit—she's prepared.' His gaze roamed over the embroidered embellishment at the middle of the neckline. No detail had gone unnoticed. 'It's beautiful. Really. God, Carlie would go bonkers over something like this.'

When he looked up, Lily was staring aimlessly at the dress in his hands. She reached out and tentatively zipped up the dress's zipper, patting the garment affectionately. 'You should take it,' she blurted out. 'Carlie's slightly smaller than Eden, I think. I bet it would fit her perfectly.'

'Oh, no, Lily, I can't take this—' He held the dress out to her, but Lily pushed it away gently.

'After all the help you've given Eden and me? Jason, it's the first chance I've had to give you something in return. I'd love for Carlie to have it. To wear it. It's a gift, even if it is just a hand-me-down Cinderella dress.' Her smile said that she meant it.

He looked down at the satin, bunched and creased in his hands. 'But that isn't just what it is. It's far from just a hand-me-down. It's a Lily Brentwood original. You're serious?'

'As a heart attack,' she replied. 'I've got plans for a new dress for Eden. Truly, Jason, I hope Carlie enjoys it.'

'Thank you for this.' He took great care to set the dress down across his knees. 'You know what I would really enjoy? Seeing the rest of the designs in that sketchbook.'

'Why?' No malice tainted the word, just a sincere curiosity. Lily reclaimed her seat beside him, letting her fingers dig into the edges of the sketchbook.

'I might not wear silk and satin, Lily, but I can guarantee you I understand the value of a pretty dress on a pretty lady. Not wearing it doesn't mean I don't appreciate the art of it.' He patted the satin dress on his lap. 'Obviously.'

'If you're just trying to be funny …'

Jason held his hands up. 'Serious as a heart attack,' he quipped. 'I really do want to see more of your sketches.'

Whatever Lily was searching for in the silence that ensued, staring into him as though the answers were written on his heart and not merely his face, she must have found it. With both hands, she held the sketchbook out to him.

Moving slowly in fear of spooking her, he took the book, his own fingertips brushing hers as he held on and she let go. It was her everything, he knew it. He understood it.

Three pages in, he shook his head. 'I take it back. These aren't just really good.' He tore his attention from the detailed drawings.

'They're phenomenal. Cinderella's dress was just the beginning for you.'

It didn't look like she believed him, but Lily scooched her chair a little closer to his, nonetheless. 'Thank you,' she replied. 'They're not all wedding dresses. Just formal dresses, a mix of luxury and simplicity. A simple luxury, if you will.'

'Sounds like a decent tagline to me.' Jason pointed to a strapless number with an angled skirt, shaded a deep crimson with gray and white accents along the bottom edge. 'This one's cool. I like the angle on the bottom.'

She chuckled to herself. 'It's got an angular hem with a cinched bodice.' Her finger trailed along the page. 'The accents would be small and subtle, but the sparkle they would give the dress would be immense. And then there's this one ...' Lily flipped the page for him, her explanations rolling off her tongue a little more rapidly, her fingertips indicating sweetheart necklines and lace overlays a little more vehemently. Jason didn't understand every word she said, and for a moment he wondered if maybe she was duping him, making up words and descriptions in order to get him back for pretending to teach her the names of automotive parts.

But as he cast a glance from the page to the side of her face, he realized the chances were slim that she was making it up on the fly. Because she wasn't teaching him a damn thing.

She was spilling over with the freedom of finally not having to keep the excitement these sketches stirred within her a secret.

When she stopped for a breath while flipping to the next page, Jason took the opportunity to get in a few words of his own. 'You've never shown these to anyone, have you?'

Lily deflated almost immediately, leaning more heavily on the chair arm. 'I used to, but after a while, being told time and time again that designing clothes was a pipe dream kind of weighed on my psyche. Until recently, I only kept doing it because I wanted to. Because I needed to.'

'Until recently?'

She waved a dismissive hand. 'I submitted a portfolio of my designs to a handful of companies with assistant and internship opportunities available.'

All the pieces clicked into place. 'In Chicago,' Jason finished for her.

She nodded.

Until then, it had seemed like Lily was rolling with the punches the best she could, taking things as they were thrown at her. But he saw the way her gaze shifted to stare out into the darkened, starry sky. She had taken her first active steps toward making her dream come true, and the universe had tossed her a curveball by taking advantage of her spontaneity. She was closer than she had been, but still so far.

'Your car picked a fine time to chug out its last breaths.'

'You're telling me. But thankfully, I picked a fine time to meet you, too.' It took a second for what she uttered to register, and when Lily realized how it could be construed, she cleared her throat. 'For my car's sake, I mean.'

Jason turned back to the sketchbook and flipped the page, choosing to let her curious choice of words roll off him. 'Wow, would you look at this dress.' Anything she had said was suddenly absent from his mind. All that remained was the exquisite detail of the pencil strokes and shading that came together perfectly to form the image on the page. And that's what it was—perfection. Even to his untrained eye, Jason could see that this dress design was special. 'Lily, this is the best one I've seen in this whole book.'

She was locked on the drawing the same way he was locked on her. Nothing could mask the way her eyes glazed over as she stared at it, adoringly and lovingly. 'The A-line scoop-neck dress,' she sighed. 'Floor length layers of chiffon, floral lace overlay over a silk bodice, flowing skirt that gathers at a banded waist … that's my baby, right there.'

'It's a dress made for a princess,' Jason whispered, his mouth curling into a soft grin.

'It's a dress made for me,' she corrected. 'That design is mine, for me only. Someday, I'll get to wear it.'

'You've designed your own wedding dress.' It wasn't a question. He stared at the sketch with renewed interest, picking up on the model's faded champagne hair piled high atop her head, the soft curve of her jaw. He realized then that it was Lily's depiction of herself. 'This is you.'

She smiled in return, but it didn't meet her eyes. 'I did that when I was thirteen years old. It's been tweaked and perfected over the years, but the main features have always been the same. Guess I know what I like.' She touched the page. Wistful, she breathed, 'Someday.'

'I should have known,' he admitted softly. 'I told you it was a dress made for a princess.'

When her eyes met his this time, she wasn't merely staring. Her ocean eyes searched his, flitting ever so slightly as though she couldn't take him in all at once. First his irises, then his dark lashes. Lastly, her gaze drifted downward, to his mouth, and it held there for a heartbeat, just long enough to force Jason to follow suit, wondering suddenly if he would taste the sweetness of Nancy's sweet tea on her lips.

'It's my fairytale gown,' she whispered, entranced. He didn't think she had meant to say the words out loud.

'Even fairytales can come true.'

She watched his mouth form each syllable. Jason wasn't sure if he'd said the words for her sake, or his own. Not until he'd grown silent once more did she raise her head and lock eyes with him again.

'Someday,' she replied, her voice barely above a whisper.

Only inches away, still leaning against the arm of her wicker chair, Jason thought he could feel the faint caress of her breath on his cheek. It would take only a fraction of a second to close the gap between them and lose himself in that pretty gaze.

Or find himself.

'You deserve a fairytale, Lily. I hope you realize that.'

Above the rush of his pulse in his ears, he thought he heard the hint of a gasp amongst the song of the crickets and the scent of the potted marigolds. He blinked.

It was just enough time for Lily to pull away, transforming her expression of surprise into a mask of feigned indifference. And it was feigned, because there was no mask opaque enough to hide the shock in her eyes that she tried in vain to hide.

'Fairytales don't exist,' she muttered, standing abruptly.

At least, that's what he thought she said. It was hard to tell with her back turned toward him and her head down, brushing off some nonexistent dust from her blue jeans as the sketchbook slapped down onto the porch. 'I should go inside.' She turned to him, all trace of the heavy-lidded, pensive look on her face now erased. 'Thank you, though. For the clothes and toys, and for tonight.' She hesitated, but added, 'This was nice.'

'It was.' He rose to his feet, clutching the dress tightly. So many other things crept into his mind. Things he could add. Things he should say.

We should do it again sometime.

I meant every word.

You don't see what I see when I look at you.

But the truth was, Jason wasn't sure he had really seen Lily until he had sat with her only a breath away, eyes alight with the longing that only finding one's real, true passion could ignite.

He saw her now, though. Every fleck of silver in her eyes, and every hope and dream that she hid from the world in fear that they would never understand.

All he wanted was to remind her that she wasn't alone, that she didn't have to be afraid to reveal her talents and her sparkle to the world. With all those sincere, beautiful things to say as Lily crouched down to retrieve the sketchbook, the only thing that came out when he opened his mouth was, 'No problem at all. Have a good night, Lily.'

Chapter 11

Lily

Lily wasn't a fan of things being complicated. She avoided complicated. Heck, she had run from complicated only a week ago, in search of a life that propelled her forward rather than held her back.

Yet, here she was, smack dab in the middle of what was only growing more and more complicated by the minute.

Not only had the manager at the Starbucks in Chicago called that morning to sternly advise that the barista position couldn't be held for her any longer, but the daycare spot she had secured for Eden in the city had also been tugged out from under her a few hours later. At least the woman from the daycare had been apologetic about it and said she would put her on the waiting list for the next available spot, but it was still another thread of silk in a spiderweb of complications.

If only that was where the complications ended.

You deserve a fairytale.

Those four simple words had haunted her for the past two days. Mostly because they were the furthest thing from simple, and because they weren't true. Contrary to Jason's belief, fairytales were just that—fabricated stories deeply rooted in myth. Which, to Lily, was just a fancy way of saying that fairytales were lies.

She had dealt with enough lies to last her a lifetime.

Still, having a tall, dark, and handsome man show up on her doorstep with a garbage bag of toys and clothes for her daughter, while spewing pretty words about her fashion design talents and gazing intently into her eyes on the scenic front porch of a gorgeous Victorian home ... it was about as close to any fairytale as she was going to get.

Which was precisely why she had gasped when she realized how close he was—how close she was to him. One minute her mind was full of the fabric swatches and hem detailing she was explaining to him, the next she was totally, utterly consumed by the way his lips curved and parted as he watched her, waiting, wondering.

Lily had to keep her head out of the clouds. This was not the time to get distracted or read too much into one trivial moment that might have been nothing. The more she played Tuesday night over in her mind, the more uncertain she was that she was even recalling it accurately.

And that was fine. She had more important things to think about than the way Jason's dark eyes glinted in the golden porch light, or the way his deep voice had so softly swept away her pessimism for a fleeting moment and made her believe his whispers.

So much complication.

And then there was the phone call. The one she hadn't expected. The one she had got closer and closer to giving up on as each day went by.

Lily's phone rarely rang, so when it rang two days ago during her shift at the coffeehouse, it had momentarily stunned her. Seeing the 312 area code had completely undone her. As a woman who had spent the greater part of the last six months looking up the office addresses and phone numbers of fashion design companies online as part of her research, she knew a Chicago area code when she saw one.

It didn't make her any less nervous as she dove into the back room and answered the call. Lily was pretty sure she only heard every third word from Magda, the personal assistant of Lilo Ashby, CEO of Lash Fashion. Her pulse pounded so loudly in her ears that she had to ask the woman to repeat her question a second time.

'For the design intern position,' Magda said again, just as bubbly and bright. 'Ms. Ashby would like to schedule a telephone interview with you. Are you available on Friday afternoon at two o'clock?'

Lily had agreed to the interview as coherently as she could manage. Goodness, the personal assistant probably thought she was as socially awkward as they came.

But it was Lash Fashion. Lilo freaking Ashby, one of the biggest up and coming formal designers in the Midwest, wanted to interview her for a paid internship. Lily was equal parts thrilled and mortified. Thrilled because she couldn't imagine anyone better to learn from in the industry, and mortified because she now only had one more day to shed her fanatical fangirl skin and reveal the eloquent and articulate creative being beneath it. A series of broken sentences and gushing compliments wasn't going to cut it during the interview.

No, she couldn't get distracted from what mattered. Soon, Lily would have what little cash she had made during the past week to put toward the car repairs. While Jason fixed her car, she could work on finding another backup job and securing another daycare spot for Eden. Then, she would be Chicago bound. That was where her life was waiting, and it was where she would find her own happiness. Now was not the time to lose sight of that. She was following her dream. Working at a small-town café was not a part of the bigger plan.

It was part of today's plan, however. Despite Lily's string of protests, Nancy had graciously offered—or more accurately, insisted—to keep an eye on Eden while she worked the opening shift so that the little girl hadn't had to get out of bed before dawn. With only two hours left to go before Allison was due back from the florist appointment in North Springs, Lily was already daydreaming about the moment she would be able to lay her head down on the pillow that night.

It was barely afternoon, but there had been a steady line of patrons waiting for their favorite caffeinated beverages since before ten-thirty. It was probably the only reason Sonya hadn't mentioned Jason Forrester in her presence yet as she worked alongside her, pressing buttons on the cappuccino maker and frothing milk with expert precision.

Sonya was a barista on steroids, every movement efficient and flawless. Lily felt like she floundered in the woman's wake. If she could figure out half of what the older woman knew and manage to execute the knowledge into something that resembled capability, she would thank her lucky stars. Then again, not having to fend off Sonya's meddlesome curiosities for the second day in a row was worth thanking her lucky stars over, too.

'Well, well. What can I get you?' she heard Sonya say from somewhere to her left. Lily shook a hint more cinnamon on top of the frappé she was concocting.

'Something with an electric dose of caffeine … and some of that hazelnut flavoring.'

Lily snapped her head up to come face to face with Jason. Eyes sparkling like polished ebony, he raised his eyebrows at her in greeting.

Either her lucky stars just blew a breaker, or they were shining brighter than ever—she couldn't decide.

'Oh, hey,' she said feebly. 'I didn't see you there. Rough day?' Asking for caffeine in an electric dose had to mean something.

It also had to mean something that she hadn't heard from

him since their awkward moment on Nancy's front porch two nights ago. Or maybe that was just her own brain playing silly tricks again, allowing her to think there was a moment at all, something worth remembering.

You're doing it again, she thought to herself.

'One of those days that never seems to end. I figured you must be pretty busy here. I texted you earlier.' In the same instant, both he and Lily cast worried glances in Sonya's direction, but the woman was too busy being a barista extraordinaire to pay attention, having side-stepped past Lily to place a lid on the frappé in front of her. Sonya handed it to the waiting customer, then began to put Jason's order together. It left Lily with nothing to do but switch places with her, taking up residence in front of the cash register.

In front of Jason.

Which reminded her that Sonya was a shrewd, guileful con artist. Just because she wasn't staring at them both with wide eyes didn't mean she wasn't aware of every word and action taking place between them. Jason obviously remembered that as well because he added, 'It was just about your car. I wasn't expecting a quick reply or anything.'

But he was expecting a reply or else he wouldn't have mentioned it. 'Sorry, I didn't realize.' Pulling her phone from her back pocket, sure enough, an envelope icon showed up on the screen, indicating an unopened message. She pressed it.

I wanted you to know, I went ahead and ordered Cruella's new parts. One of them was backordered, so I ordered it from an aftermarket company. I know you said to wait, but I just didn't want to see you stuck. I should have her running like a top by Tuesday. By Monday, if I can get some time this weekend. I hope you're not mad.

So, her lucky stars hadn't burned out completely, though guilt swarmed her as she considered Jason's generous gesture. 'You ordered the parts? You didn't have to do that.'

'I did. With backorders and stuff, I was worried they wouldn't show up in time. So, I made the order,' he explained solemnly. 'And they arrived in this morning's shipment.'

'You have the parts?' Her eyes grew wider.

'Ready and waiting.' He gave a halfhearted grin. 'I hope that's all right.'

It was more than all right. She was one giant step closer to finally being able to continue on her way to Chicago. Only a few more days.

Considering the interview with Lash Fashion was tomorrow, Lily thought she would feel happier about it.

'I'm okay with it if you are,' she said carefully, mentally trying to calculate the funds she had accumulated so far. 'I'm sure you're ready to be done with my car by now.'

'On the contrary. I love working on ancient Toyotas with more issues than a weekly magazine subscription.' A wink followed, and Sonya slid an extra-large paper cup in his direction. 'Thank you, Sonya.'

Lily rang up his order on the cash register, painfully aware of Sonya's pursed-lipped grin in her peripheral vision. 'Anything else I can get you?' It wasn't that she didn't want to participate in banter with him, she just didn't want to give Sonya or anyone else within earshot any more ammunition to further their misguided ideas. By the time she got off work at two o'clock, Nancy would undoubtedly know every word that had passed between Lily and Jason before Lily even stepped in the door of the bed and breakfast.

'That's everything,' Jason replied, slapping a five-dollar bill on the counter. 'Branch and Benji can fend for themselves today.'

'Oh, harsh.' Lily pressed a hand against her chest, feigning pain.

'Those guys have consumed two pots of coffee at the garage already today,' he explained as he waved away his change. 'They don't need me to enable them, that's for sure.'

Two pots of coffee. She wondered if that meant Jason had

come there to gauge her reaction to the fact he'd taken it upon himself to go ahead and order the auto parts. Maybe her lack of response to his text had worried him. Lily left the coins on the counter between them. 'And I thought I was a sucker for a good cup of coffee. Anyway, thank you, Jason. I mean that. Have a good rest of your day.'

Jason stood there, one hand on his coffee cup. He stared at her unabashedly, the smallest of grins tugging at his lips. Then, he swung his glance in Sonya's direction, nodding a silent thanks to her as well. He waited, holding her gaze with the same relentless intent, unblinking. He raised his eyebrows.

To her credit, Sonya quickly turned and made herself busy with wiping down the counter.

Jason stole the chance to lean in without Sonya's prying eyes on him. 'Check your phone in a couple minutes.' His voice was somewhere between the quietest whisper and inaudible, simply mouthing the words. Lily thought she got the message, but it was difficult to completely understand anything when he looked at her that way, holding not only her gaze but her mind, too, with his own personal brand of mischievous intent.

'Enjoy your day, too,' he said, louder than necessary. Eyes sparkling with hidden laughter, he held up his cup in a parting gesture and slipped back out onto the sidewalk. Lily couldn't help herself—she watched him until he disappeared past the sun-drenched windows that faced Main Street.

Lily turned around, fighting to keep her expression neutral. Finally, something Sonya Ritter didn't know about. Something she could keep to herself. It wasn't much, but it was hers. Lily didn't know which she found more thrilling, having a secret from Sonya, or having a secret with Jason.

Surprisingly, the older woman remained silent, topping up the stack of paper cups near the coffeemaker and wiping down the cappuccino machine until it glistened. Lily followed suit, but it only took a couple minutes for her to be wishing for the lineups of customers they'd been dealing with most of the day.

Silent Sonya was even more disconcerting than Speaking Sonya.

Sucker for punishment that she was, Lily leaned against the counter, watching the way the older woman tapped the toe of her scuffed Reebok in time with the jazz music that hummed throughout the café. 'Is … something wrong, Sonya?'

Sonya kept scrubbing at a nonexistent smudge on the counter. 'Nothing at all, dear.'

Lily crossed her arms. She had never met anyone who could say *nothing* but mean *everything*.

She swore she heard Sonya add under her breath, 'Goodness, what is with children these days?' She would have laughed if the poor woman hadn't been so incorrect as to what she obviously believed, and if she wasn't blatantly referring to them both as children who weren't doing as they were told.

'Sonya, whatever you think is happening—'

'I don't think,' she corrected. 'I know.'

'There's nothing to know,' Lily argued, emphatic.

Sonya stepped forward, and instinctively Lily had the urge to step back. The counter behind her prevented that, leaving her nowhere to go.

'Lily,' Sonya began, her tone soothing and apologetic, 'this isn't about knowing or not knowing. I don't know you well, but I don't have to. And you don't have to know Jason well. Knowledge comes with time. But a kindred connection? That's not known, it's felt.'

Lily couldn't seem to get an adequate breath in. Sonya was a lot to handle on any day, but something about her lecture was hitting home, smacking her square in the chest and forcing her to sit up and take notice. She wasn't talking about romance, but a connection. Lily wouldn't admit it to her, but she understood it. She felt it. 'You obviously *do* know Jason well.'

A glimmer of amusement flashed in Sonya's eyes. 'Well enough to know he doesn't come in here to get coffee in the middle of the day without ordering for his friends, too.' She paused, letting the point of emphasis sink in. 'He didn't come here just for coffee, Lily.' With a nod, she stepped away. 'Now, no more nonsense. And check your phone. It's bleeped twice in the past two minutes.'

Lily pulled out her phone, harboring the suspicion that the woman knew exactly who was sending her texts.

Carlie and I are going to the drive-in movie tomorrow night. Carlie wants to know if Eden would like to go with her.

The second message was sent immediately after the first.

I'd like to know if Eden will bring her mama along, too.

She read the texts again. And again, giving herself a moment to compose herself. Lily didn't dare look up to see if Sonya was watching, or if Sonya knew she was right.

But she had to be right, because Lily couldn't see how she could feel so much from a few typed words. As she stared at the screen, another text appeared.

I would've asked you face to face, but the question wasn't meant for Sonya.

No, it was meant for Lily. Only Lily. And the way he had asked, playfully including her daughter in his suggestion, meant more to her than she could explain. It was fun, and fresh, and made the question seem like something more. Like it wasn't simply a friend asking a friend. Like it might actually *be* something more. Like a kindred connection.

Like a date.

Her heart was pounding furiously, an anxious bird trapped in a cage. Lily, however, was surprised to realize that she didn't think it was from fear. At least, not all fear. There was just as much anticipation in the heady mixture stirring within her bloodstream as there was uncertainty.

There were so many logical reasons not to go. So many memories of what happened when she let someone in and let her guard down.

No rules existed for her to know what this was or what Jason truly meant by asking, and there wasn't an instruction manual as to how she should feel or what the right decision was.

It took a fraction of a second for her to realize she didn't want to be governed by that kind of fear. Not anymore. It was a drive-in movie with the Forresters. She wanted to see Jason, and Eden would welcome the chance to do something fun with someone her own age.

She knew she wanted to go. Beyond that, at the moment, she didn't know anything else. But, as Sonya had so eloquently put it, she didn't need to know right now. She just needed to feel.

Lily tapped the screen, the corners of her mouth upturned. *We'd love to.*

* * *

Danielle, Lily's best friend from Sherman, had always told her she was better at showing people the kind of person she was—strong, determined, willing to learn, and a darn good eye for the little details; Danielle's words, not hers—rather than explaining it.

'You wear your confidence and abilities proudly when you're part of a hands-on project. There's not a person who can rival you when you're doing your thing, girl. But when you open your mouth, all your confidence goes out the window like a popped balloon,' Danielle had told her time and time again. 'You can show people how amazing you are, and you can do it flawlessly. You just can't seem to explain it very well.'

Lily had been best friends with Dani since childhood. She knew she meant well with her brutal honesty. But the all-encompassing truth of her statement had never rang as true as it had on this day.

Two o'clock on Friday afternoon had arrived too fast for Lily's liking. Try as she might, she hadn't been able to nail down exactly what she thought she should say once she got on the phone with the folks at Lash Fashion. Heck, she didn't even know if the interview was with Lilo Ashby herself or with her assistant as a proxy. Lily had been so stunned when Magda called to request the interview that she had forgotten to ask.

It didn't matter, though. The moment her phone rang, showing the Chicago area code, the Queen of England might as well have been on the other end of the line. Both Lilo and Magda shared the line on speakerphone. Friendly, concise, and enthusiastic, the two women had done everything in their power to ease Lily's obvious anxiety.

Nothing could save her from herself, however. Every question put forth was one Lily had an answer for, she just couldn't seem to get the full answer out without tripping over her own words and tangling her thoughts as she tried to verbalize them. At one point, Magda even tried to help her out, offering to call Lily back in a half hour to give her time to collect herself. Lily had stumbled her way through, promising she was fine.

Yet, broken sentences fell from her shackled tongue. She couldn't get past the chains that bound her, or the sudden influx of brittle courage that threatened to snap like a twig at any second.

Lily had never been one for tests or quizzes or questionnaires. Interviews were clumped into that same tremble-inducing group. But never in Lily's life had her sheer anxiousness crippled her mind so utterly and completely as it did during the phone interview with Lash Fashion. With so much to say, so much riding on the chance to get her foot in the door and show a rising star like Lilo Ashby what she was made of, the foundation of Lily's confidence had crumbled under the pressure.

In the rubble, all she was left with was a shaky thanks for taking the time to talk with them about the internship and a promise that Magda would be in touch once they had spoken with the rest of the candidates.

Lily wasn't holding her breath.

Defeated, she spent the rest of the afternoon with Eden at the bed and breakfast. The thick cloudy skies had cleared, giving

143

way to a bright blanket of blue. A stark contrast to the gloomy state of her mood. Eden, ever the precocious child, was keen on lifting her mother's spirits. She stayed close, even as Lily folded a basket of laundry—with Eden's help, which meant the bath towels would need to be refolded once the little girl was preoccupied with something else—and refilled the toiletry baskets in the upper floor bathrooms with supplies from the basement supply closet. After that, Lily managed to unearth the old sewing machine Nancy had mentioned from the hallway closet—a boxy looking Kenmore from the 1970's—and got to work trying to mend the ripped tea towel. She took it upon herself to repair a few more while she was at it, as they looked close to succumbing to the same tattered fate.

It was busy work, but Lily needed the distraction. Needed to remind herself that she had sewing skills, and that she was good at it. If she didn't, her dreadful grief for the state of her childhood dream would take over and she would cry.

'Mama, are you sad?' Eden pushed the wooden chair up beside Lily and clambered up onto it, watching intently.

Sometimes, Lily wondered how she ever got so lucky as to be the little girl's mother. Eden was such a small being, but the compassion and generosity and beauty within her was ten times larger. Pride swelled, and her heart burst with the force of it.

'Nah, baby, I'm okay. Just got a lot on my mind.'

Fiddling with the corner of one of the newly stitched tea towels, Eden mulled over her next reply. 'You look sad,' she reasoned. 'Like when I couldn't find Bunny at Greta's.'

Gosh, it had been weeks since that incident. Eden had slopped a healthy dose of spaghetti sauce onto her beloved velveteen rabbit, and while she napped, her babysitter, Greta, had tossed the stuffed toy into the washing machine. Lily hadn't known a thing about it, and when she picked Eden up from her babysitter's house after work, she'd said nothing of the rabbit's absence. It took two full days for Eden to admit what was wrong, but not before the little girl had become a sullen shadow of herself, thoroughly believing the rabbit was gone for good. The reunion with the cleaner, softer bunny had reduced Eden to tears of joy. Bunny was perched upstairs on their bed now, awaiting its pint-sized owner's return.

Somehow, Lily didn't think a few days were going to rectify what she had lost during the train wreck of an interview. Still, she smiled at her daughter. 'Nothing to worry about, my girl. I promise. Are you ready for tonight?'

Eden beamed up at her and gasped. Almost knocking over the chair in the process, she raced from the room as though she hadn't heard her question at all. Lily heard the heavy *thump, thump, thump* of feet on the stairs, then the faint pitter patter down the upstairs hallway overhead. The sounds reversed as her daughter made her way back, slower this time, puffing heavily as she appeared again in the kitchen.

'Here!' she exclaimed excitedly. 'I'm not sad when I got this with me.'

Lily would have guessed that Eden would choose her velveteen rabbit as a consoling gift to keep sadness at bay, but it wasn't Bunny that she presented to her mother.

Eden held out the Panther de Ville replica as though it held the key to happiness.

As shocked as she was, Lily felt relief more than anything that Nancy wasn't around to witness Eden's attempt at making her smile. In less than two hours, Jason would pull up outside and whisk them away to the drive-in movie. Neither of them had ever been to a drive-in before, and Lily had to admit she was looking forward to it, even if it was *Cars 2* on the big screen.

She could just imagine the hearts and stars that would be floating in front of Nancy's eyes when she found out about the event.

Lily would not call it a date. She refused. But Nancy Bergeron would.

Holding the model car in her hands, seeing the way Eden stared at the toy with her own stars in her eyes, Lily wondered what Jason would call it.

* * *

The drive-in movie theatre was held in a five-acre field on the edge of town. According to Jason, the land was owned by a local resident who permitted the Port Landon Recreational Committee to use the spot free of charge with only one stipulation: that the space be used for something to give the younger generation something fun to do and somewhere interesting to go. If the packed parking lot was any indication, then there were a lot of children in town who experienced all the fun there was to offer.

'Mommy, look!' Eden's face was pressed against the backseat window.

Lily didn't have to wonder what her daughter was marveling at. The massive movie screen blazed light across the field, showing the colorful message in block letters that scrolled from left to right, depicting the radio channel to tune in to so that the movie could be heard. It was such a merry mix of modern and retro that Lily was just as childlike in her own wonder. 'Pretty cool, huh?'

'Wait till the movie starts!' Carlie exclaimed from the seat behind Lily. 'And Daddy makes the sound come through the car!'

Lily chuckled, casting a glance toward the driver's seat where Jason sat. 'Is that just one of your many magic tricks?' she asked wryly.

Jason steered the truck into the first open parking spot he found before pressing buttons on the dash to find the radio channel. 'You just never know what else I might have up my sleeve.'

'Hurry, Daddy, it's about to start!'

Eden let out an excited shriek, and both girls fell into a fit of giggles. Lily could only see Eden from her spot in the passenger seat, but there was no mistaking that lighthearted sound—Carlie and her daughter were friends. It was one thing to hang out in the park because they happened to be there at the same time, forced together by chance and circumstance, but an invite to a movie and simultaneous high-pitched giggles sealed the deal.

Seeing as both Jason and Lily were wearing matching faint grins that hadn't faltered since they'd begun the drive out to the edge of town, it looked like they were becoming friends, too. A movie and a smile shared—it sounded like friendship to Lily.

She kind of liked it.

'Thank you for inviting us along,' she offered, interrupted by an electronic monotone voice floating throughout the truck cab.

'*Stay tuned for tonight's feature motion picture. Stay tuned for tonight's feature—*'

The endless loop was cut off by girlish cheers from the backseat.

'Where's the popcorn, Daddy?' Carlie's feet bounced off the seat in front of her, and she clapped her hands. 'We need the popcorn … stat!'

Before Lily could laugh or question the young girl's termi-nology, Jason shook his head. 'One mistake of leaving *The Good Doctor* on television for five minutes, and this is what I end up with.' He shook his head. 'Pass me that bag by your feet, please.'

'I'll handle this.' Lily plucked the grocery bag from the floor and tore open the bag of movie theatre popcorn from the convenience store. She inhaled the buttery scent dramatically. 'Mmm, maybe I'll just eat it all myself.'

'Nooo!' Carlie tried to whine, but it was cut off by more giggling. 'You have to share!'

'Oh, all right.' Lily plucked one piece of popcorn from the bag and held it out to the little girl. 'You can have this one.'

'No, more than that!' she laughed. 'You're no good at sharing, Lily.' She jutted her arms between the front seats, squealing as she narrowly missed the bag.

'Well, then.' Lily popped the puffed kernel into her mouth, unable to contain her amusement. 'You're not very good at pretending to be mad, either. You should really stop laughing, Carlie. It'd be more realistic.'

The little girl put her hand over her mouth, but it was futile. The giggles continued to erupt. 'I can't,' she cried, still craning forward for the bag, 'You're too funny!'

'Funny lookin'!' Eden piped up beside her. The joke was enough to reduce both girls to tears, they were laughing so hard. Carlie's outstretched arms disappeared into the backseat once more as she collapsed onto the seat with Eden.

'All right, you two, we'd better settle down before the movie begins.' She cast a glance at Jason. 'You mind if I just hand it over to the girls?' she asked. 'I doubt they'll eat it all, but stranger things have happened.'

He waved a dismissive hand, grinning from ear to ear. 'Nah, let 'em have a little fun.'

'I think they already are.' Lily passed the bag into the backseat just as the monotone voice was interrupted by the opening credits of the movie. Another cheer from the backseat, garbled by mouths full of buttery popcorn. 'This is so cool,' she added in a whisper, her gaze locked on the screen ahead.

And it was. Darkness had fallen, though a hint of the day's brightness still appeared on the horizon. A four-door sedan and a large SUV flanked the truck, and Lily could see excited children bouncing and pointing toward the screen. No wind, no rain, just an unobstructed view of an outdoor movie screen and two young girls who thought it was the greatest Friday night ever.

'Agreed.' Jason unveiled a bag of Twizzlers from the grocery bag and, inconspicuously, he held a finger to his lips. He continued to speak while ripping open the bag, his voice mixing with the movie's audio and drowning out the sound of the plastic being torn. 'Carlie and I check this out almost every weekend we're together. It's always this packed, too.'

'Daddy, shh!' Carlie tapped his seat. 'The movie's on!'

'Yeah, Mama,' Eden chimed in, enjoying the chance to joyously chastise. 'Shh!'

Turning around in his seat, Jason smirked at the two cherub-faced girls. 'Who's being funny now, huh? Want to make a switch and sit in the front seat so you can see the movie better, and Lily and I can still talk without bothering you two princesses?'

The girls were unbuckling their seatbelts and clambering over the middle console before Jason even had the entire suggestion out. Lily laughed, wondering if that had been their end game the whole time.

Popcorn was already crushed into the floor where Carlie's booster seat sat, but Jason didn't mention it. Instead, he settled the girls into the front seat—Carlie in the driver's seat and Eden cross-legged on the passenger side, with two juice boxes in their cup holders and a bag of popcorn propped open between them—and removed their booster seats from the back, setting them on the grass outside the truck.

'They'll be fine there till the movie is over,' he whispered to Lily. He waved a hand toward the opened door to the backseat. 'Shh, or the cute little gremlins in the front will ground us till we're forty.'

'No, a hundred!' Eden piped up from the front, setting off another series of giggles.

'You just watch your movie, my girl.' Lily reached over the headrest and ruffled her daughter's hair.

Once all four doors were closed, the movie's audio surrounding them from all sides, Lily sighed and let her head fall back onto the comfortable headrest. 'Yeah,' she breathed, turning toward Jason. 'This is awesome. Thank you again, Jason.'

Jason didn't fit in the backseat quite as well as she did. His knees pressed into the driver's seat and the headrest was too low for him to lean back comfortably. He didn't seem to mind. 'You guys never did anything like this in Sherman?'

Lily was pretty sure it was the first direct question about her hometown he had asked her since they met. Maybe it was the happiness in her daughter's eyes, or the moment of luxurious downtime she was stealing, but Lily didn't dodge the subject. 'We didn't have a theatre in Sherman,' she replied. 'Even if we did, I don't know if I would have gone to it.'

Something sharpened in Jason's gaze, evident in the dashboard lights. 'You and your ex weren't movie-going kind of folks, I take it.'

A scoff erupted from her throat. It wasn't funny, but his choice of words was uncanny. 'My ex hasn't been around for a long time, Jason, but I guess you could say that. Part of him was always with me in Sherman, no matter where I went or what I did. So, yeah, if I'd gone to a movie theatre, he would've been with me whether he was actually there or not.'

He didn't flinch, but her forwardness surprised him. It surprised Lily, too, and she was thankful for the dimness of the truck cab. She hoped it hid the heat flushing her cheeks.

'Sorry,' she added. 'I'm not trying to ruin this night with my baggage.'

'Don't apologize for talking about yourself,' he whispered. 'Sometimes, the stuff that makes up who we are is difficult and hard to take. Doesn't mean we should push it down and keep it hidden away. It's better to get it out willingly than to have it explode when you least expect it. Besides, me and baggage, we're old friends. You can't ruin tonight by bringing baggage along with you.'

Lily didn't raise her head, just her eyebrows. 'Those are pretty profound words.'

'I'm a pretty profound guy.' The corner of his mouth lifted. 'Seriously, though, I'm just speaking from experience.' A bout of silence followed, and both adults checked to make sure the girls weren't paying them any mind. Little hands were mindlessly shoveling popcorn out of the bag, their enraptured gazes locked on Mater and Lightning McQueen's antics.

'Does she see her father very often?' Jason's voice was soft with no hint of demand. He slid down in his seat, sprawling out as much as possible and leaning his head against the headrest behind him. Hands clasped together over his abdomen, he waited.

Lily admired his bravery. She wasn't sure she would have had the guts to ask about Carlie's mother first. 'Michael left before she was born,' she confessed. 'He's never met her.'

'Damn, I'm sorry, Lily.' He stole another glance at Eden's profile, this time more curiously. 'He's missing out, big time.'

'I agree with you, but he never saw it that way. He always had big plans. Unfortunately, children weren't a part of those plans.'

'So, he just left?' Jason couldn't seem to comprehend the notion, and a mix of incredulity and horror marred his chiseled features. Lily felt lighter, somehow, knowing he was shocked by Michael's decision. It meant she wasn't crazy for still being unable to understand it herself after all these years.

She nodded. 'Within a few weeks. All the cliché stuff you hear about, like *This wasn't what I signed up for*, and *This isn't how I planned out our life*. He said it all, like I had done something to him. Like having a child was some kind of jail sentence that would prevent him from doing all the things he had said he was going to do since we were teenagers but hadn't done yet by our late twenties. That was the thing with Michael, he had big dreams, but if those dreams weren't realized quick, and with a big payoff, he moved on to the next supposed moneymaker.'

'His big dream was to be rich?'

'Not just rich, but rich quick.' She shrugged. 'That was how he measured success. Dollar signs.' It surprised Lily that she was able to pinpoint Michael's misguided aspirations so easily now. There had been a time when she wanted so badly to believe that his motivations included her and their life together that she would have given very different answers. The entire town of Sherman would have. But being the teenage golden boy of his hometown didn't allow Michael's indiscretions to continuously go under the

151

radar the way he thought they did. People noticed his flippant attitude; they witnessed his inability to hold down a decent job and his incessant desire to live beyond his means. To puff out his chest and pretend to be something he wasn't. They mentioned it to Lily, too. Worried about the hole he was digging, the vicious cycle she was caught up in as she worked tirelessly at the restaurant and he drove them further into debt while waiting for the universe to give him all the things he thought he deserved. He had not only wrecked her trust, but he'd destroyed her credit.

By the time she saw him for who he really was, Lily didn't know how to save herself from the situation her naivety had placed her in.

Then, she found out she was pregnant. A switch flipped within her. She might not have known where to start when it came to fighting for herself, but she vowed she would fight tooth and nail for the child she carried. For the life her child deserved.

She would never understand the ease with which Michael turned his back on his unborn daughter, how nonchalantly he had signed his name and stripped himself of his parental rights, like being a father was a choice, but it was a blessing in disguise. Lily let him walk away, and he had done it without a second glance. He evacuated Sherman almost immediately. She didn't ask for a dime; after all, she couldn't get blood from a stone. She didn't want his money, anyway. She didn't want anything from him. The only thing that had mattered since was the little girl their tumultuous time together had graced her with.

'Money doesn't equate to success,' Jason replied quietly.

'Or happiness,' she added. 'Or so I've heard. Doesn't mean I wouldn't like to give it a try.'

'You and me both.' His amusement was only evident for a split second. 'But not at the expense of my kid's happiness.'

'That's because you're a real father,' Lily whispered. *A real man*, she added silently.

Because that was what men did, they put their children's needs before their own. Measured their success not by money, but by moments. Memories. By the things they shared with their family.

Jason's throat moved visibly. 'I try to be. Being a father is the best thing that ever happened to me. Hands down.'

'I hear you. It was unexpected, but now, I can't imagine being anything but a mother. My own mother always told me that would happen, but I didn't believe her until I experienced it.'

'She's in Sherman?' Jason asked softly. 'Your mom?'

Lily shook her head slightly. 'It'll be three years in October since she passed away from a stroke.' Before Jason had the chance to utter the socially mandatory apology for her loss, she gave him a fleeting smile. 'I'm just glad she got to meet Eden.'

'That's good.' He paused. 'You said at Nancy's that your mom got remarried when you were a kid, so you've got a stepfather, then?'

'Mom was wonderful, but unfortunately she wasn't very lucky in love. My own dad left when I was three, moving to Lansing. I lost contact with him years ago. And let's just say that my love affair with satin and silk that came from Mom's second marriage lasted much longer than the union itself. It was just her and me after that.' She sighed. It felt freeing to talk about her own life, the parts that were hers and hers alone, no matter how unorthodox those parts might be. 'My mom was a good mother.'

'So are you,' Jason reminded her. 'Just in case you forgot.'

'Like you do?' she challenged, one corner of her mouth lifting. 'You're a good father, too, Jason.'

'It's hard only getting to see her every second weekend.' He cast a glance toward the front seat of the truck, where his daughter laughed unabashedly at the cartoon movie. Her effervescence was a stark contrast to the pain glazing over her father's eyes. 'I'm no fan of your ex and his decision, but there's one thing he said that rings true to me—this isn't how I planned out our life.'

'I take it your split from her mother wasn't amicable.' Lily matched his soothing tone, taking note of the way he had spoken of the girls without using their names so as not to catch their attention.

'It wasn't,' he admitted. 'I think I thought I could show her that we could have it all, right here, together. I think I was so hellbent on it that I'd convinced myself that things were working out between us better than they actually were.'

'Sometimes, we only see what we want to see,' Lily whispered. 'I'm just as guilty of that. But I don't think we did anything wrong by believing in the people we loved.'

'I thought you weren't an optimist?' He leaned over and nudged her shoulder.

'I might not like it, but in the end, I believe in love. I believe people are good.' She shrugged, not wanting to sound like an over-romanticized walking cliché. 'Besides, I wasn't always a pessimist.' She smiled. 'Sometimes, the old ways manage to crack through the foundation.'

'Well, I'll be damned,' Jason whispered, a taunting smile playing on his lips. 'You're a closet optimist. I didn't see that coming, either.'

'Don't get used to it.' She shifted, allowing her limbs to sink into the soft seat fabric. 'Were you and Natalie together long?' She winced at having to mention the name aloud, but Lily's intrigue outweighed, barely, her fear of the unknown. She had confessed the truth about Michael to Jason. Maybe talking about Natalie would be just as cathartic for him.

'A while,' he replied. 'Three and a half years. Engaged for the last six months of it. But it's been about two years since she decided this wasn't where she wanted to be.'

'In Port Landon, you mean?'

'With me.' He averted his gaze, focusing on a frayed thread on the knee of his jeans. 'She didn't want to be stuck in a small town anymore. Said there wasn't enough to hold her here.'

'My gosh, I'm so sorry, Jason.' Lily's heart ached for him. He had tried to make a life with someone that wasn't meant to be, desperate to hold on to a sliver of hope that things might get better. That things might be different. She knew a thing or two about that.

'No need to be sorry. It was a long time ago.' The tight set of his jaw announced that it hadn't quite been long enough. 'We both made mistakes, and we both held on too long. I think that's what it comes down to. Foolishly, I hoped getting engaged, showing her how serious I was about her and our family, would fix things. And just as foolishly, I think Nat said yes just to give us one last shot. To try.' He shook his head at the silliness of it all. 'But things didn't change. They couldn't. I couldn't leave my hometown. I had my own business, my own home, and people depended on me. Nat depended on me, too, but in the end, there was no way I could give her what she wanted.'

'And what was that?'

'Someone else,' he said, a sad grin forming on his mouth. 'Everything she disliked about the small-town life was everything I was. Everything I *am*. She wanted more than Port Landon had to offer her. I thought I was the kind of man who would give her anything she asked for, but she proved me wrong. I couldn't give her a different version of me, but only because it didn't exist. Still doesn't.'

'You shouldn't have to compromise who you are to be with someone else.' The urge to reach out and squeeze his arm was almost debilitating.

He nodded, somber. 'I know. Nat moved to North Springs when she was only two.' He nodded toward the front seat. 'I don't even know if she remembers what it's like to have me around for more than a couple days at a time. I think that's what bothers me most. Technically, she sees her mama's new boyfriend more than she sees me, I think.'

Lily didn't even know what to say. There weren't words in the English dictionary that expressed how deep her sorrow went for Jason Forrester. It was one thing to be Michael, a man who signed over his legal parental rights to his own child and left his family without looking back. It was another to be a man with only a fraction of the life he so badly wanted, unable to stitch the tattered fabric of his heart back together because the missing threads were from something that would never be able to exist again.

'I can't fathom what that must be like,' she whispered. She bit down on her tongue, willing herself not to utter another apology.

'And I can't fathom how a man walks away from his unborn child, so I guess we're even.' He tilted his chin up slightly.

'Even? This isn't a competition.'

'You're right. But if it was, we'd both be neck and neck for first place in the Saddest Single Parent Story award.'

'Please tell me that's not a thing.' She covered her face with her hands, feigning dread.

'It better not be,' he chuckled. 'Because I'm not sure I'd want either of us to win.'

'Me neither.' Against her better judgement, Lily reached out and touched Jason's arm, hoping he found some semblance of solace in the gesture. 'If it's any consolation, I think you'd be in the running for Best Dad In The World, too. Especially if your daughter gets to vote.'

'In the universe, actually.' He grinned wryly. 'I happen to think you're doing a pretty good job as a mother and a father. That's got to be a tough gig.'

'Some days you feel like you've got it all together, running a well-oiled machine. Others, your kid is eating strawberry Pop-Tarts straight from the packaging and you're telling yourself it's a serving of fruits. We're all just doing the best we can do with what we've got, Jason.'

'And what have you got?' he asked, his voice barely above a whisper.

Head still leaned back, he faced her, watching her every move. His eyes never left hers, and Lily didn't know when his fingers landed on top of her hand, touching just above her wrist. He was just there suddenly, his warmth seeping into her skin and keeping her grounded. Time ceased to exist. Nothing was real except the moment, and the feeling within it.

'I've got my dreams,' she replied with a trembling breath. 'My baby girl. And I've got Port Landon, for now.' The corner of her mouth lifted. 'Which, as it turns out, isn't half bad, after all.'

'And me,' Jason added. 'I know this wasn't part of the plan, but you're not alone in this, Lily.'

Her breath caught, unsure what *this* was. Did he mean her blundered trip to Chicago, her unexpected stay in his hometown? Or was he talking about this, right now, the way he robbed her of her breath as well as her cynicism, giving her reasons to believe he was the furthest thing from her plan but a pivotal part of a greater one?

'I know,' was all she managed to squeak out, and her voice cracked with the weight of it. She didn't know what she was agreeing with, or whether it mattered. All that did was that Jason was there, his hand resting on hers, telling her something she didn't understand but wholeheartedly believed. Every word that fell from his lips, only inches from hers, was rooted in truth and as intoxicating as aged red wine.

Jason's shoulders moved as he raised his head slightly, his dark gaze reflecting the neon glow of the movie screen. He came closer, his gaze searching hers as his thumb caressed the top of Lily's hand.

'I know,' she said again, this time more solidly, if for no other reason than to give herself—to give them both—permission to fall.

'Mama, shh!' Eden craned around in her seat, shaking a finger defiantly. 'The movie's on!'

Lily and Jason both snapped away from each other as though lightning had struck between them. And perhaps it did. Lily didn't know how else to explain the smoldering embers left searing her hand where Jason's fingers had been only moments before.

She cleared her throat. 'Sorry, baby.' She waited for the little girl to whirl around in her seat before Lily chanced a look in Jason's direction.

The same embers warming her skin were alight in his eyes, paired with a crooked grin that would haunt her just as much as the ghost of his touch. Lily had said that she couldn't fathom what Jason was going through. But right then, in the darkness of the truck cab, she was struggling with the idea that anyone would want more than this tiny town had to offer.

Or more than Jason.

Chapter 12

Jason

There was a domino effect to everything in life; Jason believed that, deep in his gut. It was impossible to know which event or action was to blame for the next sometimes, just as it was futile to try to think of how things might have been different if he had simply knocked over a different domino from the beginning.

Call it confusion or just a plain thick skull, but he couldn't figure out how fixing a white Corolla with one wheel in the grave had led to uncovering his grandfather's car, which led to offering up some of Carlie's belongings because he knew money was tight, which then led to sneaking an offer to come to a drive-in movie past the oversized ears of Sonya Ritter and coming so close to kissing Lily that he could still feel the faint brush of her breath against his cheek.

What in the world had he been thinking?

From the start, he knew Port Landon was only a stop in her journey. He knew it when she stared at him for the first time as the headlights of his truck highlighted the disappointment in her eyes. He knew it when she took the job at the coffeehouse so she would make money quicker with the hopes of leaving town faster. And he knew it when he sent that text message, using Carlie's budding friendship with Eden as an excuse to invite Lily along to the movie.

He knew it, but it didn't mean he fully realized the expiry date on their friendship. Now, it was all he could think about.

Well, that, and the kiss that never happened.

Something happened, though. There was no other way to explain how he could have let his guard down and spoken about Natalie to her as though he had known Lily for years instead of days. He felt the difference, the shift that had unsteadied the foundation of his defenses. Obviously, he wore that difference like a brand-new baseball cap, because his eagle-eyed mother seemed to see it as well.

'What's gotten into you?' Bettina Forrester could rival the likes of Sonya and Nancy when it came to her shrewd observation. She didn't miss a thing, but unlike the two overbearing sisters, Jason's mother only spoke of her thoughts and feelings when asked. And when they involved her son. 'You seem … distracted.'

Jason felt distracted. Setting another place at the oak dining table in his parents' cramped kitchen, a heady disconnect flooded his body, like the part of him that was moving was completely separate from the part that was overrun by his thoughts. He had never been an overthinker. Now, it felt like that was all he did.

'Just thinking about Carlie.' It was a low blow, but he knew that mentioning his daughter would ease Bettina's insistent chatter.

The Sunday evening dinners at his mom and dad's apartment were just as much a part of his routine as the drive to and drop off at Natalie's place in North Springs. Fridays were good days for him—he was gifted the entire weekend to be with his daughter. Sundays were the opposite, the day he had to give her up again for real life. The only two things that made that trade-off bearable were knowing the countdown to seeing her again would start once more and getting a big ole' homecooked meal at his parents' place.

'Did you two do anything fun this weekend?' she asked.

Roderick and Bettina's two-bedroom apartment was small, but the cozy ambience made up for the lack of room. Little things reminded Jason of the childhood home he'd once grown up in— the home he now owned himself—despite the apartment being nothing like it. His Grandma Mary-Jean's crystal platter graced every Sunday dinner table spread, the familiar framed photo of his parents from their twenty-fifth wedding anniversary that had once hung on the wall beside his dad's recliner now took center stage on the electric fireplace's mantle, flanked by candid shots of Carlie and himself. The dinnerware was still the chipped, faithful Corningware he had eaten every meal from as a child. All the pieces were there, they just fit a different puzzle. It wasn't home, but home was there, in the details.

Placing forks onto the bamboo placemats, then knives, Jason nodded. 'There's a glittery painting of a unicorn on my fridge, as well as a handful of glitter ground so far into the living room carpet I might never get it out.' He smiled, lost in the memory and the table setting task at hand. 'And *Cars 2* was playing at the drive-in, so we took Lily and Eden—'

He froze. Across the open-concept room in the kitchen, his mother did, too.

It was too late; the mistake had already been made.

'You and Lily took your daughters to a movie,' she finished for him, barely able to contain the glee in her aqua eyes. It wasn't a question, but a nudge. She dragged out the last word, urging him to continue. Which only meant one thing.

'You already knew.'

Bettina tapped the soup ladle down on the spoon rest, stepping away from the pot of homemade potato and bacon soup, big enough to feed an army. Watching her in the kitchen always amazed Jason. Her eyesight might not be 20/20, but in her own

161

environment, with her own belongings and her internal familiarity to guide her, it seemed inconceivable to think his mother couldn't see her surroundings with the same vivid clarity he did.

She shrugged. 'I may have heard about your date.'

'It wasn't a date.' He wanted to ask who was to blame for his mother's intel, but it was probably better for him not to know. There was no stopping the information highway that ran straight through Port Landon.

'You took a pretty girl to a movie,' she reasoned. 'That's a date.'

Jason pointed at her in warning. 'Carlie asked if Eden could come with us; they're friends. I couldn't very well not ask Lily to come along. She has no one else.' The lies toppled off his tongue far easier than he expected.

'And Lily, she's your friend?' A challenge burned in her gaze, daring him to argue differently.

It was a fight he wasn't going to win. If there was anyone who could read him like a book and predict what he was going to say before he said it, it was his mother. Bettina knew him better than anyone, which was both a blessing and a curse. 'Yeah, I guess she is.'

Bettina grinned as she placed the salt and pepper shakers on the table. 'What a pretty name … Lily.'

Inside, Jason cringed. His mother was already swooning at the mere thought of a love interest in his life. Except, that's not what Lily was. 'Mom, Lily's leaving in a few days. I should have her car done by tomorrow, then she'll continue on to Chicago. Obviously, your secret sources forgot to mention that part.'

'Oh, I know about all that business.' She waved a hand, swatting away the truth like a pesky housefly. 'If you like the girl, what's a few hours, Jason?'

'Everything.' He had completely forgotten to adamantly deny his interest in Lily, too flooded with memories of just how much difference distance made the last time he tried to love someone. 'North Springs is closer to Port Landon than Chicago is, and I still couldn't make it work with Natalie.'

162

'Jason, she's not Natalie.'

Hearing his ex-fiancée's name on his mother's lips was equivalent to hearing a curse word. Bettina didn't say her name if she didn't have to.

'Not only that,' she added, 'But I don't think she *wanted* things to work between you two. I know that's hard to hear, son, but Natalie didn't want to be with you, just as much as she didn't want to be in Port Landon. And if that was the case, then the girl didn't deserve either of you.'

He scoffed. Leave it to his mother to personify their hometown. Port Landon wasn't the one who had been left with a broken heart when Natalie left. Still, he knew Bettina was right. Jason drove back and forth to North Springs all the time, for Carlie and for his parents.

Maybe there was a subconscious part of him that had known it wasn't meant to work out between them, either.

Natalie knew the bigger truth of it, though—there was a difference between driving to the city and being there for brief stints and uprooting one's life to live there. Jason wasn't about to walk away from his home and his business—from his *identity*—to become someone he didn't recognize. Just as his parents still had ties to Port Landon long after they had moved into the city to be closer to Bettina's doctors, Jason had ties to the town as well, and those ties were wrapped tightly around his heart, keeping him whole.

Natalie had realized he wouldn't leave before he realized she wouldn't stay. Jason could only thank the heavens above that their split hadn't been messier or more complicated than it needed to be, and that she had willingly remained close enough that he could still be in Carlie's life as much as he was. He would be grateful to her for that forever.

'I know she's not Natalie.' It was easier to focus on that part of his mother's monologue. 'But that doesn't change the fact that Lily is leaving. Or that I've only known her about a week.'

Ten days, he immediately corrected himself, *but who's counting?*

Jason looked out the window, hoping to see his father's SUV across the road in the apartment complex's parking lot. Roderick Forrester was a man of reason, not to mention a man of few words in many circumstances. Jason should have known his mother had something up her sleeve when she sent him out to the store for milk so close to supper being ready.

Clarity dawned on Bettina's face, and she rounded the end of the kitchen counter that separated the kitchen from the dining room, hands on her hips. 'Is that what this is really about?' she asked. 'That you haven't known her long enough for it to make sense? Oh, Jason, there isn't enough time in this crazy world to make love make sense.'

His hands flew up, though as a halting gesture or in surrender, he wasn't sure anymore. 'Slow down. No one said a thing about love.'

She winked, and it was the most uplifting and terrifying thing he had ever seen.

Shaking his head, Jason straightened the napkins on the table and set about placing the salad bowl in the middle of the spread. 'You don't understand.' He didn't look at her. 'You and Dad knew each other since you were kids.'

'And you think that made falling in love easier?' Bettina stepped back around the counter and turned the dial on the stove, lowering the heat of the burner to let the soup simmer. Then, she took a seat at the table, fixing her son with an incredulous gaze. 'I knew your father around town, yes, but we didn't socialize in the same circles, Jason. He's four years older than I am, and that's a lot when you're a teenager. We knew each other in passing, but nothing more.'

'But you knew each other,' he insisted, driving his point home.

His mother steepled her fingers in front of her. 'Let me ask you something. How much do you know about, say, Krista Belton?'

Bewildered, Jason shrugged. 'Not much, really. The usual stuff, I guess.' He'd gone to school with Krista from kindergarten onward, and the woman now worked at her father's insurance office on Main Street, a closet-sized office attached to the bank.

'But you've known her your whole life,' she pushed.

'That's different. I'm not interested in Krista.' Jason could have choked on his own tongue.

Unfortunately, his mother's Cheshire cat grin was already in place. 'And maybe that's because you don't really know Krista. The spark isn't always evident from a distance, Jason. It wasn't until I was talked into going to the county fair with your aunt and her friends—all of whom quickly ditched me after I said I wasn't going on that confounded Ferris wheel—and wound up on a bench with only my coveted cotton candy to keep me company. Your father was alone when he walked by that bench, having just been stood up by his friends, too. He asked if I was all right. That was it, all it took. I'd known him for more than seventeen years, but I met him—the real him—that day.'

'I had no idea.' Awestruck, he stared at his mother, seeing her through different eyes. 'I always thought you guys just ... always loved each other. That it was love at first sight.' It sounded naïve, even to his own ears.

'It was,' she said, nodding. 'From that day forward, we haven't looked back. We knew, then. It just took all those years to get to the point where we saw each other for who we actually were, not who we saw from afar.'

Jason simply shook his head. 'Do I dare ask what this has to do with me?'

His mother's head tilted slightly, taking him in with all the warmth and sympathy awarded to a timid stray kitten. 'I don't live with regrets, you know that. Regrets don't do anybody any good. But if I had to say I regretted anything in my life, Jason, it's that I would have found your father sooner so I could have loved him longer.' She reached a hand out and found her son's fingers, squeezing them with a strength that belied her age. 'There'll never be enough days in this life for me to love that man the way he deserves, and I can only pray that you'll let yourself meet someone—and I mean really meet them—so that you know what it's like to love like that.' A ghost of a smile pulled at her mouth. 'Besides, you're already interested in what you do know of Lily. You're halfway there.'

Halfway where, exactly? He didn't get the chance to ask. Humming a bluesy jazz tune, Roderick Forrester opened the door, milk jug in hand.

Bettina gave Jason's hand an affectionate pat and stood to go fetch the milk from her husband. He watched as his mother took the jug from him, but not before Roderick leaned down and tapped the side of his stubbled face, earning him a peck on the cheek from the woman he had adored for more than forty years.

* * *

It never ceased to amaze Jason how having dinner with his parents put his mind at ease. Something about being there, his mother at one end of the table and his father at the other, always managed to bring him as much comfort as if he were sandwiched between the two of them in a tight hug. It was his time to just be. Not a business owner, or a friend, or even a father—he could just be who he was without any pretenses or responsibilities.

The familiar home cooking wasn't a hard pill to swallow, either.

Coffee cup empty and a healthy—or unhealthy, depending on how you looked at it—dint in the plate of ginger cookies in the middle of the table, he wasn't only stuffed to the gills with good, hearty food, but also brimming with contentment, something Jason didn't often find.

'Do you know if plans have been made for Carlie's birthday?' Roderick pushed his chair away from the table, sprawling out in it as he savored the last few mouthfuls of his coffee.

It was bound to come up. Still, Jason winced. 'I haven't really asked Natalie about it, yet.'

Over the past few weeks, his daughter's upcoming fifth birthday had rarely been far from his mind, but he hadn't broached the subject yet with his ex-fiancée. Carlie's big day landed during the week, two Wednesdays from then, but he didn't know what to say to Natalie. In all truth, he had hoped she would be the one to bring it up when he dropped Carlie off a few hours ago. She had said nothing, and neither had he. 'I'll call her tomorrow night after work and get the details.'

Natalie had never kept him from seeing Carlie, and she wasn't vindictive or spiteful when it came to allowing Jason time with his daughter.

It was his own pride that got in the way. He struggled every time he had to ask permission to whisk his own flesh and blood away for an afternoon that wasn't a part of the usual schedule, or every time he had to attend a birthday or holiday in a house that wasn't his, with people he didn't know. Being a third wheel—or fourth, or fifth—at his own daughter's milestone events broke his heart all over again every time it happened.

But he did it for Carlie, and he would continue to do it for her. Because she was what mattered. His own ego didn't stand a chance against that kind of love.

His mother and father exchanged a stricken glance. 'Jason …' Bettina began.

Whatever well-meaning statement she was about to make was interrupted by the loud blip of Jason's phone. Tucked onto the seat of the chair beside him, Jason hurried to read the text message. Rude, perhaps, but he wasn't ready for what he knew his mother would undoubtedly say.

Hey, hope your day's been good. Was just curious about the status of Cruella. Mine, not yours. She ended it with a winking emoji.

So, Lily was getting restless. The memory of their almost kiss flooded his mind as he typed back, *I should be able to get 'er done by tomorrow, if that's okay.*

No winking emoji accompanied his words.

'Jason,' Bettina tried again. 'I think some things have to change, son.'

He looked up from the phone and witnessed two sets of eyes, both full of thinly veiled emotion. 'I know.' His voice cracked. The lopsided division between Carlie's two lives weighed on more than just him. So did the fact that it was his own fears—probably irrational and fallacious, but fears, nonetheless—were the reason for such a divide. He had once risked everything by asking a woman to marry him in the erroneous hope that it would keep their family together, and it had ultimately ended with a jagged rip down the middle of their family photograph. Two houses, two separate lives.

Asking for anything more than what he already had could start the gears turning of a mechanism he didn't want to move. It could have dire consequences.

Yes, he knew he had to do something, say something. But it was a risk, and he knew the damage risks could create.

Another electronic blip of his phone saved him from having to endure another moment of their obvious discomfort.

More than okay. There's no rush, actually. I've been thinking some things through, and until I pay off my debts and get some money saved up, I was thinking I might stick around for a while.

Another message arrived within seconds, an obvious afterthought.

If that's okay.

Staring at the screen, Jason's vision swam, turning the words into fuzzy clumps of black on white. His parents might as well have been a million miles away, though Bettina's comment echoed through his brain, loud and clear. *Some things have to change.*

His fingers trembled slightly as he tapped out his reply to Lily. *More than okay.* He paused, then hit send.

When Jason raised his head this time, he agreed with his mother on a visceral level. Some things did have to change.

They already were.

168

Chapter 13

Lily

She would never admit it out loud, but Lily's decision was made as much from want as it was circumstance. She didn't yet know the full cost of the Corolla's repairs—Jason had only given her ballpark figures without including labor—but she didn't yet have enough cash saved up to pay him and still replenish her bank account a little more. Not to mention she was back to square one, looking for a job and an apartment in the city.

Lily was being honest with herself, now. Fleeing from Sherman on a wing and a prayer had been reckless. Silly, even. Thinking she could simply land her dream job and secure an apartment of her choosing had been even more ridiculous. Things were never that easy, and she should have known better.

Which was why she was going to stay in Port Landon for a little while longer. Because it was easy. Too easy, in fact. She had a roof over her and her daughter's head, she had a job to go to every day, and her car was going to be good as new once Jason was done with it.

Jason. Another reason to stay in Port Landon, and another thing she would never admit out loud.

He had been about to kiss her, she was sure of it. Heck, she'd wanted him to. The way his eyes had glittered with the reflection of the dashboard lights as he kept flitting his gaze toward her mouth, saying all the things she never realized she longed to hear until the soothing sound of them graced her ears.

You've got me, he'd whispered. *You're not alone in this.*

No matter how many times she played it over in her mind, it didn't seem to lose its potency, or its conviction. She didn't distrust the truth of his words. However, Lily did wonder about her own interpretation of them. Intoxicating as it was, it was possible she was reading too much into it all. *You've got me* could be purely platonic, and *you're not alone in this* could be as friendly and encouraging as *Good job!* and a gold star. It was possible she was completely wrong about his intent to kiss her as well.

'Goodness gracious!' Lily hissed under her breath, entering the coffeehouse through the rear door. 'Enough.' She was going to drive herself absolutely crazy if she didn't stop all the overanalyzing and overthinking.

Lily's running shoes made an awkward squeak as she halted mid step, coming face to face with Sonya's quizzical stare.

'Oh, sorry, Sonya, I didn't know anyone was back here.' The back room was reserved for break time and storage. It was meticulously organized and tidy, but any of the hip, homey vibes had been saved for the front of the coffeehouse where customers milled about. Because of its stark walls and lacking ambiance, staff usually only retreated back there when they needed to. There was just too much to like about the front of the coffeehouse to waste a precious minute in the back.

'Which means you were, in fact, talking to yourself,' Sonya concluded. 'I'm not sure if that's better or worse. Should I be worried?'

'No, but maybe I should be. What's going on out there?' Tossing her purse into one of the battered lockers by the door, Lily heard voices coming from the front counter. Which wasn't unusual, except that there was something about the octave in which people spoke, and the rapid fire of words she couldn't quite make out.

Something was up.

Sonya huffed out a sigh. 'Whatever kind of day you're having, it might not seem quite so bad once you hear how Paige's is going.' With that, the older woman retrieved a plastic-wrapped roll of paper towels from the top shelf of the supply wall and trudged back out into the mayhem. The door dividing the front from the back swung on its hinge, and Lily clearly heard Allison's voice ring out, 'I just can't believe this is happening.'

As hesitant as she was, Lily had a job to do. She followed in Sonya's wake, silent and afraid of what she was walking into.

The coffeehouse was about half full, but a quick scan revealed that everyone already had cups in front of them. They were sticking around for the ambiance.

Allison stood behind the counter, hands pressed against it so hard her knuckles were white. Paige was cross-legged at the booth closest to the counter, her head in her hands. The mood in their corner of the café was so riddled with tension, Lily didn't know if *she* wanted to stick around.

Sonya, crouched behind the counter, rose to her full, stocky height. She joined the other two pairs of haunted eyes in staring at Lily, as though she had just entered their worst nightmare.

'Are you … okay?' Lily didn't know who she was asking in particular, but it seemed like a good place to start. She scanned Allison's and Paige's long faces, giving them both a chance to respond.

'Far freaking from it.' Allison's shoulders slumped as she stared toward the booth at her cousin. Lily had never witnessed her boss so devastated before, let alone utterly defeated. 'Paige's dress isn't coming.'

It took everything in Lily's fashion-loving heart to resist gasping and reaching for a chair before her legs gave out in despair. 'By not coming …' Maybe she was mistaken. She *had* to be mistaken.

'The boutique in New York used someone else's measurements to make my dress,' Paige replied weakly. 'They're dreadfully sorry about the mix-up—' She made crude air quotations with her fingers, '—but unfortunately they won't be able to make a new dress in time for the wedding.'

Lily's heart ached for Paige. A woman's wedding dress was a symbol of new love and new life, a whimsical piece of the puzzle that transformed every inner little girl into the princess they someday hoped to be, even just for a little while. To think that Paige had handed that important part of her special day over to someone and that they had made such a heartbreaking error was catastrophic. 'I'm so sorry, Paige. There are no words for how sorry I am.'

'Mistakes happen.' But the statement was as empty as Paige's words were flat.

'Is there a seamstress in town? Or maybe there's a place in North Springs where you can find a replacement?' Lily didn't know much about the city, but as the closest bigger center, there was a chance.

Allison offered up an undignified snort. 'There is, but I'm betting our pictures are tacked up behind the register after the kerfuffle we caused trying to find my wedding dress. Come on, Paige, even you've got to admit that's funny.'

Paige shook her head. 'That poor, poor sales associate. Gosh, what was her name? Mary, Mindy …'

'Mira!' Allison snapped her fingers. 'That's her name. You know, I could call there, just to see. If Mira answers, she might have to up her blood pressure pills or something, but I'll risk it.'

'Who's on blood pressure pills?'

In perfect synchronicity, the four women swiveled to gape at the owner of the deep, masculine voice. Lily's cheeks burned at the sight of him. Too many witnesses, too much tension already. The last thing she needed was Jason Forrester added to the mix.

Paige offered him a halfhearted smile. 'Hi, Jason. We're just talking about the wedding, that's all.'

He raised his eyebrows. 'And you need blood pressure medication already? Paige, you haven't even married him yet.'

She rolled her eyes. 'Very funny. But since I currently don't have a dress to wear down the aisle, blood pressure pills might be something I'll need to crush into my coffee pretty soon.'

Hands shoved in his pockets, Jason wore a look of bewilderment. 'I thought you had one coming from the Big Apple or something?'

He leaned against the counter, facing the bride-to-be. Which meant he faced away from Lily. As she took in his profile, Lily could see that his body exuded calmness, but his eyes were sharp as he treaded lightly. He was a man in an emotional woman's conversation, uncharted territory, and all it would take was one wrong comment to send any one of the women surrounding him into hysterics.

'There was a mix-up,' she explained. Paige shrugged, and Lily's respect for the woman soared. Not everyone would deal with an honest-to-goodness mistake with such grace and understanding. It was her custom-made wedding dress in question, after all.

'And you don't have a dress.'

'It's just under two weeks till my wedding and I don't have a dress.' Paige whirled around and rested her forehead on her arms, sprawled across the tabletop. 'Just saying it is sending me into a downward spiral.'

'Then don't say it,' Allison quipped. 'We're going to get this figured out. Lily, can you get Paige one of those café mochas she loves so much?' Lowering her voice, she added, 'Toss a shot of espresso in there, too. She needs a shot of something stronger, I think, but it's the best I can do for now.' Then, Allison was gone, rounding the counter and sliding in across from Paige in the booth, her phone at the ready. She was undoubtedly seeking out the North Springs bridal boutique number, preparing to give poor Mira a flustered trip down Memory Lane.

Lily stared hard at the coffeepot in her hand. It pained her too much to glance at the poor woman in the booth behind her. Thankful to have something else to focus on, her mind raced. And now, it wasn't only because this was the first time she had seen Jason since she'd texted him yesterday with her plan to stick around town a little while longer, or because she didn't know how to judge his reply.

More than okay. Not exactly the answer she expected. Yet, it set the butterflies fluttering in her stomach into a full-fledged frenzy. Sure, he was mimicking the words she had used in her previous message, but it was more than that. The inclination was there. He wanted her to stay just as much as she wanted to.

Right?

The butterflies that swarmed her now were due to more than Jason's presence. A woman sat behind her, desperate for a café mocha and someone to help her salvage an important part of her fairytale wedding. A woman who had been kind to Lily, just as the rest of the town had.

There weren't many things Lily could help others with around these parts. She was an outsider, with a dwindling cash flow and little tangible belongings to offer up. But this was one time when she could help. When she could repay a little of the abundant generosity Port Landon had shown her. When she could show others—and herself—what she was capable of. What her dreams her made of.

'I can do it.' The words came out quieter than she meant them to.

Jason was closest to her, and his dark eyes widened ever so slightly. He didn't say anything, but she could see the truth in his gaze. He had been thinking the same thing.

She thought she saw him nod. Just a slight dip of his head. *Yes, you can*, he seemed to silently encourage her.

She whirled around, focusing beyond him toward the booth where Paige and Allison sat. 'I can do it,' she repeated, louder this time.

The words were out. There was no going back. No matter what the likes of Michael Pennington, or even Lash Fashion, believed, Lily had to believe in herself. In that moment, she did, wholeheartedly.

Sonya was the first to recover from her surprised stupor. 'You make dresses?'

Lily turned back to the drink on the counter and sprayed a dollop of whipped cream on top of the café mocha, using it as a moment to stamp down her own budding shock. Part of her was still surprised that she'd spoken up at all. But there was another part, a bigger part, that trembled with anticipation, aching to get a sewing machine in front of her and make something magical. 'I make a lot of things.' She nodded at Sonya. There were some things Nancy hadn't mentioned to her sister during their gabfests, it seemed.

Paige was up and out of her seat so quickly that one would have thought Lily had a ready-to-go dress hidden under the counter.

Lily slid the coffee mug toward the bride-to-be.

'You've designed weddings dresses before? And turned those designs into wearable clothing?' Allison enunciated each word, clearly and concisely. There was a beacon of hope standing before her in the form of Lily Brentwood, and the woman took her maid of honor duties seriously. She was going to make sure there was no room for any more misinterpretation in the name of her cousin's wedding.

Lily thought of the flowy cotton sundresses she had first begun with a few years ago, starting with something she deemed simpler, with less structure and more room for error as she learned different sewing techniques and found her own personal groove. After those sundresses came her first attempts at bustiers, with side boning and elegant beading and overlays. Only once she mastered the intricate workings of those did she attempt her first full-length gown. Currently, eight completed examples of her unique designs sat folded in a sealed plastic tote, stowed away in a storage locker she had yet to see the inside of. Just thinking about it, she winced, praying her creations were okay. 'I have, a few times,' she replied, nodding again. 'But—'

Allison jutted one long finger out, shaking her head. 'No buts. You're telling me that you can design and create a wedding dress for Paige.' It wasn't a question. 'In less than two weeks. That's a feasible timeframe for such artistic things?'

Lily loved Allison's way of talking. Never belittling other people's capabilities or likes, even if she didn't understand it. Allison realized that whether it was ornamental needlework or creating the perfect cup of coffee with intricate foam art, the end result took time and was still someone's masterpiece, therefore worthy of respect. 'I can do this, Allison.'

Paige touched her hand to her cousin's arm. A patient gesture, calming. It said, *Easy, tiger.* When she leaned on the counter, fingers steepled at her lips while she calculated the best way to approach the crisis at hand, there was a surprising lack of urgency guiding her next words. 'Lily, there is absolutely no pressure for you to do this.'

Days ago, she had blown the only interview to come from the numerous job applications she had submitted to Chicago companies. This was a chance to show the world what she could do—possibly her only chance. The prospect of being able to create a wedding dress for Paige made her heartbeat quicken, but it had nothing to do with pressure.

Lily, she realized in that moment, just wanted to make Paige's dress. She wanted to give in to her passion and let her creativity take over. If she could tap into that desire, it didn't matter if this was her only current prospect or one of many. She would be doing what she loved. That had to count for something. 'I know you haven't even seen anything that I've designed and—'

'But I have.'

In the sudden chaos, she had almost forgotten he was there. Now, Lily stared at Jason with wide, curious eyes. So did everyone else.

'I'll vouch for her designs.' His eyes locked with Lily's, unwavering. 'You'll love her work, Paige. I do.'

In unison, Allison and Paige squealed, two excitable teenagers trapped in adult bodies.

'Oh, Lily, this is perfect!' Paige insisted, bouncing on her heels. 'I'll pay whatever it takes, and I promise not to be a Bridezilla.'

Her heart pounded hard against her ribcage. 'Oh gosh, I'm not worried about that at all—'

'Then, that's that!' Paige interjected. 'Lily's going to make my wedding dress! Right here in Port Landon!'

Lily gawked around the room at the sea of faces as they cheered excitedly, all eyes trained intently on her. Like she was doing them some kind of favor. She couldn't hear past the blood rushing in her ears, and there was a sense of tunnel vision overtaking her senses. Once her gaze landed on Jason, everything else seemed to momentarily fade into the background. His words resonated within her, threading themselves into the fabric of her being and becoming a part of her.

He'd said he loved her work. Vouched for her talent to the people he knew and loved. Jason had taken a chance. For her. They all were, Paige in particular.

No, she wasn't doing anyone a favor—they were the ones helping her. Showing her that a little belief went a long way, and that even the most validated fears were no match against the power of community.

Or the power of love.

Chapter 14

Jason

Finally—finally!—Lily Brentwood was beginning to comprehend her own talent. Beginning to take a chance on herself. Jason could see it written all over her face how much it shook her to utter those words: *I can do it*. But it was only because she didn't seem to see the magic that propelled her passion—or was it that passion that made it magic?

Jason did. He saw it as clear as any sunny day, as blatantly as any neon sign. He believed that everyone else would see it, too, if Lily offered them a glimpse.

It had been more than a week since he had first laid eyes on Lily's sketchbook and he couldn't get the designs out of his head. Once Paige saw Lily's work firsthand, she would be just as enthralled.

Enthralled, that was a good word to use in relation to Lily. There was no other way to describe his connection to her. With her schedule at the coffeehouse, and his own time spent at the garage, coupled with the looming wedding dress deadline, he didn't see her every day. In fact, her car had been repaired and ready to go since yesterday morning, but their broken conversation between a handful of texts had advised him that she could finally retrieve it today.

She was never far from his mind, though. It was both a blessing and curse—a blessing because he found himself wanting to be near her, if only for company; and a curse because Branch tended to pick up on his distracted demeanor, and he was only too keen to comment on it.

'I hear your girl's got a gig as Port Landon's very own Vera Wang.'

Torque wrench in hand, Jason levelled a narrowed gaze at his best friend. 'She's not my girl,' he stated, wiping sweat from his brow. 'As for the rest of that sentence, I have no clue what you just said.'

'The famous designer?' When Jason's expression didn't change, Branch waved a hand. 'Never mind. Kait must be rubbing off on me. I swear, that's all she's been talking about since Monday night.'

It made sense since Paige and Kait were so close. Until then, however, it hadn't occurred to Jason that perhaps Branch might have known more about the current state of Paige's dress designing than he did. 'Has Kait seen Paige and Lily?'

The corner of Branch's mouth tugged up. 'Scared she's seeing her more than you are?'

'Don't start, Branch.'

He held up his hands, blackened with grease. 'It was just a question. You know, simple conversation.'

'Is this some trick to get me talking about my inner feelings or something?'

Branch rolled his eyes. 'You're hopeless. Especially if you need to be tricked into talking about your damn feelings.'

Jason tossed the torque wrench on top of his toolbox and rounded on his friend. There was no such thing as simple conversation these days. 'Look, it's complicated, all right?'

'This ain't your Facebook status we're talking about, Jay. Just hear me out.' Branch wheeled the creeper he was perched on out a bit further from the sedan he was working on. 'I know what you said before, about how I can't understand because I've always loved Kait and my feelings for her were never in question. But Kait's feelings were exactly that—complicated. Do you remember last Christmas?' He paused, wincing. He remembered, very clearly. 'I watched her suffer in turmoil as she tried to figure it all out, without all the facts. I might not have experienced what you're going through, but I'm just saying … don't rule it out because you don't understand it. You and Lily are both conflicted, I can tell. It's warranted, but don't close your eyes and suffer in silence, especially when you might not have all the facts.'

Jason's jaw worked as he mulled it over. Branch wasn't aware of Lily's ex or the man's abandonment of his daughter—those things were told to Jason in confidence; he wouldn't tell another soul unless Lily asked him to. Lily was being cautious for a reason, and those were facts Jason did possess.

But, as much as he hated to admit it, Branch was right. There was a difference between having some facts and having all of them. Lily could be even more conflicted about him than he was about her. And that was saying something.

'Thank you, Dr. Phil,' he mocked. 'We'll now interrupt this regularly scheduled program to take a short commercial break.'

His colorless humor earned him another eyeroll. 'Yeah, you're definitely hopeless.'

The faint creak of the office door pulled their attention across the garage. Lily shuffled in, sandals on her feet and sunglasses perched on her nose. The steel spiral binding of the sketchbook under her arm caught the reflection of the sun from the window and glinted as she pushed the door shut behind her.

Branch smirked, holding his hands high. 'I don't think I need to say anything more.'

That's a first, Jason thought wryly. But his friend was still grinning from ear to ear when he trudged past him into the office.

'Getting tired of walking yet?' He chuckled, scanning the desk for the invoice he had placed there yesterday. Sometimes he wondered if the surface opened up and swallowed things whole in the middle of the night.

Lily pushed her sunglasses up on top of her head. 'It's not so bad walking in town,' she replied with a smile. 'At least it's nice out, and there's always something to see.'

'Careful, you're starting to sound like a true-blue resident.'

'Got to see the glass as half full, right?'

He glanced up. 'A true-blue resident *and* an optimist.'

Laughing, she set the sketchbook on one of the chairs by the door. 'I blame you for that one. So, you're really done with my Cruella, huh?'

'As done as I can be. She'll get you where you want to go now, at least.' Something twisted in his gut at the mention of Chicago, but Jason forced it down, ignoring it.

'That sounds promising.' Her purse made a heavy thud on top of the desk. 'It also sounds like I owe you some money.'

Jason scanned the invoice in his hand. He had shaved off as much as he could for the labor charges, having done all the work himself and not necessarily during work hours. The bill still had too many digits lined up in a row for his liking. 'You don't have to pay me all at once,' he reminded her. 'And there's—'

'Just give me the bill, Jason.' She reached out and took the paper from him, turning it so she could read it. It might have just been Jason reflecting his own feelings onto her, but he swore she paled a little as she read it. 'And you're sure you're okay with me paying in installments?' she added, still staring at the typed calculations.

'Of course. I know money is tight. I don't want you to strap yourself.'

She set the invoice down. 'And I don't want to take advantage of your generosity, though it might already be too late for that.' Unzipping her purse, Lily pulled out a brown envelope and held it out to him. 'Five hundred, that's what I've got. Allison paid me yesterday. I also heard from the hotel in Chicago—finally.' She let out a relieved sigh. 'They're refunding me all but the first night's reservation fee. So, I should be able to pay you the rest of it next week when the refund hits my bank account. They said five to seven business days.' She crossed her fingers.

'That's great that they're going to give you your money back. Took 'em long enough.' He tentatively reached for the envelope. 'This is a big chunk toward your bill. Thank you, but are you sure?'

'I mean, if it's negotiable as to whether or not to pay you …' A teasing grin played on her lips. 'Trust me, Jason. It's fine. It's your money. I'm going to pay you back every penny as soon as I can. It's hardly enough considering all you've done for Eden and me.'

He shoved the envelope into the drawer to his left. 'I just try to help when I can. I'd do it for anybody.' Even as he said it, he regretted it. But the words had already come out, sounding too generic. 'Do you want a receipt?' Hardly a smooth recovery.

She waved her hand dismissively. 'I'll get one when I've paid it all in full.' Lily looked around, which caused him to follow her gaze. As soon as their eyes met, Branch immediately turned back to his task at hand.

Busted, Jason thought. His friend was hanging on every word.

'Has it been busy today?' Lily asked.

Jason didn't believe for a second that she had missed Branch's wandering intrigue, so she was obviously going to pretend she hadn't noticed. Two could play at that game. For now, anyway.

'The phone keeps ringing and the vehicles keep showing up to be fixed, so it's definitely busy enough. Benji will be here tomorrow as well, so the extra hand will help get a few things knocked off our list.'

'Yeah, let me guess, you'll get caught up right around the beginning of autumn, just in time for folks to start calling and wanting to book an appointment to have their winter tires put on.'

Jason raised a brow, impressed. 'That's quite the guess. And very much correct.'

She shrugged. 'My cousin worked as a mechanic at a Ford dealership. I remember him saying there is no getting ahead when it comes to repair work on vehicles. If it's not repairs that need to be done …'

'It's maintenance,' Jason finished for her. 'Right again.'

Beaming, she reached for the sketchbook. 'Have you got a minute? I came to pay you, obviously, but there was something I wanted to show you.'

Obviously. His curiosity piqued, Jason rounded the desk, leaning against it with his hands in his pockets. 'If this is about the dress gig with Paige, I'm not sure I'm going to be much help.'

She grinned, flipping through the pages. 'Trust me, you've helped more than enough with that situation. And it's going well, thank goodness. Paige chose one particular design right away. There's a seamstress here in town—Shirley, I think?—who's going to help me pull it off in time. She's retired but Paige said she still does projects from home. Sounds good to me. I'll take all the help I can get.' There wasn't a hint of anxiety to be found in her expression or her words. Lily was genuinely thrilled with her role as head designer, and Jason was thrilled for her.

'I know Shirley. She knows her stuff, so I'm sure you'll both learn a lot from each other,' he replied. 'If it's not about the dress, though, then what have you got there?'

Whether from nerves or anticipation, Jason couldn't quite pinpoint, but Lily's hands trembled as she fumbled with each page, searching for one image in particular.

'This.' She held out the sketchbook, hastily willing him to take it from her. As though she might change her mind before he saw what graced the page.

Her nervous energy was contagious, permeating his pores and sending his own nerve endings into a series of tingles and crackles. Fear of the unknown had been Jason's friend for a long while, and whatever he was about to see meant enough that it had Lily in knots.

That meant it meant something to him, too.

He turned the sketch, making sure no brightness cascaded in from the afternoon sun and hindered his first glimpse. Immediately, he was thankful for the forethought.

Before him, in meticulous pencil strokes and various shadows and shading, sat his grandfather's Panther Lima. Only the car he saw wasn't just a mirror image of the car sitting out in his garage under a thick vinyl cover, it was a reincarnation of it.

To scale, Lily had taken painstaking effort to redesign the old vehicle into a reinvented version of itself. An absolutely gorgeous version of itself.

'I know that a hot rod is actually a classic American car and not a British one, and the street rod vibe has to do with the oversized engine and modifications for speed, but I thought maybe the sleek shape of the Panther Lima would be well suited with horizontal hot rods flames that stretched toward the rear of the car, depicting speed but also a fiery burst of rebellion and freedom.'

Lily's explanation came out furiously and fast, but her voice was distant, heard through a tunnel of memories and awe. Though the colors were far from traditional—classic hot rod flames would be a vivid mix of yellow, red, and orange on a black car—they were just as vibrant and even more inspiring. In her design, the car had been resurrected in a brilliant plum with metal flake, each sparkle and hint of glitter penciled individually to give the drawing depth. The flames, classic hot rod shapes reaching from the front grill, across the hood and stretching across the doors toward the back tires, were a blazing orange, but they were outlined in a feather of lime green. It gave the car an edgy look, mixing traditional with custom ideas. The rims were spoked steel, eye-catching. Jason's finger brushed across the image, awestruck by the alluring conglomerate of chrome and color.

'I've sourced the tires to an aftermarket company in California, and if you don't like the spoked style of the rims, they're fourteen inches and you can always—'

'Lily.' He breathed out her name, his voice unrecognizable to his own ears. 'You designed my grandfather's Panther. My Cruella.' It was a fact, nothing more. He was simply trying desperately to wrap his head around it.

Lily mistook his shock for disdain. 'Like I was saying, you can always change things or completely ignore my idea. It's just—'

'It's just beautiful.' Jason reluctantly tore his gaze from the automotive beauty on the page. 'Lily, this is amazing. There isn't even a word for how amazing this is.' He didn't try to mask his bewilderment. 'And I'm hearing you talk about fourteen-inch rims and American muscle cars … Lily, you didn't know a fender from a ball joint.'

Her sigh of relief coincided with her laughter, creating a gasping chuckle. Lily shrugged. 'You can learn anything on the Internet with enough research.'

Jason could picture her, huddled over her phone at Nancy's dining room table, the room dark save for the eerie glow of the screen. One hand scrolling through diagrams and articles and photos found on search engines, the other scraping delicately across a blank page, turning the blank page into a work of art.

Giving his grandfather's beloved car new life.

'Not this,' he said, shaking his head. 'You didn't learn this. The names of things and the history of classic hot rod flames, sure. But no one just learns how to design something so breathtaking, Lily. Something so perfect. You've got a gift, and there are a lot of people in the custom vehicle world who would trip over themselves to get a chance to have a design like this created for them.' He swallowed. 'I have no idea how I'm going to thank you for this. But thank you.'

'So, you like it, then?'

He balked at her genuine surprise. 'No, I love it, Lily.' It wasn't a word he tossed around easily. Loving something meant you wanted to hold it in your hands and keep it all to yourself. You didn't want to let it go. It meant you felt something for it with every sense and synapse within you. With your heart.

As Jason stared into the bluish gray gaze of the woman he had never expected to find, he realized with a deep, visceral conviction that, in that moment, he didn't want to let her go, either.

Chapter 15

Lily

Two weeks was such a long time in some ways, and such a short time in others. There was a time when Lily thought she would be in the middle of Chicago by now, moving out of a hotel room and into an apartment, with a handful of leads toward internships or employment opportunities in the fashion industry.

Instead, she was exactly where her car had left her, with a job that wasn't anything like the design jobs she had hoped for and a dumpster fire of a job interview under her belt.

It had been two weeks going nowhere fast, spinning her wheels, no closer to the goal she had pushed toward in the beginning.

And Lily was surprisingly okay with it. Always a stickler for things being a certain way, going according to plan, she never stopped to realize the upside to stepping off the path and traipsing through the unknown. Even away from that path, the sun still shone and the sky was still blue. There were still flowers to stop and smell, and there were still options as to which way to go.

The key was to be brave enough to let one's plans fall apart and not fall apart with them. Only then could one see that the obvious path was not the only way to get where they were going.

Lily wasn't foolish enough to believe she ever would have come to Port Landon of her own accord. She also never would have admitted defeat without crashing and burning in Chicago.

But Port Landon saved her from all that. With its open arms and comforting ways, becoming stranded had prevented her from being burned by her own naivety and disorganization. If she had made it to Chicago, Lily was confident that, right now, she would be on her way back to Sherman, tail between her legs and heartbroken. It would have gutted her to admit how she had tried and failed so miserably.

Breaking down in Port Landon hadn't just saved her from that defeat, it had saved her from herself. All or nothing—that's how she had always worked. And if she couldn't have the life she thought she and Eden could attain in Chicago, then Lily would have retreated to her hometown and undoubtedly never tried again.

Where she was now was neither all, nor nothing. Lily was somewhere in the middle, somewhere unexpected. But somewhere she wanted to be in that particular moment.

'What in the world are you doing here?'

Lily glanced up from the locker, her hands suspended in midair as she made to shove her purse inside it. Eden was already carting her dollhouse figurines toward the door that led to the storefront, and she stopped in her tracks as well. Allison stared at her with quizzical eyes, her auburn ponytail swaying with the breeze that blew from the air conditioner vent.

'I'm … working?'

'The heck you are.' Allison shooed her toward the back door. 'Shirley called my cell because she didn't have your number. The fabric and lace you ordered is available in North Springs. She drove there early this morning and picked it up as soon as the shop opened. Let the dressmaking begin, Lily!'

188

'It's here?' Somehow, it still hadn't sunk in that she was doing this. Working alongside someone she didn't know, on a dress design that had come from her own mind and would be brought to life with a needle and thread.

'We won't talk about the expedited shipping charges,' Allison replied. 'But seriously, go on. I've got the front counter under control, and I'm sure you need all the time you can get to pull this off for Paige.'

She fought to keep her expression neutral. Her boss was right, she did need all the time she could get. She also needed the money from the coffeehouse job to pad her bank account. She still owed Jason a hefty sum of cash as well.

The logical part of her brain told her there were only so many hours in a day. The timeframe was limited for Paige's dress; it was the following weekend. She had the weekend and the workweek to finish it.

The Lily Brentwood from two weeks ago might have fought Allison on it, stating she could work her shift and then burn the midnight oil in hopes of completing the dress while also earning her coffeehouse wage. But she felt the difference that those two weeks had made. She was thinking with more than logic.

She was thinking with her heart. And that part of her reminded her that there was no reason to run, no need to work so hard that she didn't enjoy the here and now.

Frankly, she wanted to work on that dress. Yearned to. Having the creamy satin under her fingertips, hearing the soft whir of the sewing machine as it transformed the spool of fabric into a luxurious gown …

'If you're sure that's okay, then I'm all for getting started.'

Allison held up her hands. 'There's not a soul in this place that won't wait an extra couple minutes for their coffee if it means that Paige will get the gorgeous wedding dress she deserves. Everybody's talking about it.' She beamed, as though it was a good thing.

Lily tried not to think about it. She didn't need the pressure. She was good enough at putting pressure on herself.

'I'd better get going, then. Shirley knows I'm coming?' The elderly woman Lily had been introduced to was well into her seventies, but a couple minutes of watching the woman work at her sewing machine at the beginning of the week had proven that her age was no match for the expertise she harbored. Her movements were as quick and fluid as her voice was calm and confident.

She could do anything on enough cups of tea, Shirley had said. Lily believed her.

'She's ready and waiting.'

Lily was tugging her purse from the locker when Allison spoke again.

'You're coming to the wedding, right? You've got to see your own design during its moment of glory—Paige said so.'

It had never occurred to her that she would see Paige walk down the aisle. Allison's mere mention of it, however, lit a flame of want inside her. She ached to see her own design on the wedding runway. 'I would love that,' she admitted. 'Can't say no to Paige.'

'There isn't a person who would right now.' Clapping her hands like an excited child, she emitted a stifled squeal of delight. 'The whole town's going to be there, you know.' Her lips pursed together, suppressing a grin. 'Everyone.'

'That makes sense,' Lily replied, cautious, afraid to step on a proverbial landmine. She had a sinking suspicious she knew what—or rather, who—Allison was referring to. 'I'd better get go—'

Lily's cellphone bleeped loud and shrill, announcing an incoming message. Pulling it from the back pocket of her jeans, she saw only five words and a time.

Meet me at the pier, 7 p.m. A winky face was the only signature.

Lily stared at Jason's words. Just another thing to add to the long line of unexpected events lately.

'Who's that?' Allison asked, one eyebrow raised.

Too quickly, Lily stammered, 'Oh, uh, Shirley.'

Allison didn't hold back, letting her laughter spill out like a tipped pitcher of sweet tea. 'Please, girl. Not only has Shirley never sent a text in her life, there's nothing that old woman could say that would have you grinning like a freaking fool. Tell Jason I said hello.'

* * *

Shirley Jacobson's house was as tiny and sturdy as its owner. Only two blocks from Main Street, from the driveway Lily could still hear the occasional splash of waves hitting the docks in the harbor. The house was more like a brick cottage with its sloped steel roof and matching grid-patterned windows peeking out onto the street on either side of the royal blue door.

Stepping over the threshold was like stepping back in time. There was only one thing inside the house that had been manufactured after the late seventies—Shirley's sewing machine.

Lily had sighed out loud the first time Paige brought her there to introduce her to the elderly woman. Entering the bedroom at the back of the house that had been converted into a sewing room had been a milestone for Lily. Since she was retired, Lily thought perhaps the woman's designated sewing area would reflect that, expecting small and homey.

Shirley's home office, however, would have rivaled any top industry mogul's creative lair. Spools of countless silks and cottons and fleeces were propped up against each other, lining one wall. Hooks jutted out, displaying rolls upon rolls of lace and ribbon. A huge rolling cart with multiple compartments sat with some of the drawers ajar, revealing a mosaic of beads, stones, and other embellishments. And the sewing machine sitting atop the antique Edwardian desk was a gleaming, top of the line Singer. Shirley Jacobson could have created almost anything in that room, for anyone.

'Let's see this dress design that's got Paige all in a tizzy,' Shirley had said during their first encounter. Standing in the middle of Shirley's room of creative chaos, Lily had put the sketchbook into the woman's wrinkled hands. She held her breath, focusing on the dark spider veins that crept along her fingers as she regarded the drawing with raised eyebrows. A glance in Paige's direction proved she was holding her breath as well.

'This dress,' Shirley glanced up, regarding Lily carefully, 'you're going to want ivory silk charmeuse.'

Lily nodded, though the woman didn't ask. It was all outlined there on the page. Even if it wasn't, Shirley would have known it was the best choice. Less expensive than mulberry silk, it offered up the smooth finish and lustrous sheen, the perfect fabric for the design Shirley was scrutinizing.

'I don't have it here.'

Lily and Paige deflated together, their shoulders sagging.

'Well, I suppose that there are other alternatives we could look at,' Lily replied, trying to be as accommodating as possible and keep her tone light. Paige didn't need to know how distressed Lily would be if they were forced to attempt the design with polyester charmeuse instead. The fabric might look similar, but it was less ideal, tending to fray during handling and pucker at the seams.

'I said I don't have it here,' Shirley stated, 'But I never said we wouldn't order it.' She pointed a long, gnarled finger at the sketch. 'We'll design this dress exactly as it was intended. It's beautiful, Ms. Lily.'

That was the moment Lily knew she adored Shirley Jacobson.

The adoration only built as she spent more time with the elderly woman. By the time Lily showed up on her doorstep, there was already a pot of coffee on for her, a pot of tea for Shirley, and the various materials, threads, and measuring devices at the ready. Shirley was just as keen to get started as she was.

Though generations spanned between them, Lily was awestruck by the ease with which they collaborated. In between cutting and pinning this, and measuring and draping that, Lily heard about Shirley's life in Port Landon—born and raised, thank you very much—and the love of her life, her late husband, Alvin. Listening to her talk about him, one never would have known he'd been gone more than fifteen years.

'Nothing divides love,' Shirley advised her wistfully. 'Not time, not distance, and certainly not death. I love that man just as much now as I did when I was twenty.'

Lily was still thinking about that when she bid Shirley goodbye, hoping to get some supper on the go for Eden before she took the little girl with her to meet Jason. Her daughter wore her weariness of having spent an exciting afternoon at Shirley's in the heavy lids of her eyes, but there was no way Eden would miss getting to check out the boats in the harbor with her and Jason.

'Hurry, Eden. We're going to need a miracle to eat supper and get there on time.'

Her cellphone rang just as she buckled Eden into her car seat and climbed into the driver's seat of her car. Shifting in her seat to retrieve it from her back pocket, she fumbled and dropped the darn thing. It slid off the console onto the floor by her feet, landing screen up.

That was the moment she realized, in her haste, that she had pressed the button and answered the call. Mortified, Lily plucked it from the floor.

'Hello?' Lily asked, breathless.

'Ms. Brentwood, is that you?'

Lily gasped. She couldn't have hidden her shock, but she knew that voice. Had dreamed about it since the week before. It was a voice she never expected to hear again.

'Th-this is Lily.'

'Marvelous! Must have been a bad connection or something. This is Lilo Ashby, dear. We spoke last week.'

'Yes, ma'am, I remember. Thank you again for the interview.'

Lily squeezed her eyes shut, fearful her politeness would be conveyed as sucking up.

'Oh, Lily, I should be thanking you. Between your portfolio and your sincerity, I'm thrilled to have had the chance to speak with you. That's why I'm calling, dear. I do apologize for ringing you after hours, but I just simply couldn't wait until tomorrow. I've spoken with my staff, Lily. We'd love to offer you the internship at Lash Fashion.'

The rest of Lilo Ashby's words registered sporadically after that. Lily wasn't just shocked anymore, she was purely, inconceivably astonished.

'I'm sure you have a lot to think about, darling,' Lilo said. 'Do take your time, but we'll need to hear your decision by the end of next week. Toodles!'

Lily stared at the screen of her phone long after the call ended. All this time, she had wanted a foot in the door into the fashion industry, a spot where she could begin to make her mark and gain ground as a budding designer.

'Who was that, Mommy?'

This was it, what she had been waiting for. Not Port Landon, and not a flighty crush she had on the man who had become her white knight in a moment of need. Besides, with the exception of a few pretty words and what might have been an attempt at kissing her—which was merely a heat of the moment thing, she decided—Jason had been pretty clear that what they had was simple friendship. Nothing more. Believing it was anything more wasn't just presumptuous—it was potentially dangerous. To her daughter, and to Lily's own fragile heart.

'Our miracle,' she replied.

She needed to do what was best for her daughter, and for herself. And that's what the internship offer was.

Her priorities hadn't changed, even if her heart had.

Chapter 16

Jason

Inviting Lily to the pier had been a spontaneous decision. It was like everything had built up inside him—his mother's comments, his conversations with Lily herself, his dubious thoughts and feelings about, well, everything—and the only way to lessen the pressure was to see her again. The custom paint job she designed for his grandfather's car was a tipping point, pushing him over the edge and forcing him to press the buttons and send the message.

He would be at the pier at seven o'clock, with her or without her. Either she would respond and say she couldn't make it, or she would show. His message hadn't offered her a choice in the matter, but the decision was hers, just the same.

There was something about the pier in Port Landon that soothed Jason, always had. Especially as the day was giving way to night, when the lights from the boats began to flicker to life, spreading columns of cascading brightness across the otherwise darkened waters.

That's what the harbor was to him, a beacon of light on his darker days. When things were closing in on him, hurting his heart and tying his resolve in knots, Jason would retreat to the pier. His own simple sanctuary. Usually, he left the pier feeling lighter than when he'd arrived.

He stared out across the water. The docks were filled with boats, thick rope tethering them to the shore, but many were still milling about in the harbor, coming and going at a steady pace. In an hour or so, when the last of the stores closed and the diner turned its sign, there would be more traffic on the waters than on the roads. The pale face of the moon had appeared, though the sun had yet to retreat to slumber. People moved in and out of his peripheral vision, their chatter a constant, comforting buzz amidst his incessant, swirling thoughts.

'Boo!' The word hit him at the same time the impact did. Jason's knees buckled as he let out a loud *oompf!* The reaction was enough to elicit a delighted giggle from the five-year-old hurricane that slammed into him.

'You're little but you're mighty, aren't you?' He crouched down. He stared at Eden as though for the first time, suddenly aware of how seeing her, with Lily only a few steps behind, seemed to free a web of bliss within him that had been tangled and forgotten. 'You two made it here just in time.'

'For what?' Eden glanced around, obviously expecting something unmistakable and over the top.

Lily caught up, her champagne hair and loosely stitched cardigan waving in the breeze that blew in off the water. Curiosity tainted her gaze.

'To watch the sun go down.' Jason ruffled the girl's hair as she scrunched her cherub face into an expression of disappointment.

'But sunset isn't until, what, nine o'clock?' Lily said.

'Oh.' The corner of Jason's mouth curled upward. 'Looks like we'll just have to wait, then.'

Lily laughed, shaking her head. 'Well played.'

'I thought so.' He turned to Eden. 'You ever watched the boats come in through binoculars?' Jason pointed toward the tower

196

viewer mounted to the other side of the pier. He was already moving toward it as Eden shook her head. With a little adjustment, he lowered the binoculars as far as they would go and boosted Eden up onto the metal base around it. 'You grip the sides and turn the whole thing,' he instructed. 'You can look at whatever you want.'

'Whoa,' the little girl marveled. 'I can see on that boat!' She unlatched one hand from the steel handle and pointed emphatically.

Jason grinned. 'Carlie says she can see up the captain's nose, she's so close.' It earned him another high-pitched giggle, one that made him feel buoyant. He suffered the same sensation when Carlie laughed that way, so innocent and unbound.

Lily watched them, amused, as he stepped away and gave Eden the reins. 'So, do you come here often?'

Chuckling at the clichéd pickup line, he nodded. 'Actually, yeah. I bring Carlie out here every weekend she's with me.'

'Is that why we're here?'

Her question stalled him. Why *did* he want her there so badly? He'd been out there plenty of times alone. He wasn't trying to substitute his time with Carlie. There would never be a substitute for that. And he didn't usually mind the solitude after dealing with people throughout his workday.

What was different enough that he had felt compelled to have her there, with him?

'Just wanted to share the sunset with someone.' He leaned against the railing. 'I can't let you miss out on one of Port Landon's greatest features.'

'Wouldn't want to miss that, then.' Lily matched his stance, arms rested on the wooden rail. 'How is Carlie?'

'Ready to burst from excitement about her birthday on Wednesday. I've never seen a kid so excited about a cake in her honor.' He laughed.

'Wow, only a handful of days away. You'll go to North Springs, then? I'm assuming there's a party.'

He nodded slowly, carefully. Jason didn't want his answer to come out wrong. 'There's a party with some of her friends during the day. Natalie's family's putting it on.'

Lily's gaze locked with his. 'You don't go, though?'

'My parents and I will have a little celebration during my next weekend with her. Two cakes are better than one, I always say.' He tried to make light of it, but he could see that Lily didn't quite buy the façade. 'It's hard to be a part of everything from here when I have the garage to run and people depending on me,' he added. Even as the words came out, they were hollow.

'I'm sure if you told your coworkers it was for your daughter's birthday party, they'd understand if you took the afternoon off.'

She was right, of course. Branch would be the first one in line to kick his butt out the door and send him on his way toward North Springs. 'Probably,' he admitted.

'Everyone knows what Carlie means to you. Your devotion is kind of hard to ignore.' Her eyebrows raised, daring him to argue such an obvious fact.

Correct again. He nodded.

It was a long moment before Lily spoke. 'Maybe I'm overstepping by saying this, but perhaps you could talk to Natalie about this?' Lily suggested softly. 'I could be way off base, but it sounds an awful lot like you feel excluded from your daughter's life. Does she know that?'

Jason stared at her. Then, he stared at her some more. He thought about how little he had confided in Natalie since their breakup. *No,* he thought, *she doesn't. Because I didn't even fully know it until you put it out there in front of me.*

'I try not to rock the boat,' he confessed.

It was her turn to stare at him with wide, disbelieving eyes. 'She's your daughter, Jason. You have every right to be a part of Carlie's milestones and triumphs and mistakes. It's called life. No one can take that from you, especially not because you and her mother are no longer together.'

He wondered if her solid stance came from years of not having someone else to fight for inclusion in her own daughter's life, or if it came from not having anyone who wanted to.

Either way, Jason's truth came from fear, nothing more. He knew that. 'I am a part of all of that. Just not the way I want to be. But back then, I didn't know what would happen if I asked for more. I worried about what would happen next. If we have to go to court for custody—'

'Wait,' Lily interjected, standing straight as a fencepost. 'This schedule you guys have got going on, it's not court ordered?'

Jason shook his head. 'It was Natalie's first suggestion when she left, and I just agreed.'

'You … agreed.' Confusion marred her every syllable. 'Jason, why?'

'Because I was already losing everything I cared about,' he admitted. 'I couldn't have what I really wanted—my little girl at home with my every night.' He shook his head, struggling to say aloud the debilitating worries he had carried with him for two years. 'I planned to talk to Natalie about it once things settled a bit. It just never happened. Fear has got the best of me. It might be irrational fear, but it's fear nonetheless.' He turned to her. 'The court system isn't going to side with a father, Lily. Who's to say they won't give me an even rawer deal than the one I have now? That's a chance I can't take.'

Something akin to sympathy poured from her gaze. Or maybe it was pity and Jason just couldn't tell the difference. Feeling exposed after confessing his biggest fear, he wasn't sure he had it in him to try to decipher it.

'Jason, you and Natalie … you're on good terms, right?'

He didn't hesitate. 'We are. We both just want what's best for Carlie.' Natalie was a good mother to their daughter. He would never argue that fact.

'And the Natalie you know, the one you see now that the dust has settled on your breakup and you've come to terms a bit with where you three are at … would she keep you from Carlie?' Each word came out soft and gentle, guiding him toward the light at the end of the tunnel.

He paused, allowing himself an honest moment to strip away all the trepidation and anxiety that shadowed his thoughts and judgment when it came to his beloved daughter. As the haze cleared, only one answer remained. 'No. Natalie has never been that kind of person.'

'Then, I really think you need to talk to her,' Lily reasoned. 'You've got to try to work out a schedule that allows you a more equal role. You deserve that. So does Carlie.'

'My mother would sure love that. My parents live in North Springs and they don't see her nearly as much as they would like.' Which was his fault. Another thing he knew for a fact, and that riddled him with guilt and anxiety. His insistence to appease Natalie had drawn lines in the sand that not only kept him away from his daughter, but his parents as well. Because, while he wanted the best for Carlie, they wanted the best for him, which meant appeasing him, no matter how cowardly his requests might be.

'They just want to be grandparents to their granddaughter. I get that.'

He nodded. 'Me too. Especially since Mom has glaucoma. Who knows how long she has left to actually see her granddaughter.'

'Oh, Jason, I'm sorry.' Lily's hand suddenly rested on his, though he didn't register its movement until the warmth permeated his skin. 'Please do yourself a favor and talk to Natalie. You said yourself she wants what's best for Carlie, and that includes having you and your family around more often. I'm sure she will understand that.'

He nodded, fixated on her hand clasped around his on the railing. 'I will,' he vowed, looking up to meet her gaze. 'Thank you, Lily.'

'Don't thank me. I just listened.'

'Maybe that's all I need, someone who knows how to listen.' He didn't move a muscle.

Someone like you, he added silently.

Neither did she. 'Maybe.'

Jason could feel the tingle on his tongue. There was something he should say, some poetic idiom that tied his hurricane of emotions together in a tidy bow and delivered them clearly and memorably. Something he could give Lily that made her realize how she made him feel.

But were there even words when he was this apprehensive about what was going on in front of him? He was stuck on a constant see-saw that had him rising toward the sky and reaching for the happiness he found in Lily's presence one minute, then falling away from it the next, full of uncertainty that left him shying away from her, despite his feelings. A vicious cycle, leaving him more and more confused each time it repeated itself. He could hardly explain his feelings to her when he could barely admit them to himself.

Jason wasn't a fool. He was falling for Lily Brentwood. Where he was amidst that fall was what he couldn't seem to wrap his head around.

Was this what love was really like?

Love. Even the word tasted acrid at the back of his throat. He didn't throw the term around, and the only thing he was certain of, when it came to it, was that he would never understand the complexity of it.

He reminded himself that understanding something and feeling it were at two opposite ends of the spectrum.

He had never been this completely entangled in his own feelings before, never experienced this kind of roiling emotional upheaval. Maybe that meant he had never experienced this kind of love before. The kind he wasn't looking for but had found, anyway. The kind that scared him to possess, but was scaring him more and more to lose. He wasn't good at showing it, but it was there, nonetheless, holding fast and gripping his heart in its fist.

'Are you going to Cohen and Paige's wedding?' His voice came out hoarse. Strengthened by a moment of courage, he turned his hand over underneath Lily's, letting her palm rest on his. He marveled at how small and soft her hand looked against the backdrop of his rough, callused skin.

She nodded. 'I was surprised when I was invited, but yeah, I'll be there. You?'

He nodded. 'Going to see the reaction firsthand, huh?'

She knew he was talking about Paige's wedding dress. He had heard the dress mentioned numerous times around town since Lily agreed to make it. By now, it had grown its own persona. People were just as intrigued to see the dress designed by her as they were to see the town's resident baker and veterinarian tie the knot.

'Maybe,' she said wryly. 'Pessimist or not, I'm still a sucker for a good wedding.' She gave his hand a slight squeeze before slowly dragging it away.

The sensation of her fingertips trailing across his palm stayed with him long after her touch was gone. This was what he loved about Lily—the way they didn't need to say things out loud for them to be spoken. The ease with which they existed together. The touch of her hand said just as much to him as the custom sketch she had drawn in her limited extra time.

Lily could feel there was something between them, too. She must.

'Carlie's going with me,' he added. 'My parents will be there, too, so I figured why not give her a reason to dress up in one of her party dresses and dance the night away. Especially since it's only a few days after her birthday. Five-year-olds get to go to wedding receptions, you know.' He nudged Lily playfully as he turned to watch Eden, still scanning the harbor for boats to spy on.

'I'll have to keep that in mind.'

'Mama, there's a pirate ship!' Eden exclaimed, practically hanging off the handles of the tower viewer. Her curly pigtails bounced with each jerk of the binoculars. 'Ahoy!'

Jason chuckled, but Lily bowed her head. 'Children,' she choked out. 'They say what they mean, and mean what they say. Even if it doesn't make sense.'

'If there's anything I've learned, Lily, it's that things don't have to make sense to be true.' He was beginning to believe that more and more each day.

The smile she offered him rivaled any fiery sunset he would see that evening.

'Come on,' she chuckled, pushing away from the railing. 'Let's go rescue that poor tower viewer from her clutches. And do me a favor, Jason?'

'Name it.'

She narrowed her eyes. 'You might be right, but don't tell *her* that things don't have to make sense to be true, or else we'll be out here till dawn searching for buried treasure.'

* * *

It was pitch black outside before Lily carried Eden up the front steps of the bed and breakfast. The beauty of the disappearing sun had been lost on the little girl, not only because she wasn't old enough to see the value in such natural wonders, but because two and a half hours of watching so-called pirate ships in the harbor and making treasure maps on the back of old receipts from Lily's purse with a ballpoint pen had exhausted her. Eden had been curled up on the bench by the pier, her head on Lily's knee and covered with the plaid shirt Jason had worn over his T-shirt, for the past half hour.

'You sure you don't want me to take her?' Jason asked, following her up the porch steps. Lily and Eden had walked to the pier, but he had insisted on driving them back to Nancy's. He hadn't wanted to wake the girl if they didn't need to. He also wasn't ready for the evening to end.

'I'm good as long as you get the door.' She grunted out the words, stepping aside to allow him access to the door handle.

Jason swung the screen door open wide just as Nancy whipped the inside door open, ushering them in.

'Looks like she couldn't handle the nightlife of our tiny town.' Nancy's wispy outfit swayed as she gracefully shifted from one foot to the other, letting Lily pass by. The silky scarf in her wild hair seemed to drift down into the busy kaleidoscope of colors in her billowy dress and robe, getting lost within the patterns. Bright green reading glasses were perched atop her head.

'I'm going to take her upstairs,' Lily whispered. 'I'll be right back.' Draped across Lily's shoulder, Eden's eyes fluttered but remained closed as they disappeared upstairs.

'What a lovely evening.' Nancy's eyes fluttered as well, but for a very different reason.

'It was a nice night.' He left it at that. Seeing the woman so eager for something, anything, to latch on to only gave Jason greater satisfaction at offering up little in the way of elaboration.

'So, was—'

'Jason?'

Lily's head poked over the banister at the top of the stairs.

'Everything okay?'

'Eden wants to say goodnight. She's adamant.'

'I'll be right there.' He kicked off his shoes. It was impossible to miss Nancy's tight-lipped expression.

Upstairs, he pressed a reassuring hand against Lily's back in the doorway. 'It's okay,' he whispered to her, then entered the bedroom.

The room was just as he remembered, a gazillion pillows on an oversized bed. This time, he knew the angelic little face would be in the middle of the downy comforters and feather pillows, and he jokingly sat down on the edge of the bed with a little bounce, ruffling the linens and eliciting a giggle from Eden. She looked on the verge of sleep, barely awake. Yet, the girl clung to the model car with one hand. The other was rested atop the crisp, white covers, fingers fluttering in a gesture to stay conscious.

'You need to get some shuteye, little girl,' he said softly. 'Shut those peepers.'

'Peepers.' A stifled chuckle followed. 'Night night, peepers.'

Jason reached out and held her hand. It was something he always did for Carlie, and the gesture always managed to render him awestricken at how small and fragile a child's hand was compared to their larger-than-life personalities. 'Night night, Eden.'

He gently let go and made to stand, but tiny fingers wrapped around his wrist with surprising strength.

'You're my friend, Jason.' *Jathon*. His name, coupled with her lisp, tugged at his heart strings.

'You better believe it.'

She released her grip, curling her fingers under her thumb with only her pinky outstretched. 'Friends forever.' Her voice was thick with impending slumber. 'Pinky promise.'

He watched her for a moment, took in her rounded cheeks and her heavy-lidded eyes. She fought like a trooper to keep them open, and each time they widened for a fraction of a second, the grayish depths pleaded with him to make her this one promise, and to keep it.

Eden wanted him to stick around. Forever, even though he knew she had no concept of what that meant. He wasn't sure he knew the vast concept of forever, either. Maybe no one did.

What he did know was that he wanted her and her mother to stick around as well. How in the world did he say that, though?

He couldn't expect openness from others if he didn't put his feelings out there and open himself up to them, too. And if it was easier to tell a child he adored her than it was her beautiful, talented mother, so be it.

Things didn't have to make sense to still be true.

'Friends forever, sweetheart,' he said, wrapping his finger around hers. 'Pinky promise.'

Chapter 17

Lily

As a child, Lily was afraid of many things. She didn't like insects for the most part, and anything creepy-crawly tended to send a shudder racing up her spine. Snakes were worse; the mere sight of one made her heart beat so fast and so hard that she was sure it would burst from her chest. Watching fifteen minutes of the movie *It* made sure she feared even the most docile of clowns, and there was no way she would ever look at cornfields the same after a few of her friends pulled a prank on her as a teenager.

But nothing scared Lily the way hearing that promise to Eden fall from Jason's lips did.

Worried her daughter would rope him into reading a storybook or talking about the model car in a bid to fend off sleep, she had crept up the stairs. She heard Eden's request just as she reached the doorway.

Her daughter's little voice was enough to suck the air from Lily's lungs and render her immobile. She couldn't move, couldn't speak. She could only listen. Lily wasn't sure what she wanted Jason to say in response, but his choice to make such a heartfelt promise to her five-year-old evoked more fear than any colorfully painted face or centipede.

Lily didn't mention the promise when Jason retreated from the bedroom, turning the light off in his wake.

'There, she'll sleep now,' he whispered.

She was glad to hear it, but, somehow, Lily knew that her daughter would be the only one sleeping tonight.

She was right. Hours after Jason left, hours after she had thanked him for a wonderful evening at the pier and gently brushed off Nancy in a bid to be by herself, Lily lay awake beside Eden. Sleep was the furthest thing from her mind, too consumed by her rampant thoughts. Her daughter's soft, even breaths were the only thing keeping her calm, allowing her to remain under the covers and stare at the stucco ceiling instead of wrapping herself in her borrowed robe and wandering through her borrowed house in the middle of the night.

The entire life she had begun in Port Landon was exactly that—borrowed. To say otherwise would be to kid herself. Whenever she spent time with Jason, Lily forgot that fact for a little while, permitting the companionship she hadn't known she so badly craved to take over her rational mind.

But it was temporary. All of it. She had known that since the moment her car chugged to a halt. So did Eden, and Nancy, and Jason. They knew, just as she did.

And still, Lily had been the one to forget the very fact she had been trying so hard to convince others of. No wonder folks were having such trouble believing her. She didn't consistently believe herself.

It was time to change that. Time to remember that there was an internship waiting for her in Chicago, that her life started when she accepted the job and pointed her car toward the city. To stay sitting in Port Landon any longer than necessary was merely spinning her wheels, preventing the inevitable and the life she had dreamed of. Port Landon was never part of her plan.

Neither was Jason. She needed to remind herself of that, too.

His promise to Eden—he meant well. But promises were sacred in a child's eyes. Preschoolers were still innocent to the indiscretions and pain brought on by the world around them. They didn't understand that adults could be anything but their knight in shining armor, the ones who bandaged their skinned knees and wiped away their tears. Adults could do all those things and still break a promise as simply as they'd first uttered it without meaning to.

Jason had spoken his promise to Eden from a place of comfort, with the desire to ease a child's mind and lull her into a much-needed sleep.

However, Lily saw it for what it was: a broken heart in the making. The promise was dangerous.

So was staying in town any longer. It pained Lily to realize she was the one who had put Eden in such a situation, giving her a chance to grow fond of someone, especially when that someone in question had meant well. When that someone in question was so worthy of such fondness.

But there was a time when Michael Pennington meant well, too. His broken promises had come from a different place, one of greed and a narcissistic sense of entitlement. Eden's father was nothing like Jason Forrester.

Yet, both men wielded promises they couldn't deliver, that would ultimately crush the trusting and naïve mind of a little girl.

And Lily had no one to blame but herself.

Friends forever, sweetheart. Pinky promise. Lily heard those words as though a ghostly presence was whispering them into the darkness. Forever was a long, long time. Especially to a child.

She needed to stop the vicious cycle. No more pretending the stopover in this tiny town was anything but temporary, and no more chances for Eden to get hurt in the process.

It was time to leave Port Landon.

* * *

With the coffeehouse closed, Lily was thankful for the long Sunday that stretched out before her. She was going to need every second of it to get Paige's dress closer to a finished state. Shirley was a godsend, working on bits and pieces of it even when Lily wasn't there. After seeing the elderly woman in action, the way her hands looked so frail yet moved with such innate capability as though the sewing machine were nothing but an extension of her own arms, Lily trusted her wholeheartedly to create the dress exactly as it had been designed. It didn't mean she didn't want to be a part of the process as much as possible, though.

Nancy had insisted that Eden spend the day with her while Lily went to Shirley's. Something about a girls' spa day. Seven colors of nail polish sat in little glass bottles on the kitchen island, and Lily prayed that, by the time she returned, one of those vibrant shades wouldn't be permanently splotched on the hardwood floors. The décor in the bed and breakfast was timeless, but even someone as eccentric as Nancy couldn't make a slime lime spatter match an antique pre-1900s hutch.

Lily looked forward to the day to focus on her creative endeavor. Spending hours bringing one of her designs to life with the aid of an expert was something most people only dreamed of. A full day of thinking about silk, lace, and the perfect pintuck meant not having to recreate yesterday, which had been a full day of thinking about paying debts, making plans to leave, and—

'Jason.'

Bounding down the front porch steps into the sunlight, Lily had been smiling to herself, too engrossed in the tulips and dahlias that filled planters on either side of the stairs to see that Jason's Dodge Ram had pulled up at the curb. He was out of the truck before she registered his presence.

'Hey, Lily.' He wore the crooked smile that Lily had come to recognize as the perfect accessory to whatever outfit he might be wearing. Today, that happened to be a pair of worn jeans and a black T-shirt that accentuated his broad shoulders. 'I found this in my truck. Must be from Friday night at the pier.' He held out Eden's long-sleeved Paw Patrol shirt, the one she had worn over her T-shirt to fend off the harbor breeze.

'I didn't even realize. Thank you.' She slung the shirt over her purse to toss in the passenger seat of her car. 'You're up and about early. I hope you didn't come here just because of that. It's the weekend, Jason.'

'What can I say, I'm a morning person.'

'That's just the coffee talking.'

He chuckled. 'Touché. And is the caffeine the reason you're so chipper this early?'

'I'm headed to Shirley's to work on Paige's dress. For the whole day. What's not to love about that?'

'Sounds like a perfect day for you,' he said. 'I've got to admit, I'm excited to see this dress. Someday, I'll be able to say I knew you before you were famous.'

'You're getting a little ahead of yourself.'

'Maybe, maybe not.' His cheeky grin remained as he shrugged. 'If nothing else, you're famous in a small town.'

'Like you,' Lily quipped.

'Like me.' Hands in his pockets, Jason rolled a stray pebble around with the toe of his boot. 'Port Landon's as good a place as any to get your start. Who knows, maybe it'll turn into something bigger down the road.'

There was something about the way he said it that made Lily's stomach twist. She recognized the acidic taste at the back of her throat—guilt. *Tell him*, she willed herself. *Be honest with him.* 'Fame in Port Landon is a little different than fame in the city.'

'You just wait and see. Another few weeks, after folks see Paige's dress and what you can really do, it's anyone's guess where we'll be by then. I might have to grab a number in order to get my chance to talk to you.'

Another few weeks. Where we'll be. *We*, he'd said.

'Jason, there's something I should tell you.'

211

'That sounds ominous.' He laughed, but it was tainted by hesitation.

'I should have told you when I first found out, but I—'

'It's okay, just tell me.'

She could almost see the fortress being constructed, the way his breathing slowed and his posture tightened, steeling himself against whatever came next.

'I heard back from one of the companies I applied to in Chicago.' Her voice came out weak, riddled with the guilt of not telling him sooner. 'They offered me an internship.'

'You got a job in Chicago. Lily, that's great.' His words didn't match his expression. Or maybe it was the other way around seeing as Jason's face gave nothing away. If he was surprised or elated or sad, he didn't show it. In fact, his words suggested congratulations, as did the smile he wore, but there was something she couldn't put her finger on that made the words sound flat, made his smile resemble a mask of sorts.

Was she imagining it? No, it wasn't a fabrication. It was hope. Hope that he wore the joyful mask for her sake. Hope that he wanted her to stay just as much as he wanted her to go.

He ran his hand through his hair. 'When did you find out?'

Her face burned. 'Friday, before …'

'Before we went to the pier.'

'I wanted to tell you. I should have.'

He waved a hand. 'You don't owe me an explanation, Lily.' Another chuckle rose from his throat. 'You don't owe me anything.'

'You're wrong,' she insisted, taking a step toward him. Surely, he could see that wasn't the case at all? 'I owe you everything. I wouldn't even be able to leave if it weren't for you.'

Jason took a step back. 'I was just doing my job. I'd never dream of leaving someone stuck here if they didn't want to be.'

Immediately, Lily wondered if he was hopeful, too. Hopeful that she would correct him and confess that she wanted to be there. That she hadn't felt stuck in Port Landon since those first

212

trying days. It was the truth, yet the words caught in her throat like thick cotton. 'I know you wouldn't,' she replied. 'It's not that I don't—'

'When do you leave?' The intensity in his dark eyes belied his outward calm demeanor. She didn't know how to interpret it, but it was enough to make her second-guess her previous assumption about what he might be thinking or waiting for.

'I …'

There were so many things she wanted to confess to him, whether he was willing to hear them or not. There were so many reasons to go, but also so many reasons to be there, right where she stood.

I want you to ask me to stay, she realized. *With you. Ask me to reconsider. To make this work. I want you say something. Not that you were just doing your job, but something, anything, that proves I'm not the only one who wants to hold on to what we've found in each other.*

'After the wedding,' she breathed out, choking down every other wistful phrase. 'I've still got a dress to make and some loose ends to tie up.' She cringed at her choice of words. Her nerves were getting the better of her. It was impossible to wrap up the life she'd begun there with a neat little bow and stow it away like a forgotten memento.

'That's not far off.' Jason's throat moved as he contemplated it. 'This time next week, you'll be gone.'

'If I take them up on their offer,' she clarified quickly. She chanced another step in Jason's direction, her heart beating like a frenzied bird in a cage. With a sigh, a plea left her lips. 'Tell me what you're thinking, Jason. I feel like I'm making a mistake, somehow.' Hysteria built like frothing water against a dam. 'What do you think I should do?'

There it was. A chance offered up to him on a silver platter to open up to her, to tell her what he was concealing behind the mask of detachment. She didn't want him to make the decision for her—she would never ask that of anyone. But she didn't want to have to wonder what he would have said had she failed to give him the open invitation to reveal what was in his heart. 'Let me in, Jason,' she added in a whisper, as much for herself as for him.

It could have been the bright sunshine that made him blink rapidly, once, twice, then again. Jason's chest rose and fell, sighing out an audible breath. Lily anticipated his response as his lips parted. He took a tentative step forward, closing the gap between them.

Then, the mask he wore slipped, unveiling a flicker of sadness. Jason held his hands up, palms out, as though to prevent himself from getting any closer. As though, like a moth to a flame, he didn't trust himself to keep a safe distance.

'Take the job in Chicago, Lily.' He strode back to his Dodge Ram and left her standing there, more alone than she had ever been before.

Chapter 18

Jason

There's an expression regarding assumption and what it makes those who assume. Whoever *they* are that coined the phrase knew exactly what they were talking about.

Lily was leaving Port Landon. And with good reason. He would never begrudge her the chance to chase her dream as a fashion designer. Hell, those folks in Chicago would have been crazy to look at her portfolio and not want to offer her a job. Jason believed in Lily's talent, and he believed in her drive to achieve her goal.

He also believed in their connection. Despite everything, he had begun to feel like they were getting somewhere, together. Getting closer. Unfortunately, Chicago would undoubtedly pull her farther away, undoing whatever loosely knotted ties had been formed. He'd known it was coming, yet it still pained him in a way that defied his common sense.

It wasn't the fact that she was leaving that hurt him the most, though. She had known about the job offer before meeting him at the pier. He thought of the way her hand had held his as she prodded him about talking to Natalie and getting a fairer

215

schedule figured out for Carlie, the way she had looked into his eyes and whispered *Maybe* when he suggested that all he needed was someone who listened to him the way she did.

He had really thought they had grown close enough that she would have shared such a huge revelation with him. He had thought she would want to tell him, as a friend.

As maybe more.

So much misinterpretation on his part. He had been out of the dating game so long, and so wounded by his own failed engagement, that Jason couldn't even distinguish romantic interest from old-fashioned kindness. What they had was friendship, blossomed on the foundation of a broken car and their daughters of the same age. The connection he had latched on to was based on the mirror image he saw in her; a generous soul broken by the actions of another, determined to rise from the ashes of that heartbreak and find oneself again.

The difference was that Lily was on the path and actively seeking rebirth. Jason was still treading water in the same cesspool of presumption and small-town expectations.

Lily never meant to hurt him, he knew that. But knowing she didn't tell him at the pier, that she obviously had been going through the interview process at the same time she casually suggested that she might stay in Port Landon for a while—it all sounded a little too familiar to him. Saying one thing, while planning for an escape in the shadows. Presuming one thing, while turning a blind eye to the truth.

He sighed. He had taken it all a little too personally, and he had assumed too much. It wasn't Lily who had hurt him, not really.

He had done that all by himself.

Jason clicked the button on the computer mouse. Again. 'Come on, you piece of—'

'If you were hitting me like that, I wouldn't work for you, either.' Branch's boots thudded loudly on the scuffed linoleum of the garage office. He headed straight for the coffeemaker. 'Is this

216

your problem?' He pointed a thumb at the coffeepot, still half full from the morning. 'Caffeine withdrawal. At this point, maybe you should just put a straw in the pot and drink straight from it.'

'Very funny.' Jason crashed his finger down on the mouse again. 'This damn computer is frozen again. Third time this morning.'

Branch poured creamer from the fridge into a mug of coffee and held it out to his friend. 'There's always been a delay on the invoice printing screen, Jay. It's your patience that's the issue, not the computer.'

'I'm just trying to get some work done.' Jason set the coffee cup down beside the mousepad. Even the sweet scent of hazelnut and sugar did little to soften his mood.

Pouring himself a cup, Branch raised his eyebrows skeptically. 'You only do mountains of paperwork when you're one of two things,' he reasoned. 'Ticked off, or trying to avoid me.'

'Can it be both?' Jason leaned back in his chair. 'I'm not in the mood for one of your lectures.'

'I don't lecture, I teach.' Branch leaned against the doorframe, eyeing his friend over the rim of his coffee cup. 'What wisdom do you need from me today, young grasshopper?'

'We're the same age, idiot. And I just said I don't want to talk about it.'

'Want and need are two different things.'

'You're not going to let up, are you?'

'If the roles were reversed, would you?' Branch glared at him, daring him to say otherwise. After a lifetime of friendship, there was no question that they had helped each other through some hard times.

Jason let out a long breath. 'Lily is leaving.'

'Ah.' His friend nodded, as though no further explanation was needed. 'I hadn't heard that.'

Imagine that, Jason mused. *Something the gossip grapevine hadn't got a hold of before me.* He found a sliver of comfort in knowing he wasn't the last to find out, at least.

'She was offered a design job in Chicago,' he continued.

'That's great. You and Kait have both said she's pretty talented. Sounds like she deserves the chance to show the bigwigs what she's made of.'

'Yeah,' he replied. 'You'll never hear me say she doesn't deserve it.'

Branch eyebrows raised. 'So, that's why you're upset and taking it out on the computer?'

'No.' Jason leaned forward, shaking his head. 'I'm not upset that she—'

'Even though you knew she was leaving weeks ago?'

'It's not that. She didn't tell me—'

'You're upset that she didn't tell you fast enough?' Genuine bewilderment veiled Branch's gaze. And when he said it like that, Jason felt the first shards of guilt for being frustrated and hurt in the first place.

'I guess it's just that I was with her at the pier and she knew about it. She never said a thing.' It was the best explanation he could put into words. 'I thought she would want to tell me something like that. I thought a lot of things.'

Branch mulled this over, taking a sip as he thought it through. When he set the mug down beside Jason's, still untouched, he held up his hand, two fingers raised.

'There's a lot of guessing and thinking in that answer, buddy. Let's break it down, shall we?' Branch waggled one finger, eliciting a vexed groan from Jason. 'Lily waited to mention the job offer. Did you ever stop to think that maybe it was just as hard for her to tell you about it as it was for you to hear it?'

The shards of guilt grew in his stomach, forming jagged, stalactite-like swords that pierced his resolve. He stared at his coffee mug, watching the steam billow upward and tangle in the cool air before dissipating. Jason said nothing.

'On top of that, you said you thought a lot of things.' Branch ducked his head to confirm his friend was listening. 'What kinds of things?'

Jason's jaw tightened. The moment he said the words, they would be out in the wild and he would never be able to rein them back into captivity. He would step off the steep precipice, unable to claw his way back up. 'I thought ...' He raised his head. 'I thought there was something between us.'

'Did you tell *her* that?'

Of course not, because he hadn't even admitted it to himself until now. 'Technically, no. I mean, I thought she knew. I thought it was obvious.'

'You're right. You really did think a lot of things.' Pulling up one of the vinyl-clad chairs reserved for customers to the desk, Branch sat down, elbows on his knees. 'You can't be upset that Lily doesn't realize you love her when you never told her, Jay.'

'I don't—' Jason stopped himself before the kneejerk denial left his lips. He needed to stop. Stop denying, stop hiding, and stop waiting for the universe to right all his wrongs for him. 'I won't hold her back, Branch.'

'Of course you won't. You're too busy holding yourself back to do that.'

Branch's statement hit him like a punch to the gut.

'Seriously,' his friend continued. 'You're so hellbent on making sure you don't get hurt by somebody else, that you're hurting yourself in the process, man.' A plea accompanied his words, begging Jason to listen, truly listen, to what he was saying. 'So you made mistakes with Natalie. We all make mistakes. Would it be a mistake to take a chance and tell Lily everything you just told me?'

Being honest was a double-edged sword; his feelings would be laid out on the table, but at least Lily would know where he stood and what the last few weeks meant to him. 'I want her to follow her dream,' he said.

Even if it doesn't include me. Jason didn't understand how he could mean something so wholeheartedly and still be riddled by so much pain because of it.

'No one's questioning that,' Branch replied evenly. 'But you should at least find out what Lily wants, too. Maybe her answer is different than it was a few weeks ago.'

'Maybe.'

Branch rolled his eyes at Jason's noncommittal response. 'Lily can't make decisions without all the facts, and you can't deal with those decisions until the facts are all out on the table. You've got to be brave enough to ask her, though.'

Was it really that simple? With a start, he realized that it was, and that it wasn't the fear of his feelings being unrequited that frightened him most in that moment, but the chance that he could let Lily walk away and never truly know what might have been.

'Besides,' Branch added, 'a little happiness would look good on you, and not only when you're with Carlie.'

Carlie. His reason for everything. 'She loves Lily and Eden, too,' he said. It wasn't until it was out of his mouth that he realized the insinuation. Branch didn't miss a beat.

'Good.' He smiled wryly. 'Then, that's all that matters.'

Jason let his friend's advice sink in. Blanketed by silence, his sigh sounded loud and demanding. 'It's so hard to want her to stay and want her to go at the same time.'

'If that isn't the definition of love, I don't know what is, Jason.'

The use of his full name clutched his windpipe and squeezed. Only six months ago, Jason had been the one advising his best friend about being honest with the woman he loved. About taking the chance and being sure that no stone was left unturned in his bid to make her realize how much he still loved her. Branch and Kait had found love after more than a decade apart.

Jason would never know if he and Lily could do the same if he wasn't brave enough to be honest.

'Friday, on the pier, Lily told me I should talk to Natalie. See about getting more time with Carlie.' If he was going to be open and honest, he might as well start now, when it would earn him a second opinion on something he should have spoken of a long time ago.

'So, she's not only pretty, she's smart, too.' Branch stood, dragging the chair back by the door. 'Lily's a keeper, Jay. Anybody can see that. You've both got trust issues and can't seem to get out of your own way, but you've got valid reasons, too.' He picked up his coffee mug from the desk. 'Reasons are what you guys need. She needs a reason to want to keep our tiny town on her radar, and you need a reason to look past your fear disguised as logic.'

Eyebrows raised, Branch challenged him to say differently. Jason kept his mouth shut.

'She's not a mind-reader, and you're not just someone she'd be settling for if she stuck around. The sooner you realize those two things, the sooner you'll be ready to try and make this work. And that's what this is about; not staying or going, but making it work. For both of you.' Branch tipped his Lakers cap toward Jason and retreated into the garage, coffee in hand.

Jason stayed rooted in his seat long after he disappeared. Much could be said about the way a childhood friend could get through to a man like no other. They had never been the kind of people who said what the other wanted to hear. Instead, Branch—when he wasn't being a goof-off—said the things Jason needed to hear.

Jason was making mistakes. Big ones. Ones that were being repeated as though history were stuck in a hamster wheel.

Branch was right. Lily wasn't a mind-reader, and he needed to open himself up to her if he expected the same. Fear disguised as logic; it's what had governed his every move over the past two years.

No more.

His cellphone was cool against his fingertips as he scrolled through his contacts and pressed the button to make a call. Her voice was polite and welcoming when she answered, something Jason had never allowed himself to notice before.

'Hey, Nat,' he greeted her. 'Can we talk?'

* * *

221

A special kind of havoc was reserved for a child's birthday party. A group of eight young girls, moving as one like an uncontrollable hurricane, emitting chaos and leaving colorful, sparkly mass destruction in their wake, all while shrieking and giggling with complete and utter delight.

To an adult's senses, it was catastrophe. An impending evening's worth of cleanup and probably meltdown once the partygoers all retreated home and the birthday girl began to crash from her sugar high.

It was also bliss.

Standing in Natalie's living room, back against the wall so as not to get caught up in the swirling birthday tsunami, Jason beamed. He had stood in this very spot a few times before, during past birthdays and Christmases and Easters, but those times had consisted of futile attempts to fade into the background, to give Natalie and her boyfriend, Shane, a wide berth. Seen through the shredded fabric of Jason's heart, he was an intruder in the life his ex-fiancée had made for herself without him, a reminder of how close they had come to embarking on a marriage that undoubtedly would have exacerbated, instead of resolved, their disharmony. He had believed himself merely one of Natalie's mistakes, a blip on the radar she would just as soon erase than have it continue to circle needlessly, now that she had made it out of the line of fire.

'It's good to see you.'

Jason turned at the sound of her voice. Natalie's hair was short, cut in a pixie style. Eyes as bright and green as gemstones, they glinted as she smiled. It was good to see her too, so happy and energetic.

Two years ago, it wrecked him to have to let her go. Now, through the lifting fog of his own pain, he saw that it would have killed him to be the reason for her to lose that vibrancy he'd once loved so much. 'You too. Thank you for this.'

Together, they both watched the antics unfold in the middle of the living room floor. Eight preschoolers chattered and chuckled while Disney princess wrapping paper and pink and silver ribbon burst randomly from the midst of the ever-moving pile. Bettina Forrester sat in the middle of that conglomerate, the glue holding it all together. Carlie jumped up and patted a bubblegum pink bow into her grandmother's hair, and Jason had never seen the woman so full of joy. Across the room, his father, Roderick, tinkered with the ornate cake pedestal, confirming it was perfectly level and situated in the correct position for his granddaughter's mountainous cake.

'Don't thank me,' she said. 'I'm just glad we got to talk the other day. I've been worried about you.'

'Me?' Jason snapped his attention away from the girls to stare at her incredulously. 'Why?'

Natalie's emerald eyes grew dim. 'I know that what happened between us—what I did—it hurt you. I'll never expect you to forgive me, or to understand. Heck, maybe I'll never understand why I let it go on so long.' She waved a hand, fighting to stay on track. 'This isn't about me, or about that. But afterward, you … weren't you anymore.'

'It broke my heart, Natalie.' There was no other explanation, and he wouldn't hide the truth. He'd done enough of that lately. 'But, believe me, I don't blame you for what happened. We've both made mistakes.'

She nodded, a relieved sigh escaping her lips. 'I know, but I'm still sorry.' Her arms curled around her waist, the sequined hem of her tank top clenched in her fists. 'It was more than that, though. You shut everything and everyone out. I get it, I do. So much changed so fast. But the longer it went on, I was so scared that it wasn't just your heart that was broken.' She paused. 'Your spirit was, too. All the fight in you, all the little things that your friends and family loved about you, was gone.'

A long breath escaped his lungs, leaving him deflated. Jason hadn't realized Natalie had noticed his shattered psyche, much less given a damn. Maybe he hadn't wanted to. 'I guess I lost myself there for a while.'

'Well, whatever it was that helped you find yourself again, I'm thankful for it.' She nodded toward the middle of the room, where Bettina was now holding up Carlie's brand-new plush tiger, roaring playfully and trying to touch her granddaughter's pink headband with its paw. 'So is Carlie,' Natalie added. 'You're still good to pick her up on Friday?'

Jason's throat was thick and dry as cotton. 'You bet.'

'I'm sure you two will have a great week together.' Natalie touched his arm. A familiar gesture, an affectionate one. 'I'm really glad you called, Jay. We're glad to have the real you back. All of us. I mean that.'

She drifted back into the kitchen, leaving him in the company of thoughts he never thought he would think. While he had feared he'd held Natalie back too long, stealing the spark once lit within her, Natalie had feared she had stolen his will, leaving him too battered to continue the war.

There was love there, still, even if they were never meant to be. It gave him hope. Instilled a sense of contentment he hadn't remembered existed.

Whatever helped you find yourself again, I'm thankful for it, she'd said. He was, too.

As Jason's mother cast a glance at him from her chair surrounded by her granddaughter and friends, her eyes seeing and savoring and taking in everything around her, etching it into her memory to keep it safe and hold on to it long after she saw no more, Natalie's words collided with ones Bettina had spoken to him only a handful of weeks ago.

I want to see you happy.

He wanted that as well. Happiness, such a subjective emotion, yet affected by so many objective things. Jason realized now what happiness was to him—his family. Every crooked, gnarled branch of the tree. Family wasn't all straight lines and blood ties, and it wasn't only who was still before us in the immediate vicinity.

His family wasn't perfect, but it was all he had. And it was his reason to find happiness and hold on to it, no matter how outlandish or unexpected or downright crazy it seemed.

And Lily made him happy.

It wasn't something that had helped him find himself; it was someone. Her. She was his reason. All he had to do was find a way to be her reason, too.

Chapter 19

Lily

Lily had been to a lot of weddings in her life, but she didn't think any of them had ever been planned with such an intriguing mix of elegance and simplicity.

She also didn't remember ever seeing a dog walk down the aisle with the ringbearer.

It was interesting to attend a wedding ceremony amongst folks she didn't know well. All the weddings she had attended in Sherman were for relatives and friends she grew up with, people she saw every day and knew how they were faring without having to ask. A few weeks ago, she hadn't known any of these attendees existed.

Sitting in the back pew, however, Lily wondered if anyone remembered that they hadn't known her a few weeks earlier. Everyone called her by name as they passed, and no one hid their anticipation at seeing Paige Henley become Cohen Beckett's wife while wearing a Lily Brentwood original.

'It's just as much Shirley's pride and joy as it is mine,' she repeated more than once, and each time the person she was speaking with would pat her arm affectionately and reply with some variation of, 'Oh, honey, she said you'd say that.'

Lily would have agreed with anything at that point. After what was possibly the longest week of her life, she had finished Paige's wedding dress yesterday afternoon, just in the nick of time. With Shirley running entirely on Earl Grey tea, and Lily's fatigue compounding enough each day to make her wonder if sucking on coffee beans would be more effective than drinking prepared brew, the final touches had been added to the hem, confirming that the intricate beadwork and lace matched the ribbon Lily had sewn by hand to wrap around the stems of Paige's bouquet.

The dress had turned out perfectly. As yet, she had only seen it on a mannequin. When she delivered the dress to Paige the day before, Allison was there, the bride's helpful and supportive shadow. The two women had disappeared into a bedroom with the garment bag in tow, leaving Lily to stare awkwardly around the apartment while Paige tried the dress on. The calming sage walls and open concept did little to ease her anxiety. If her measurements had been off, if the drape of the skirt didn't fall the way it was intended, if there was even a thread out of place …

Allison had appeared, shutting the door behind her with a soft click. 'You have no idea what you've just done.'

Lily's face fell, unable to read her expression. Heck, she could barely hear the woman through the blood rushing in her ears. 'Is it …'

'Perfect.' Allison broke into a blinding grin. 'It's freaking perfect, Lily. You should see it.'

'Well, let me see it, then!' Suddenly, the urge to witness the finished product on the bride-to-be was overpowering. Anxiety fled, quickly replaced by delirious emotion.

'Paige says you have to wait.'

'You can't be serious.'

'What the bride says, goes. It's bad luck to see her before the wedding, anyway.'

'That's for the groom, Allison!'

Allison's Cheshire Cat grin widened. She was enjoying every minute.

'Paige really isn't going to come out here and show me.'

'We'll see you at the wedding tomorrow.'

How sneaky, she had thought. There was no way to get out of attending the wedding, now. Not that she had wanted to, though it had crossed her mind fleetingly over the past week.

Lily hadn't seen Jason all week, not since he'd bluntly told her to take the job in Chicago. Words failed her every time she tried to come up with a decent text message, and she had been too timid to go to the garage again and face him. It occurred to her she could simply send the cash she owed him with someone else, paying off her balance in full and giving herself a clean slate, but she hadn't been able to bring herself to do that, either. Just like her confliction when it came to going to Cohen and Paige's wedding, she was just as conflicted about paying off the balance on her car repairs and not having another reason to see Jason.

Now, she had lots of chances to see him, as she sat there in a borrowed dress from Paige's closet. The strapless red number fit her like a glove, hugging her hips and making her feel as though she should be on a glamorous runway and not hidden away in the last row of a small-town church. And it was good she wasn't there for any other reason than because she wanted to witness her design in its moment of glory. It was also good that she felt pretty in the red dress and wasn't wearing it for anyone but herself, and that she wasn't there in hopes of seeing Jason and levelling out the tumultuous landslide that had crashed down between them.

Because Jason was nowhere to be found.

Granted, he had said he would be at the wedding, not the ceremony itself, but Lily still found herself disappointed by his absence.

Which only made her feel sillier about the whole thing.

Jason Forrester wanted her to take the job in Chicago. He had left no room for misinterpretation, no room for discussion. Lily was thankful, in a way, seeing as how she had so wrongly read all the other cues.

Looking back, she saw how clearly she had wanted to believe in things that weren't really there, to hear things that weren't actually spoken aloud. Hindsight was both a gift and curse, and Lily was most definitely her own worst enemy. She would never learn. The clarity with which she saw her mistakes now was crystal clear, only adding to her foolishness.

After all, Jason had never given her a concrete sign that he'd ever wanted more between them than friendship. She hadn't offered him that, either, to be fair. Not really. It was a game they had played, talking around the subject, seeing their connection in their peripheral vision but never looking at it head on.

At least, she thought that's what it was. She didn't know what to believe anymore.

She needed to stop trusting herself to make the right decisions when it came to men. There was a reason she had sworn off them before her disaster of a road trip—speaking of that, maybe she should stop trusting herself to make decisions at all—and she needed to remember that.

The organist began to play a pretty melody Lily didn't recognize, and one by one the wedding party made their way down the aisle. She recognized Cohen, looking dashing in his crisp black tux, a burst of color at his breast pocket where a deep red rose and baby's breath were pinned. Christopher, Allison's husband, followed as his best man, his arm linked proudly with the maid of honor, who just happened to be his wife. The bridesmaid dresses donned by Allison and Paige's other friend Kait were beautiful; flowing satin amethyst gowns with sweetheart necklines and short sleeves that sat just off the shoulder. The classic crimson roses clasped in their hands only added to the stately elegance.

Cohen's son, Bryce, was next, beaming as he marched up the aisle beside Jazz. A murmur of delight spread through the crowd as the brindle boxer, wearing a tiny corsage on the back of her collar that mimicked the bridesmaid's bouquets, wagged her tail the entire way to the front of the church.

All the tittering halted the moment the organist delivered the first majestic notes of 'The Wedding March', and a mass roar of shuffling feet and shifting bodies echoed throughout the room. Sun streamed through the elongated stained-glass windows, bouncing off the satiny ribbons adorning each flowery decoration fastened to the end of the pews. Anticipation crackled through the air like igniting embers as the attendees bent one way, then the other, trying desperately to catch their first glimpse of the bride.

Lily held her breath as a collective gasp fanned out across the pews.

Suddenly, there she was. There *it* was.

Paige appeared at the back of the church, so close that Lily could take one large step and touch the extravagant bouquet in her hands. But Lily didn't move. She couldn't.

It was a dress that she had designed in her mind and constructed with her own bare hands. A roll of silk charmeuse that had been handcrafted into a gown fit for royalty, embellished with intricate beading and delicate lace.

Seeing it on Paige, though; it looked different. Because it wasn't just a garment of fabric and thread anymore, it was a part of Paige. The dress was made for Paige just as much as Paige was made for the dress. They were one and the same, and together, they were perfect.

Arm in arm with her father, the bride stepped forward and began her trek toward the groom. All the sounds around Lily seemed distant somehow, lost amidst the pounding of her own pulse and the overwhelming flood of emotion. A quick glance in Cohen's direction at the front of the church proved he was just as overcome by the sight of his wife-to-be. He had every right to be moved to tears. Paige was breathtaking.

Suddenly, all the long hours and cups of coffee and aching

hands over the past week were forgotten. Only Lily's pride remained, swelling from inside her and threatening to spill over through the tears that brimmed her eyelids.

'Good job, sweetheart.'

Gaze locked on Paige, now only a few feet from her future husband, Lily whirled around. Sonya Ritter had reached out from the pew in front of her and touched her arm, smiling from ear to ear.

'What a beautiful, beautiful bride,' she added in a whisper. 'And a gorgeous dress.' Sonya bent down and tapped Eden's shoulder, who stood beside her donning the fanciest sundress Lily had been able to find amongst the bags of clothing borrowed from Carlie. 'Your mama made that dress,' she said, pointing. 'It's pretty perfect, huh?'

Wide-eyed, Eden turned back toward Lily, entranced. 'Princess perfect.' *Pwincess perfect.*

In that moment, Lily's heart soared so high that she didn't even have it in her to be disappointed that her young daughter had wanted to stand with Sonya instead of her.

The older woman didn't wait for Lily's response, turning around to face forward as Paige's father kissed his daughter's cheek and watched as she stepped toward the man who would vow to love her until the end of time.

A shuddering breath shook from Lily's lips. Wiping away a stray tear that was destined to ruin her mascara if she wasn't careful, she fought against the intense undercurrent that threatened to sweep her away. It wasn't merely the sight of two people standing before one another and declaring their unabashed love in front of their family, friends, and community.

It was Sonya's words. Her praise, and the term of endearment that accompanied it.

Lily had heard the congratulations but not the voice. And when she had turned around, seeing Sonya, her disappointment—for a fleeting moment—had been even stronger than her triumph.

231

Because she had thought the praise was coming from Jason. It wasn't until she heard the compliment, that she realized how great her desire was to see him, to share the moment with him.

And he wasn't there.

Somehow, Lily knew his absence was her fault.

* * *

The wedding reception was as entertaining as the traditional ceremony was glamorous. A switch had been flipped, taking the festivities from timeless and classic to rollicking and spirited.

Without a formal invitation, Lily had no way of knowing the reception was being held outside. She found it a bold move, considering Mother Nature could have chosen to rain on their parade, literally. Once she followed the crowd toward downtown and witnessed the locale chosen for the party, she saw that it wasn't just a bold choice, but the right one.

The pier looked nothing like the one she had stood on a week ago. Sure, the wooden railings and boards beneath her feet were there, but the Port Landon pier had been transformed into an oversized outdoor pavilion. Garden lights with large Edison bulbs were intertwined with twinkling fairy lights, illuminating the sky despite the sun only beginning to sink into the west. In a few hours, they would rival any stars that dotted the clear, cloudless sky.

The DJ had set up in one corner, with enormous speakers strategically placed to deliver tunes onto the pier and across the water. Tables with white linens and tall glittering centerpieces lined one side of the pier's deck, but it was left mostly open and ready for the guests to dance the night away.

The warmth of the day was thwarted by the breeze off the water, creating a comfortable temperature and constant air movement. Lily welcomed the breeze. The wedding party did, too, judging by the way Allison was fanning herself with her rose bouquet on the way to the DJ's table. Still very much in maid of honor mode, Lily's employer's hands gestured this way and that as she filled the DJ in, patting the long-haired man on the back and offering him a contagious smile before flitting back toward the rest of the wedding party. Allison had long since mastered the art of delivering instruction while remaining warm and friendly. There was a reason she was a boss, and a darn good one.

A long table sat at the mouth of the pier, topped with countless plates of appetizers and finger foods encapsulated in pretty faux-crystal lids. A tower of plates was perched at one end, a huge etched crystal bowl of punch at the other. Lily was still staring at the setup when the music began, a soft instrumental tune that floated on the breeze and out into the harbor, causing the guests to sway with the melody as if by instinct.

Lily was certain the majority of the town was in attendance. Yet, the party was far from raucous. The crowd divided into smaller groups, the odd person flitting from one clique to the next, but folks seemed to move as one, their conversations and greetings mixing together to create a constant hum like bees in a beehive lying in wait for their queen. Lily didn't fully comprehend the melded sounds until the music abruptly stopped, sparking a shift in the crowd, all looking toward the DJ in silent anticipation.

'It is my pleasure, on this perfect summer evening, to introduce to you, for the first time, Mr. and Mrs. Beckett!' The voice boomed over the loudspeakers. The entire pier erupted into thunderous cheers, and Lily clapped her hands, overjoyed for Cohen and Paige as they made their way from the shore onto the pier, Paige's rose bouquet held high in blissful victory.

Allison pointed toward the DJ, and on cue, he pressed a button, sending the upbeat sounds of a well-known Black Eyed Peas song thumping across the pier.

Lily, determined to stay on the sidelines, watched the couple's descent from the east side of the pier. Her fingers touched the tower viewer. It was a gesture to steady herself, but feeling the warmed metal beneath her fingertips, remembering how ecstatic Eden had been to witness the boats glide across the lake, so close she could reach out and touch them—it unbalanced her.

This is happiness. She watched as Cohen and Paige mingled with their beloved community. One finger traced the binoculars as she stared toward the mouth of the pier, watching Sonya twirl her daughter around, the momentum billowing out Eden's skirt and making her beam with glee. The older woman had been adamant that she introduce her friends to her favorite pint-sized coworker, and neither Sonya or Eden had let the other out of their sight since.

Eden was happy here, she thought.

Lily found herself pressing her eyes to the viewfinder, lost in the memory of that magical evening on the pier with two of her favorite people.

I was, too, she realized.

But it was too late for that, now. So centered on what was in the distance, she hadn't stopped to see what was right in front of her. The small town of Port Landon, the good people who took her in and treated her as their own …

'Jason.' Still peering through the viewfinder, Lily realized that she was looking but not seeing, her mind a million miles away. But she could no longer see the harbor, her view blocked by a dark suit and a shy waving hand.

She stood, staring straight into the espresso eyes of Jason Forrester. He was barely recognizable in a black suit and deep blue shirt. A small bundle of wildflowers was clasped in one hand, his other still suspended in mid-wave.

'Wow, Lily, you look amazing.' He smiled crookedly but there was a hint of nervousness at its edges.

'You do, too.' Everything sounded distant, at the end of a tunnel she couldn't see. 'I … I didn't think you were coming.'

'I'm late, I know.' He must have suddenly remembered the flowers in his hand, and Jason stepped forward, offering the pink, blue, and yellow blooms toward her. 'I'm sorry.' The up-tempo song faded, giving way to a slower tune Lily recognized as one of her favorites, a ballad by Edwin McCain.

'You have nothing to apologize for, Jason. I should be the one—'

'Don't you dare.' He held up a finger. 'Will you dance with me?'

The wildflower bouquet still clutched in one hand, she let Jason lead her out into the middle of the pier. Out of the corner of her eye, Allison had substituted her signature high-powered dance moves with a chance to slow dance with her husband. She meant to seek out Paige and her new husband to see if they were relishing in the slower pace of their day, but Lily was too engrossed in the way Jason's hand rested at the small of her back and the spicy scent of his cologne that lingered in the air.

'Paige's dress is stunning, Lily,' he said, words meant only for her. 'You did a fantastic job.'

'I guess I work well under pressure.'

'Maybe, but you're also extremely talented,' he replied, his gaze never leaving hers. 'You deserve all the success you've got coming your way.'

'Jason.' She had to address the elephant in the room—er, on the pier. 'About Chicago—'

His hand was between them in an instant, his finger pressing gently against her glossy lips. 'I was wrong to react the way I did when you told me about the job offer. I did mean what I said,' he explained. 'I do think you should take that internship in Chicago. I do. You deserve it, and they'd be lucky to have you. That's the truth.' He paused, inhaling deeply as though to steady himself. 'But there are a lot of lies I've been telling myself lately, too. The biggest one is that I could simply watch you walk away. But I can't, Lily.'

Her mind spun like a top. She nodded, unsure how to say any of the things she was thinking. How to verbalize any of the things she was feeling.

'I want you to chase your design dreams. More than anything.

Before you go and do that, though, I want to show you something.' Jason lowered his hand, but Lily had already felt the tremble of his finger before it left her lips. 'Lily, do you trust me?'

Four words. A simple question awaiting a simple answer. In Lily's mind, there was only one honest response to give. 'I do.'

Chapter 20

Jason

In his head, the day was supposed to play out very different than it did. Jason had stared at his invitation to Cohen and Paige's wedding countless times, deep purple cardstock with golden foil calligraphy and one solitary red rose blooming from the right-hand corner, so he was well versed of the timeline. Wedding ceremony at eleven o'clock, then a gap of time in between until the outdoor reception started at four due to wedding photographs being taken offsite.

He knew, and still he had managed to miss the ceremony entirely. Thankfully, he believed both Cohen and Paige would understand once they heard his reasons.

Lily, on the other hand, didn't understand at all. How could she? His reason was her. She just didn't know it yet.

Seeing her there on the pier, it was as though the crowds of guests had parted, revealing her to him. Lily kept to herself, allowing the party to go on around her as though she were merely a bystander. No one could overlook her, however. Not in that dress. With her champagne hair styled in a graceful knot, only the tiniest wisps of blonde free and blowing lightly in the breeze, and the strapless, knee-length dress that showed every soft curve and striking angle, Lily Brentwood was the definition of natural beauty. Watching as she stepped toward the tower viewer and peeked through the binoculars, he wondered if she was where he was, then, reminiscing about the day they had spent in that very spot with Eden, watching boats churn the glassy waters as the sun gave the sky over to the moon.

She uttered his name as though he were a ghost. Either she hadn't expected him to show, or he had appeared like a figment conjured up from her own thoughts. He hoped it was the latter.

He ignored everything after hearing his name on her lips. The music, the floral decorations and twinkling lights, the massive wedding cake being rolled out toward the appetizer table that could have only been created by the bride herself—somehow, he wasn't surprised Paige had trusted no one else with her wedding cake, and by the looks of it, the fondant red roses and deep violet and blue lace designs were nothing less than the Cakery's finest—and the fact that his parents and daughter were nearby watching his quest for forgiveness as it unfolded; it all paled in comparison to the relentless need coursing through him to give Lily exactly what she deserved from him. Honesty.

Do you trust me? It was no small question. He wouldn't have blamed her if she'd said she didn't. Or that she couldn't. The woman had been through hell, and trust was earned. He had taken what little he'd gained and crushed it with his own fear-induced defenses.

'I do,' she replied. And whether it was merely the acknowledgement that she did, in fact, trust him, or the fact that those words were uttered during a fairytale wedding, it was the greatest gift he could have received.

'Then, will you come somewhere with me?' He didn't attempt to hide his shaky hands or quivering voice. He wouldn't hide from Lily, not anymore. 'I know we're in the middle of a wedding and—'

'Yes,' she replied, her gaze never leaving his. 'I know you enough to know that you wouldn't ask if it wasn't important. So, yes, I will, Jason.' She nodded as though affirming her conviction to herself as much as him. 'But Eden—'

'She's safe with Sonya,' he replied quickly. Too quickly.

Lily's brows drew downward. 'How did you know she was with Sonya?'

Jason watched as the realization washed over her. She had been hoodwinked, and Sonya's insistence that Eden spend time with her was merely a part of the plan.

'Sonya knows where we're going,' she stated.

'Trust me,' Jason replied, 'Having to confide in Sonya Ritter was not my first choice. But Eden knows her well, and she'll be comfortable with her. Carlie's here with my mother, too, so they'll be able to play together. Are you okay with that?'

Jason followed Lily's gaze in the direction she had last seen Sonya and Eden. The dance floor was so full that they were barely able to make out the bright pink of the little girl's dress.

'Okay,' she said with a nod. 'I trust you.'

He could tell she was reminding herself of that fact just as much as him.

'Come on.' Reaching for her hand, Jason led her off the pier, following the wooden railing in hopes of being able to sneak by without raising too much attention to their departure. 'If you want to make it out of here unscathed, don't make eye contact.'

He was only half joking.

Once their feet hit the rocky ground, Jason clutched Lily's hand a little tighter. It took a minute for him to realize she wasn't wearing spiky heels or outlandishly high boots that would make her trek across the gravel treacherous. The wedge-soled sandals on her feet were reasonable, only providing her an extra inch or so of height. A logical choice.

He wondered what she would think of the choice he was about to give her.

'Jason!'

He stopped in his tracks, caught red-handed implementing his escape route. Lily, not expecting it, crashed into his arm. He thought he heard her apologize, but only managed a steadying hand to keep her upright.

His mother stood only a few feet away. He had left Carlie with her at a table on the other side of the pier when he arrived and didn't expect to face her until he and Lily returned. Seeing her there, standing tall in the new dress she had purchased specially for the wedding, he was frozen. Not in fear, because he vowed to never let fear dictate his actions again, but in awe.

Seeing her as she stood there, seeing him; in that moment, it meant everything.

Something so trivial, something many never even gave a second thought to. But Jason saw the way Bettina Forrester grinned, a wide smile that reached her sparkling eyes, so full of love and gratitude and hope that Jason couldn't fathom a moment where he didn't have hope again. There was too much of it radiating from his mother, permeating his illogical fears and erasing them with ease.

Bettina swung her gaze from her son to Lily. The intensity of her stare seemed to transfix Lily, just as it did Jason. Was she holding her breath? He felt like he was.

Lily didn't know much about his mother, only the vague particulars of her diagnosis. Bettina, however … well, there wasn't anything Jason hadn't shared with her. She knew all of it—not just how they'd met, but about the drive-in and the design of his grandfather's car, too. His mother had been the one to stand beside him during the past week, listening to him as he explained his irrational fears and guiding him when he blatantly asked her what he should do.

She knew the truth—he loved Lily. As Lily had so eloquently said, she knew enough about him to trust him. Well, he knew enough about her to love her. It was new love, just beginning to bloom, but love just the same. It surprised him as well as Bettina, but his mother had held on to that truth like a lifeline as she partnered up with him to pull off the surprise he wanted to show Lily.

Bettina Forrester saw it all. And as Jason smiled at her, his hand tangled with Lily's, she nodded. 'Thank you,' his mother said, her voice thick. She placed her hands affectionately on Carlie's shoulders. 'Thank you so much.'

Lily's eyes were wide as she realized the older woman was speaking to her. Entranced, her mouth opened but nothing came out.

'Come on,' Jason whispered. 'I'll explain later. But we'd better go before someone sees us.'

He pulled Lily along toward the road, where vehicles lined both sides in perfect rows.

'I … Jason, is Carlie wearing …'

'The Cinderella costume you made. Yes, she is,' he laughed. 'It was her number one choice. I told you before, I pick my battles. Hurry.'

Jason's Dodge truck was farther up the street than he remembered, and by the time they reached it he felt bad for dragging her away from the party. His haste was for good reason, he reminded himself. Lily had told him last week she was leaving after the wedding. If he didn't do this now, he might lose his chance.

'Jason, will you at least tell me what's going on?' She whirled around at the passenger door, staring up at him with bewildered eyes. 'Was that your—'

'My mother.' He nodded.

'She …' Lily stared back in the direction they had come from. 'She was thanking me, wasn't she? But why?'

'Look, Lily.' He took the wildflowers from her hand and set them on the side of the truck bed before clasping her hands within his. 'There's a lot I've got to explain, and I will. My mother knows a lot more about you than you do about her. Let's just put it that way.' He offered her what he hoped was an encouraging grin. 'You just made my mother one of the happiest women in the world. All I want is a chance to do the same for you.'

Lily looked desperate for information. Surprises obviously weren't her thing. But after a moment of searching his gaze, she must have found that sliver of trust once more because she nodded and allowed Jason to open the truck door for her. She climbed in without a word, momentarily defeated.

He laid the wildflower bouquet across her lap. Jason hoped she realized that this was one battle he was picking, because it mattered. And he wasn't going to let it end without a fight.

Chapter 21

Lily

They rode in silence. Jason tapped his fingers against the steering wheel, but it wasn't a rhythmic sequence in time with the radio. Each tap was sporadic. One, then two more, no pattern.

He was nervous.

That made two of them, then. There were a lot of ways this evening could have gone in Lily's mind, but none of the scenarios she would have come up with on her own included Jason showing up and whisking her away from Port Landon like a bandit on the run. He wasn't speeding by any means, and his driving was far from erratic, but she caught the way his gaze flitted back and forth between the road and the clock on the dashboard.

'Jason, I really think you should tell me what's going on.' She had a few things she needed to tell him as well, but considering his dramatic escape from Cohen and Paige's wedding, she preferred to let him explain himself first.

Jason flicked on his signal light for the next exit. 'I can do better than that,' he replied quietly. 'I'll show you.'

Lily sighed, leaning back in her seat. She saw the hint of a smirk play on his lips just before she turned away. Glaring out the passenger side window gleaned her more information than Jason did. The city limit sign for North Springs passed by on her right, a large spotlight gleaming to illuminate it.

'North Springs,' she said quietly. They had been driving longer than she'd realized. 'Jason …'

He reached across the console and cupped her hand in his. 'Three minutes, then you'll understand.'

She hoped he was right, because this didn't make sense at all. A week ago, he had stood before her and told her to go to Chicago as planned. Then, an hour prior, he had stolen her breath away by confessing that he didn't want to lose her.

Where North Springs fit into all this, she couldn't comprehend.

The soft glow of twilight basked the asphalt streets in iridescent grays and blues. Cars still lined both sides of the streets, and people still poured out onto the sidewalks from stores and pubs and apartment buildings. Unlike the quieter town of Port Landon, it didn't seem to shut down by eight o'clock.

'This is it.' Jason's voice cut through the silence as he navigated the truck into an angled parking space outside a classy boutique on Sunview Avenue. The street was lined with similar little shops, small businesses with eye-catching window displays and ornate signage. Further up the row, a posh-looking bistro was still open and in full swing, patrons floating in and out of it in a constant stream.

Lily scanned the sidewalk as Jason killed the engine. The nose of their vehicle pointed at Bridgette's Jewelry and Gifts. Fed up with the secrets and games, Lily stared at the gold and silver in the window display. 'If you're looking to buy me something shiny, Jason, sorry to burst your bubble but it looks like it's closed.'

She heard a strangled chuckle to her left. She turned to see him run his hand through his hair. Wisps stood up on end and stayed there.

'I'm not saying I wouldn't buy you something shiny, Lily, but that's not the reason for this trip.'

Lily unbuckled her seatbelt and craned around, staring at him squarely. 'Then, what *is*?'

He pointed out the window. 'That.'

Lily followed his finger passed the jewelry store. Beside it, a vacant storefront sat, its huge front windows darkened and lined with paper to obstruct the view inside. Big double doors, wooden and carved with a calligraphy *F* were closed, and a large *For Rent* sign hung crookedly in the window. Her eyebrows drew down.

'Come on. I told you I'd show you.' He clambered out of the truck before Lily even had time to fully register what he said.

Ever the perfect gentleman, Jason opened the passenger door for her and held out a hand to help her to the ground. With him still in his suit and her still wearing the strapless dress that undoubtedly cost more than the rest of her wardrobe combined, Lily felt as though she had walked onto the set of some romantic comedy movie. Addled by nerves, she awaited the punchline, wondering if it would be at her expense.

'Why are we here?' She needed to say something to fill the silence as Jason ushered her toward the dark storefront, rummaging in his coat pocket as her shoes made a *clip, clap* sound on the concrete.

'Because this is the middle of North Springs,' he explained. 'And because I want you to see, really see, the options that are available to you.'

Lily had no idea what he was saying. She wondered if he realized how cryptic and frazzled he sounded. 'That doesn't really tell me anything, I don't think.'

'Okay, then let's see if this does.' The key in his hand fit perfectly in the brass lock, and the righthand door clicked open easily. A trio of teenagers passed by as he opened it, laughing at something someone said. Jason didn't so much as blink in their direction, focused solely on Lily as he waved a hand. 'Ladies first.'

Inside, the rental space was wide open and stark. Lily stared at the white walls and the glass cabinets pushed to one side of the room, cloaked in dark shadows. The fluorescent lights burst on a moment later, revealing the built-in shelves along the back wall, and the doorway near the back of the room that led into another smaller room. The nondescript counter jutting out to her right divided the open floor from the glass cabinets behind it. A set of keys still hung in one of the cabinet locks, waiting for someone to turn it and slide the glass door open.

Lily whirled around. 'What is this, Jason?'

'One of your many options.'

'I don't understand.'

'It's yours,' he replied. 'If you want it.'

'What?' She couldn't possibly have heard him right.

'It's yours,' he repeated. Jason closed the gap between them. He didn't reach for her, but Lily swore she could feel the heat emanating from him, seeping into her and calming her growing anxiety. 'I told you that my parents live here in North Springs. Today was the first time you've met my mother, but it wasn't the first time she'd heard of you.'

'You talked about me, to your mother.' Lily struggled to process this. What it meant, where he was going with it.

He nodded. 'If I hadn't, I might never have been able to realize what's been going on in my brain,' he admitted. 'And my heart.'

Funny he would mention that particular organ, because Lily's own heart was pounding frantically.

'Lily, I need you to know that I believe in you, and in your talent. Seeing Paige's dress today was only proof of what I already knew you could do.' He waved a hand around the room. 'So, when my mother told me about this spot, I came to check it out. The rent's not bad and the clientele on this strip … there's a well-established jewelry store beside it and a high-end bistro on the corner. It would be perfect for you to open your own bridal boutique.'

Her eyes widened. 'Jason ...' She breathed out his name, at a loss for words.

'I don't mean immediately. I don't even mean you have to rent it now. But places like this exist, and I want you to know that I want to help you attain one of them if it's something you would want. Now, or eventually.'

She spun around, taking in his words and the vacant walls around her that cried out to be adorned with fancy dresses and pretty shoes.

'I understand if you feel it's not enough, Lily,' he continued quickly. 'I know it's not Chicago. And I am not saying don't take that internship, so please don't take it that way.' He pleaded with her to understand the muddled explanation he was having such a hard time getting out. 'I just wanted you to see that you've got options, and they're everywhere, not just in Chicago at the first company who showed interest in your designs. Paige has contacts in New York that she's ready to utilize, and there's room to grow here. To design what you want, how you want, and be in a place where people will see it. I'll help you any way I can.'

She was still seeing the vacant space through his eyes, with elegant gowns showcased in window displays and books of fabric swatches lined up on the back shelf. With sparkly tiaras displayed in the glass cabinets and Lily standing in the middle of it all, the designer. The owner.

It was her dream, but with a twist. Because it sounded a lot like it had become Jason's dream for her as well.

'You found me a place to open a boutique.'

'Someday, if that's what you want. And technically it was my mother that did,' he corrected wryly. 'I can't take all the credit.'

'She sounds like quite the woman.'

'You have no idea. She's extraordinary, and just like me, she wants to help you, too.'

'But why?' The question burst from within her as though it had been building for ages, gaining momentum and inflating in her chest until it broke free. 'Why would she go to all this trouble to help me, Jason?' She stared at him, pleading for clarity. 'Why would you?'

'Because of how I feel about you.' His throat moved visibly, but he pressed on. 'I never expected you, Lily. I never expected this.' He motioned between them. 'I'm the worst person when it comes to showing it or dealing with it. I know that. Hell, I've proven that. But you said you knew enough about me to trust me. Well, I know enough about you to love you. To know that this could be the beginning of something really good. Maybe it doesn't make sense, but that doesn't make it any less true.'

The words brought her back to the pier, where she first heard them from his lips. He had been trying to tell her then, in his own convoluted way. Just as she had been trying to tell herself.

Feelings; they were so complicated and overwhelming. It was so easy to feel something and be unable to convey it clearly. So much had been said between them, channeled through their crossed wires only to have the resultant message become muddled and incoherent. The back and forth, the maybe and maybe not—it was complicated, and confusing, and sometimes tortuous.

But it was still love.

'Jason, I … I can't rent this space.'

His smile faltered. 'If it's the rent, I will—'

'Jason.' She cut him off, stepping forward. 'North Springs isn't where I want to be.'

For a fleeting moment, Jason all but collapsed in on himself, shoulders sagging. Lily didn't think she would have seen the glimpse of despair if she hadn't been so acutely aware of his every move. 'We can try to make this work while you're in Chicago, then.'

She shook her head. 'We don't have to.' Lily reached for his hand, the key still folded in his palm. 'Jason, I turned down the internship at Lash Fashion.'

'What, why?' He stared as though seeing her for the first time, bemused.

She chuckled lightly at his childlike puzzlement. 'For two reasons, actually.' Her hand squeezed his, finding the strength she needed in his touch to explain. 'You're not the only one who's been talking to Paige about her contacts in New York. Goodness, what she must be thinking right now knowing that both you and I asked her the same questions but for different reasons.' She laughed, then. No wonder Paige had been so adamant during their conversations throughout the week, knowing both sides. 'She's going to help me build my own business. Shirley, too. I've got quite the little team in Port Landon.' She reached up and caressed the edge of his jaw affectionately, silently telling him that he was a part of that team as well. 'So, I'm going to stay in Port Landon and slowly build my business from there. With the Internet, it's possible.'

His confusion gave way to complete and utter shock. 'You're staying.'

The corner of her mouth lifted. 'I am. With Cohen and Paige moving to the new home on their acreage, Paige is going to rent the apartment above The Cakery to Eden and me. I'll work out of there for now, and if I need more room, I'll save for a storefront. In Port Landon. Because that's where I want to be, Jason. In your hometown.' With a wry grin, she added, 'If that's okay.'

'More than okay.' Jason's arms were suddenly around her, encircling her waist and holding her with a gentleness that belied his strength. 'What's the other reason?'

'The same reason we're standing here, now,' she whispered. Words meant only for his ears. A secret she was desperate to share with only one man—him. 'Because I know enough about you to love you, too.'

There was so much more she wanted to say—that she wasn't just choosing the town or the job or anything else, that it was him she wanted, and whatever other craziness came with him. But as Jason lowered his mouth to hers and kissed her tenderly, she realized the truth.

He knew.

'Want to go back to the wedding?' His forehead pressed against hers, he grinned. 'I think I owe you a dance.'

'I'd like that.' Although, she had to admit, standing there in his arms was a pretty perfect place to be, too.

'My mother might be a little overwhelming,' he warned. 'But she would love to see you.'

'I'd love to meet her,' Lily replied, meaning it. 'And we can celebrate with Eden and Carlie. Because there are a lot of things to celebrate right now.'

Jason's face lit up. 'I can't think of anything I'd love to do more.' Hand in hand, he led her toward the door.

'A dance party with the girls,' she said wistfully. 'Sounds like a memory in the making.' Lily giggled as Jason stopped and tugged her to him once more.

'One, in a long line of them.' He kissed her again, soft and surreal. 'Let's go home, Lily.'

Epilogue

Jason

Six Months Later ...

'That should be good!' Jason switched his gesture from inching the flatbed truck closer toward him to halting it. The brake lights lit up as the truck groaned to a stop. Branch climbed out of the driver's seat and made his way to the back, eyeing up the tarp-covered cargo strapped to the bed.

'Lily's going to kill you,' he chuckled, unable to take his eyes off it.

'Or love me.' Jason smirked. He was still surprised that he had gone and done it without telling her. He hoped he wasn't overestimating Lily's fondness for him.

'She already loves you, idiot.' Branch tugged on one of the tie straps. 'The question is, will she love this car?'

Checking his phone, Jason shrugged. 'She gets off work in a few minutes, so I'm sure we're about to find out.'

'Well, if she doesn't,' Branch said, grinning despite the icy chill, 'I'll be glad to take it off your hands. I'm already thinking it could use some wide white walls and a few engine modifications—'

'Get your own project car.' Jason's thick winter jacket rustled as he shoved his friend away from the covered vehicle. 'I've got plans for this one.'

And he did. He just hoped Lily looked at it and saw what he saw. It wasn't just a car. It was a symbol of how far they had come, the future they would have together.

'Help me get her unloaded, will you?'

Together, they spent the next twenty minutes getting the car maneuvered into the vacant spot in Jason's garage behind the repair shop. He didn't miss the way Branch eyed up the patina on the hood or the rusted mirrors before they slipped the cover over it once more. His best friend was itching to get his hands dirty and restore the vehicle himself.

It was one thing to own a car that Jason had wanted since he was a teenager, but it was even more fun to own one that Branch had coveted just as long.

'What are you two up to?' Lily stood in the doorway, watching them suspiciously as her breath puffed out before her. 'It's freezing out here.'

Jason practically jumped out of his skin. He whirled around, confirming that things were where they were supposed to be. 'Lily, hey. I thought you were going home before you came here.'

Smooth, he thought. Out of the corner of his eye, Branch looked downright delighted that the mere sight of her sent Jason into a nervous frenzy.

'I did, and there was a note saying your mom brought Eden here. It was hard not to notice the tow truck in the driveway, though, so I got curious.' Her narrowed gaze announced that her curiosity had heightened into full-fledged wariness. 'What's that?'

Purse slung over her shoulder, she strode across the garage, passing by the covered Panther Lima on her way to him. Jason was hit by the aromatic scent of coffee beans and sugar wafting

252

from Lily like a seductive perfume. Her casual shifts at the coffeehouse were few and far between since she formally opened her online dress shop and began offering her sewing services to Port Landon residents, but she enjoyed both Allison and her job so much that she couldn't bring herself to walk away from the café entirely. Allison was only too keen to keep her on the payroll.

Branch held up his hands in mock surrender, his feet already moving toward the door. 'That, my dear Lily, is my cue to leave.' He offered Jason a pursed-lipped smile that said, *Buddy, you're on your own with this one*, and disappeared out the door into the wintry afternoon.

'Gee, that's not ominous at all.' Lily stared after Branch for a long moment before turning back to Jason. 'Jay, what's going on?'

'It's the weekend, you just got off work, and you haven't even given me a kiss yet, that's what's going on.' He enveloped Lily in a hug, kissing the top of her head before pulling away just far enough to be able to press his lips to hers.

'Good coverup, but you still haven't answered my question.' The worry creasing the corners of her eyes had eased slightly.

Jason's cell blipped loudly from the workbench.

Saved by the bell, literally. 'One sec, sweetheart.' He untangled himself from her and reached for the phone, sending a brief text before setting the phone back down. 'Okay, moment of truth.'

'Again, ominous.'

Jason rolled one of his adjustable stools toward her. 'Here, sit.' Lily didn't take her eyes off him as she obeyed, letting her purse slide to the floor.

'This wasn't how I was going to show you this, you realize that, right?' Jason closed the door, blocking out the December chill. 'I had elaborate plans and—'

'You're stalling, and it's making me more nervous by the minute.' Lily's mouth curled at the corners. 'If this is some kind of Christmas surprise—'

'It's not,' Jason assured her. 'Actually, I'm sure it's no surprise to anyone.'

'What isn't?'

'That I love you, Lily.' Jason crouched down in front of her. Even the coldest days had no chance against the warmth he saw in those pale ocean eyes. 'That I loved you before I even realized it myself.'

'Oh, Jason ...'

A series of raps on the garage door echoed off the walls, and they both snapped their gazes toward the sound.

'Come in!' Jason called out.

The door burst open, and a herd of wild five-year-olds came galloping in. Okay, not a herd, but Carlie and Eden were stomping so hard in their winter boots, their incessant giggles so shrill, that there may as well have been twenty of them instead of two.

'Right on time,' Jason laughed. The girls came to an abrupt halt beside him. Eden pressed her hand to her mouth, as though holding in a secret. Carlie bounced on her heels, practically vibrating with excitement.

'On time for what?'

'Girls, will you do the honors?' Jason was thankful he'd already crouched down. His own dizzying anticipation was making him slightly lightheaded. Eden's puffy jacket concealed the little box perfectly, and together both she and Carlie opened it, revealing the sparkling solitaire diamond ring encrusted with smaller diamonds on each side.

'Will you marry Daddy?' Carlie swayed on her heels, suddenly shy. Jason swelled with pride. She had recited the question perfectly.

The gasp that emitted from Lily was loud. Her hands flew up to cover her mouth. Eyes wide, she gaped at the ring, then Jason, then the girls, disbelieving and overwhelmed.

Jason shifted his weight to one knee and gently pulled the delicate ring from the box. 'As I was saying, Lily, I love you. All

254

of you. The parts I know, and the parts I have yet to learn about. I love you, and I want you to be my wife. Lily Brentwood, will you marry me?'

He didn't think it was possible for her glistening eyes to widen further, but they did. At first, all she could muster was a jerky nod. Through the sobs, Jason finally heard the word he had been wishing for.

'Yes,' she cried. 'Jason, my goodness, yes!'

He didn't see her move. One second she was sitting on the stool, barely holding her emotions together, the next her arms were wrapped around him, hugging him tightly and threatening to bowl him over with her exuberance.

'I love you,' she whispered. 'I love you so much.'

'I love you, too,' he replied. 'Let me put the ring on your finger before the girls spontaneously combust.'

Laughing, Lily pulled away and held her trembling hand out.

'Six months ago, I met you and taught you names of automotive parts that weren't real,' Jason explained. 'Eden, what's our name for your mama's diamond ring?'

Eden tittered, removing her hands from in front of her mouth. 'Her chrome plated piston ring.' *Chwome pwated pithton ring.* The words got to him every time.

Lily choked on her laughter, wiping her eyes as Jason slid the ring on her finger. A perfect fit. 'I can't believe you girls knew about this!'

'There is one thing they didn't know about, actually.' He couldn't bring himself to tell them everything. Frankly, it was a miracle that two five-year-olds had managed to keep his proposal a secret. He didn't want to push his luck. 'Technically, two. I've got a few more tricks up my sleeve.'

He stood, planting a soft kiss on Lily's forehead before heading toward the covered cars. Two vinyl covers hiding two very different vehicles, but they both represented the same things to Jason.

Promises. Changes. Family.

'I've done everything I could lately to keep you guys out of this garage,' he explained, untucking the corners of the cover that masked the Panther Lima. 'I didn't want to spoil the surprise.'

'What surprise?' *Surpwise.*

Jason grinned. 'A long time ago, Eden, I made you a promise. Do you remember what it was?' Six months wasn't very long in the eyes of an adult, but he would have bet his paycheck that the little girl saw it as a lifetime ago.

Eden looked to Carlie, who was just as bewildered, then back toward him. She shook her head.

'In the summer, I promised you a ride in Cruella. I said we'd all go together someday. Do you remember that?'

Fidgeting with her fingers, her gaze rounded. 'Yeah.'

Fueled by his own excitement, Jason nodded, pleased to have three sets of eyes watching him with such rapt attention. 'It's my grandpa's car,' he reminded her. 'Been in the family for a really long time. Now, I want to share it with *my* family.' Jason stepped forward, dragging the cover off the car.

Lily almost knocked the stool over as she scrambled to her feet. 'Jason, oh my goodness!' Carlie and Eden uttered a mix of *whoas* and *wows*, but Jason still heard Lily's exclamation under her breath. 'It's my design.'

The 1981 Panther Lima was no longer a mix of rust and battered steel. Lily's hand-drawn design had jumped off the page. Plum purple with metal flake, the car glittered like it was encrusted with the same sparkling diamonds as Lily's ring. Yellow, red, and orange flames stretched from the grill across the door, feathered in brilliant lime green. The fourteen-inch spoke steel rims were polished to perfection, just as Lily's design had suggested.

'Jason, how …'

'I called in a favor to a friend in Lansing,' he explained. 'Had the car towed there last month. I didn't do the work myself the way I planned to, but I think my grandfather would understand.' His arm snaked around her waist, holding her to him. 'Things don't always work out as planned, but it doesn't mean they don't work out like they're supposed to.'

Lily beamed up at him, pressing her hand to his chest. 'She's beautiful, Jason,' she whispered. 'Your grandfather would be so proud.'

Jason wondered if she could feel the relentless beating of his heart against his ribcage. 'I think you're right.' On one of his grandfather's good days, he vowed to show the elderly man what had become of his car. To reveal what love could do.

'Can we take her for a spin?' Carlie squealed from the other side of the car.

'In just a sec.' He stole another glance down at Lily. 'With the Lima done, it's like the end of an era. I want to begin a new one.'

'What do you mean?' Lily raised an eyebrow.

He released her and headed toward the other covered car. 'The Lima was my grandfather's car. The car he wanted to build with his family.' Jason reached for the vinyl corner. 'This is the one I want to build with my own family. Our family.'

Peeling the cover away, he revealed a sun-faded two-door sedan.

Carlie shrieked with delight at the sight of it. 'Daddy, what is that?'

'That, sweetheart, is a 1949 Ford Business Coupe. Also known as a Shoebox Ford.'

'It looks like something out of a black and white movie,' Lily chuckled, circling it. 'You want to restore this ... with us.'

Jason followed her, enthralled by the way her fingertips grazed across the rounded hood and up over the edge of the murky windshield. He could almost see the wheels turning as she stared into the car, seeing what it could be with time.

With love.

'We can all be a part of it. You, me, and the girls. After all, you're the one who reminded me that a hotrod should have a little American muscle.' He winked. 'We can take all the years we need to make it what we want.' He reached for her hand, kissing her knuckles gently. 'Making memories along the way.'

257

Lily cupped her other hand over his. 'I'd like that. The four of us.'

'The four of us.' He leaned in, brushing his lips against hers. 'You wouldn't believe the ideas I have. I mean, once folks see the custom design you did for the Lima, I think you'll have people knocking down the door to have their own cars redesigned, so get ready. But, on top of the spectacular custom design you're going to have to create for *this* one, I'm thinking a four-inch roof chop, and maybe Branch was right about the white walls. For engine modifications, a Weiand supercharger will increase performance, and Offenhauser heads—'

'Jason, I have no idea what language you're speaking, or if that stuff's even real.'

He grinned, wide and sincere. 'You and I both know things don't have to make sense to be real, Lily. All you've got to do is trust me.'

'And I do.' Lily brushed the edge of his jaw with her thumb. 'Let's go for a ride in Cruella.'

'I thought you'd never ask.'

Acknowledgements

As always, thank you to Erica. This journey wouldn't be the same without you. Thank you to Belinda and the rest of the HQ and HarperCollins teams for all you do. To Dennis, thank you for being my rock. Thank you to my parents for believing in me so unconditionally.

Thank you to Jazz, who's been by my side through it all. Heaven gained you as an angel during the edits of this book. You are loved and so, so missed, my girl, now and always. You'll always be the star of Port Landon in my eyes.

Thank you to the readers and bloggers for all the posts, shares, reviews, and kind words. The book community truly is the best.

Keep reading for an excerpt from
The Forget-Me-Not Bakery …

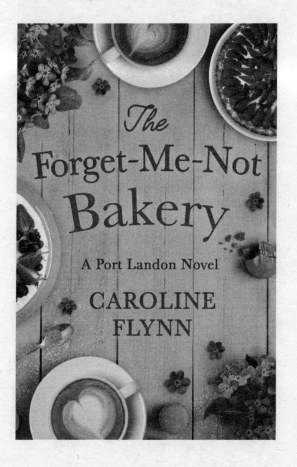

Prologue

Cohen

Eight Years Ago …

There are days that change everything. Change our lives. Change us.

Cohen Beckett didn't understand the razor-sharp truth of that statement. Until now. Now that he stood at the edge of the room, surrounded by all the people he knew and just as many that he didn't, aching with the painful loneliness of a man stranded on foreign ground without a soul in sight. Now that he was left behind, to carry on living a life he didn't know how to live alone. Now that his family of three, content and constant and perfect, was only a family of two.

Cohen didn't remember who he was before Stacey. Try as he might, he couldn't summon up recollections of his time before he'd met her by chance at university, all wide-eyed and beautiful and ready to take on the world. It seemed like a lifetime ago, yet those days, in the beginning, as he careened over the edge and fell madly in love with her, were etched in his brain with a sharp vividness that made them seem like only yesterday. He prayed that haunting vividness would never dull.

Before that, though? Nothing. The realization left him cold, and scared of what it truly meant. The thought niggled at him that he hadn't yet begun to live, to do and be anything worth remembering, until he'd met the woman he would call his wife. And if that was the case, he wasn't just scared. He was petrified. Because he would never be that man again, the one he saw reflecting back at him in Stacey's pretty emerald eyes.

Stomach in knots, shoulders tight with the facade of strength he fought to wear nobly, Cohen ached for another glimpse of his beloved wife's stare in his direction. The smile on her face that forced her long-lashed eyelids to squint with the sheer authenticity of it in the gold-rimmed picture frame beside her matching casket, the smile that seemed to follow him from across the room no matter where he stood, was a poor substitute for the beauty now housed in that closed box. No picture could do Stacey Beckett's smile justice. No memory, regardless of its clarity, would ever do *her* justice.

He'd found his one. The one who was his best friend and his lover and his rock. It pained him to think about whether he'd managed to be those things for her, adequately and fully. His chest constricted as he hoped with every fiber of his being that he had been. It hurt even more to realize that his love for her hadn't been enough to save her, hadn't been enough to protect her in the first place. The rational part of Cohen's brain understood that he could never have prevented the fluke accident that stole Stacey from him and their young son, but there were moments during the darkness of the seven nights that had followed her death when his rational mind didn't stand a chance against the grieving, guilt-stricken part that took over and threatened to drown him in his own numb disbelief.

'Dr Cohen?'

In the distance, as though through a thick veil of cotton but more accurately of dazed distraction, a voice filtered through to him. Cohen turned, and Sonya Ritter stood near him, her back turned to protect him from any oncoming folks intent on bestowing their condolences. Judging by the added lines that marred her forehead and the slight narrowed angle of her eyelids, she had said his name a few times without gleaning a response. Sonya knew nothing of impatience with him, though. As Port Landon's designated mother hen and knower of all that went on within the town's limits, the short elderly woman had taken her role more seriously when the tragedy of Stacey's passing befell their little town and rocked their community to the core. The woman was a fixture in their tiny town, and a friend to all despite her overzealous nature and overbearing personality. But she'd been a godsend to Cohen in the past week. He didn't know how he would have gotten through any of this without her. Didn't know how Bryce would have gotten through it.

Bryce. His son. The last remaining thread to Stacey that he could touch and hold. Only two years old and left without the beautiful mother he adored. Cohen didn't know how to quantify the torturous pain he was battling, but he was sure it was multiplied a thousand times over with the added weight of the grief he harbored on his young son's behalf.

'Sorry, Sonya. What were you saying?' He shook his head, desperate to hold himself together. Not for Sonya; she could handle whatever emotional turmoil Cohen – or anyone else, for that matter – tossed at her. The woman was strong and sturdy as an oak tree despite her age. It wasn't her he worried about.

The toddler in her arms was another story. The little boy he now lived solely for. Not because anything or anyone had ever come before him in his father's eyes, but because he was all he had left.

Sonya looked uncertain of Cohen's current emotional stability. She wasn't the only one. But she thankfully kept her sentiments to herself. Cohen didn't know if he could stand to hear *Are you okay?* or *How are you holding up?* one more time. People meant well, but it didn't make having to form an answer any easier.

'The director says he's about ready to start the service,' she informed him. 'I figured you would want Bryce with you?'

Bless the woman's heart. She was giving him an out, phrasing it as a question and allowing him the chance to admit he couldn't handle sitting in the front row of his wife's funeral, with his son in his arms asking why Mommy's picture was on display but she was nowhere to be found. It was going to be hard. Damn hard. There would be tears eventually, though the icy numbness that spread through him like a biting frost hadn't allowed those tears to fall yet, and there would be moments when Cohen wouldn't know how he was going to get through them.

Today was one of those days. One of those moments. That changed everything. Changed him.

But he couldn't allow this to swallow him up. He couldn't let it, as easy as it would be. Bryce needed him now. More than ever. And Cohen needed Bryce just as urgently. He held his hands out, his fingers twitching with the instinctive urgency to feel the solid form of his son against him.

'I wouldn't want him anywhere else.' He hugged the boy tight to his chest as Sonya gave Cohen's jacket lapel a gentle pull to straighten it, then she pressed her lips together and headed back toward the rows of chairs, leaving him with only his thoughts and his son to keep him steady. He had more faith in his two-year-old than his own frazzled mind to level him out.

'You all right, buddy?' Cohen pressed his thumb into Bryce's palm, squeezing his fingers gently. The boy's eyelashes fluttered before his eyes fixed firmly on his father.

Stacey's eyes.

'I want Mommy.' Bryce played with the edge of Cohen's pocket, flipping the fabric up and down, his gaze flitting from it to Cohen's face then back again. Waiting for an answer. Waiting for his daddy to fix this.

Cohen felt desolate, helpless. But, despite his throat constricting, thick with all the things he couldn't find the strength to say and all the things he couldn't change, Cohen leaned forward and kissed Bryce's forehead, his soft skin warm against his lips.

'I know, my boy. Me too.' He shifted his son in his arms, needing him to focus his waning attention on him, needing him to understand the sincerity of the words he fought to say out loud. 'But we're going to be okay, me and you.' He pressed his forehead to his son's, swallowing hard past the lump in his throat, desperate for his son to believe him more than he believed himself. 'We'll get through this,' he choked out. 'Together.'

Cohen just wished he knew how.

Chapter 1

Paige

Present Day ...

Paige Henley had heard a lot of things about Port Landon. Mostly from her cousin, Allison, a long-time resident, and mostly that the tiny town was largely made up of people with big hearts and even bigger mouths. It ran on gossip and small-town gumption, and not always necessarily in that order. Of course, that was just gossip, too, when she really thought about it.

But she knew one thing for sure. When the folks of Port Landon talked about The Cakery's grand opening later on that evening, huddled back into their cozy homes with their own personal choice of sugar fix, their recollection of just how well the new bakery's grand opening had gone would be anything but exaggerated hearsay. It would be the truth.

'I can't believe this is really happening,' Paige exclaimed, bending down to pull two chocolate cupcakes with mint frosting from the glass display case. Rising to her full height, she closed the takeout box and met Allison's gaze. 'I guess what I really mean is I still can't believe you talked me into this.'

Allison expertly rang the sale through the cash register and bid the customer – Mrs O'Connor from Huntington Street was how she'd introduced her to Paige – a good day before turning to her cousin, eyes gleaming so bright they sparkled. 'Oh, please. You can pretend you're still unsure about this whole venture, but you're not fooling me. Either you've laced the baked goods with some damn good stuff that's making people *think* it tastes good, or maybe, just maybe, the people of Port Landon have spoken, Paige … and The Cakery is officially a hit!'

Paige couldn't hide her smile. Leave it to Allison to decide that the only two plausible options were either real, honest-to-goodness success or the clandestine addition of hallucinogenic drugs.

She might not have had a clue what she was doing as a first-time business owner, but, by God, she was learning on the fly. And she was doing something right. It felt like the entire population of Port Landon had left their homes and jobs on this cheery sunny day to get a chance at the free coffee and sweet treats being handed out in celebration of Paige's first official day up and running on the bustling downtown street.

Or, if Paige was honest, to catch a glimpse of the newest addition to the small portside town they all called home – *her*. Most customers weren't even trying to hide that they were just as interested in the New Yorker who had snatched up old Wilhelmina Morrison's bakery within days of it hitting the real estate market as they were the baked goods that were strategically displayed about the room. It was like they'd never seen a girl from New York before. Like she was something akin to a Yeti from the Himalayan Mountains, something they'd heard of but never truly witnessed.

Well, they were witnessing her now, a real live city-girl-turned-small-town-entrepreneur, living in what she hoped would remain her natural habitat, her very own dream come true.

And that's what this grand opening day was turning out to

be – a dream come true. With Allison graciously allowing her own business, the coffeehouse too-conveniently located beside the bakery, to be solely run by her two employees so she could volunteer to help Paige 'control the impending chaos' – Allison's words, not hers – the doors had been unlocked for the very first time at nine o'clock sharp. The coffee Allison had donated for the event had been brewed and piping hot, ready to be sipped by the patrons who attended. Paige had expected there to be a handful of people who would come out, mostly for the free food that had been mentioned in the *Port Landon Ledger* advertisements, but she never would have expected the line-up of people that waited patiently outside for the heavy glass door to be unlocked, or the way the cupcakes, mini cheesecakes, and scones that had been on display had sold out in a matter of hours, leaving Paige with no choice but to begin cutting the large cakes into individual pieces and sell them by the slice so that everyone would have a chance to try the different frostings and cake flavors she'd boasted about in the ads.

If this day was any indication, The Cakery was going to need to be better stocked on a daily basis than she ever dreamed. The thought had Paige bursting with pride. Every sliver of fear she'd had about leaving her marketing career back in New York, every not-so-subtle hint from Allison that she should take a chance and follow her dreams of owning her own bakery, every doubt she'd harbored since giving her notice and selling her closet-sized condo in the heart of the city …

It was worth it. Crazy and reckless, but absolutely worth it. And it made Paige feel more alive than she had in years. Maybe ever. Even if she had to spend her evenings whipping up buttercream frosting just to keep up, she would do it, because this was her dream, and it was coming to fruition in front of her sapphire eyes.

Yeah, it was definitely worth it.

'Paige, this is Sonya.' Allison's voice cut through Paige's thoughts. She turned to see a slender woman with short, gray hair cut smartly into a bob hairstyle. She wore a black T-shirt identical to Allison's, with the round Portside Coffeehouse logo on the front. The woman looked to be at least sixty-five, which Paige hadn't expected by the way Allison talked about her.

'Oh, Allison's told me so much about you,' Paige gushed, dusting her hands on her block-patterned apron. 'You help her to run the coffeehouse, right?'

'I do what I can,' Sonya replied, nodding as she shook her hand with a surprisingly firm grasp. She leaned forward, a faint grin on her lips as she added in a whisper, 'Which is pretty much everything.'

'Easy, now. I can hear you plotting your stealthy takeover from here.' A wider grin crossed Allison's face as she placed her hands on her hips. This was obviously a running joke between the two of them. 'Taking a break, are you?'

Sonya pointed toward the brick wall to the right that divided the bakery from the coffeehouse. 'I've got Adrian running the place for ten minutes while I grab myself a treat. Got anything with peanut butter in it?'

Paige jumped into action immediately, gesturing toward the other side of the room where a long table with trays of colorful cupcakes and squares were on display. They'd been picked over a bit, but a good selection still remained. 'I put chocolate fudge cupcakes with peanut butter icing on the treat trays this morning! Help yourself to those. They're free for the taking.'

Sonya glanced back at the setup, but she quickly turned back to the front counter where Allison and Paige stood, pulling a crumpled ten-dollar bill from her pocket. 'Anything with peanut butter in it that I can *buy*?' She waved the bill in her hand.

Paige tilted her head, curious. 'Of course, but you don't have to—'

'Look, sweetheart …' The older woman leaned in as though about to reveal a deep, dark secret. 'Around here, we shop local. We help each other out as best we can. It's what we do, in case Allison, here, hasn't told you. So …' She slid the bill across the counter, her deep brown eyes never wavering. 'Sell me ten dollars' worth of sugary goodness, and let me be on my way, will you?'

Paige's cheeks burned hotly at having been put in her place by the older woman, but at the same time, her heart swelled with adoration and respect for Sonya … and for the town. 'A handful of peanut buttery decadence coming up,' she announced, pulling a takeout box from the shelf behind her and beginning to place an array of sweet treats into it. She was just about to disappear into the back of the shop where the kitchen was hidden by a wall when another voice broke into the conversation.

'Sonya, are you giving this poor lady a hard time?'

The voice brought Paige back around to see who it was. It was unfamiliar and deep, the voice of a man.

Sonya had turned around at the front counter, and judging by both her and Allison's easy smiles, they recognized the owner of that voice.

He was tall, standing over by the table of treat trays, pouring himself a cup of coffee from the large coffeepot Allison had brought over from her shop that morning. The steam billowed up from the paper cup in his hands, and his hazel eyes shone with amusement.

'You got one thing right, Dr Cohen. The lady's definitely going to be poor if she doesn't start letting us folks pay for the stuff in her shop.' Anyone else might have sounded crass, but Sonya's tone was anything but. She was blunt and to the point, but there was heart behind her words, not malice. 'Speaking of that, you'd better come up here and see what you can find to buy that sweet boy of yours, yeah?'

'Don't you worry, I've been given my orders,' he assured her, placing a plastic top on the cup before making his way to the front counter. 'I don't believe we've met, yet. I'm Cohen.'

A glass display case stood between them and he jutted his

hand out over it. His smile was the first thing Paige noticed about him, genuine. His eyes gleamed with just as much sincerity, and a gentle kindness seemed to emanate off him in waves. He wore dark stonewash jeans and comfortable looking loafers, but the ensemble was paired with a solid green scrub top that made the flecks of gold in his eyes shine all the more brightly.

'Hi,' Paige greeted him, shifting the box into one hand to shake his with the other. 'I'm Paige.' She could hear a sudden shyness tainting her own voice. 'Paige Henley.' She couldn't bring herself to tear her eyes away.

Cohen gave her hand a gentle squeeze, his gaze meeting hers and holding it for what could have been a minute but was probably only seconds. 'This town's been talking nonstop about you and your bakery, Paige. It's good to finally put a face and a name to all the chatter.'

'The novelty will wear off, I'm sure.' She had been living in Port Landon for the past three months, but for the first time, Paige idly wondered just what exactly the gossip was that Cohen had heard.

'As quickly as the sugar fix?' Cohen arched an eyebrow, a crooked grin dancing on his face.

'Well, hopefully not quite that fast.' She laughed.

The sound of a throat being cleared made both Paige and Cohen turn at the same time. Allison and Sonya stood there, their lips pursed, unable to hide their mischievous intrigue. It was too alight in their eyes to go unnoticed.

'Find something you like?' Allison asked, crossing her arms.

Paige didn't know if she was addressing Cohen or herself, but she quickly realized it didn't matter. What did matter was that she and Cohen were still standing there, her small hand enveloped in his.

She pulled her hand from his as easily as she could. 'Right.' She glanced down as she smoothed her apron out, giving herself a moment to compose herself and stamp down her embarrassment. 'Anything I can get you, Cohen?'

'That's *Dr* Cohen,' Sonya interjected, still rooted in place, watching their exchange with distinct interest.

Paige shot her a pleading glance, silently begging the woman to stop making this worse, but quickly tried to cover it up. 'Sorry, Dr Co—'

Cohen chuckled, shaking his head. 'No, just Cohen is fine,' he insisted. He glanced over at Sonya. 'I see what you're doing Sonya, and you can put the brakes on anytime.'

'I could.' She shrugged, waving a dismissive hand. 'But you know I won't, sweetheart.'

Paige wasn't sure whose expression was more amused, the older woman's or Cohen's, but whatever passed between them was a silent, mutual understanding. They had history, those two. Cohen turned back to Paige, unfazed. 'As I was saying,' he began again. 'I got a specific request from my son this morning for something that's double fudge, and I promised I would come and see if I could make good on that request before he got home from school. Unfortunately, I got behind in my appointments and it took longer to get here than planned. Am I too late?'

'I've got just the thing, *Just* Cohen.' She flashed him an excited smile, relieved that she did, in fact, have something that would fit the bill. She ducked down, intent on seeking out the cake she had in mind. Paige didn't even realize she was still holding the box – Sonya's box – in her hand until she was about to set it down and retrieve another one for Cohen.

Immediately, Paige stood up, her eyes wide as she came face to face with the older woman. 'I'm sorry, Sonya. I didn't finish getting everything for you! I'll be right back.' She whirled around, sending an apologetic glance at Cohen for making him wait as well, then scurried into the kitchen to add a slice of the chocolate peanut butter pie she'd made to have as her own dessert tonight, mortified at forgetting what she'd been doing the moment Cohen had entered the shop.

What in the world had come over her?

She knew all too well that Allison wasn't going to let her live that one down. And if her first impression of Sonya was anything to go by, she wouldn't, either.

Paige put on a brave face after slipping the piece of pie into the box and made her way back out to the counter. 'An assortment of cupcakes and a slice of gourmet chocolate peanut butter pie,' she announced, sliding the box across to Sonya. 'You'll have to let me know what you think.'

Sonya didn't bother to open the box and inspect the choices Paige had chosen. Pushing the ten-dollar bill closer to her, Sonya tucked the box under her arm. 'Trust me, Paige, I always let people know what I think.' She cast a fleeting glance from Cohen to Paige and back again, then winked. 'It was good to meet you, sweetheart.' She turned to leave, but not before adding, 'Have a good day, Dr Cohen,' as she closed the door behind her.

The void of Sonya's absence was felt the moment she left, but her words hung in the air like a thick veil. Allison had advised Paige on more than one occasion that the woman was a force to be reckoned with, but her spitfire personality was even more fiery than she'd expected.

'Now, about that order for double fudge anything …' Paige turned back to Cohen, unable to look Allison in the eye just yet, and went about cutting an enormous slice of chocolate Oreo cake with chocolate fudge icing and double chocolate fudge drizzle on top, carefully boxing it up. She added in a pair of mocha chocolate cupcakes for good measure. 'If that doesn't fit the bill for your son, I don't know what will.'

'It looks like he's going to be swinging from the rafters till midnight once the sugar in that hits his bloodstream.'

He was smiling, but Paige immediately wondered if he thought it was too much. 'I guess the doctor in you would be worried about the effects of all the refined sugar.'

'Nah, it's the dad in me that's worried about that,' he chuckled. 'Besides, I'm not that kind of doctor. I'm a veterinarian. Believe me, I understand the need for a good sugar fix every now and then. What do I owe you, Paige?'

Allison stepped back, gesturing for her to take her place at the cash register. Paige punched a few buttons, ignoring the smug grin on her cousin's face. When the amount came up on the screen, Cohen arched a brow. 'That can't be enough.'

'It's just for the cake,' she advised happily. 'The cupcakes are on the house.'

He pulled his wallet out and held out a twenty-dollar bill. 'Thanks, Paige. Looks like I owe you one.'

Paige counted out his change and handed it to him. 'You owe me nothing. I'm just glad I could fulfill the request of a boy with dreams of chocolate fudge.'

'One forkful of that chocolatey masterpiece and I'll bet you'll be seeing my son and me in here a lot more.'

'I'm looking forward to it, Cohen.'

He shoved his wallet back into his jeans pocket, his eyes gleaming when they met hers once more. 'Me too,' he assured her. 'But I'd better get back to Jazz. She's probably scaling the walls looking for me. It was nice to meet you, Paige. Have a good day, you two.' He offered a slight nod toward Allison, and then they both watched as he made his way out of the shop, the bell above the door tolling lightly to announce his exit.

With the shop empty for the first time since the doors opened that morning, Paige turned to her cousin, who was still grinning. 'What?' Paige asked, rolling her eyes. She knew exactly what her cousin was thinking. They had been best friends too long not to know. 'You're looking at me like something big just happened.'

'Something big did just happen,' Allison exclaimed. 'You, Paige Henley, just met Port Landon's most eligible bachelor.'

Dear Reader,

We hope you enjoyed reading this book. If you did, we'd be so appreciative if you left a review. It really helps us and the author to bring more books like this to you.

Here at HQ Digital we are dedicated to publishing fiction that will keep you turning the pages into the early hours. Don't want to miss a thing? To find out more about our books, promotions, discover exclusive content and enter competitions you can keep in touch in the following ways:

JOIN OUR COMMUNITY:

Sign up to our new email newsletter:
http://smarturl.it/SignUpHQ

Read our new blog www.hqstories.co.uk

🐦 https://twitter.com/HQStories

📘 www.facebook.com/HQStories

BUDDING WRITER?

We're also looking for authors to join the HQ Digital family!
Find out more here:

https://www.hqstories.co.uk/want-to-write-for-us/

Thanks for reading, from the HQ Digital team

If you enjoyed *A Wildflower Summer*, then why not try another delightfully uplifting romance from HQ Digital?